FAMILY CURSE

FAMILY CURSE

THE ENCHANTED ORCHARD™
BOOK TWO

KELLI ROBYNS

MICHAEL ANDERLE

DON'T MISS OUR NEW RELEASES

Join the Florid Romance email list to be notified of new releases and special promotions (which happen often) by following this link:

https://floridromance.lmbpn.com/about/sign-up-for-our-newsletter/

Published by Florid Romance
an imprint of LMBPN Publishing
2375 E. Tropicana Avenue, Suite 8-305
Las Vegas, Nevada 89119 USA

Version 1.00, April 2025
eBook ISBN: 979-8-89354-654-5
Print ISBN: 979-8-88878-287-3

ONE

Emma stared at her bedroom ceiling, tracing tiny spots of moonlight that slipped past the lace of her curtains. She had tried every method of calming her mind that Sadie once taught her—slow breathing, a mental catalog of the day's smallest blessings, even a whispered protective verse—but none of it quieted the restlessness rattling inside her. Every time Emma closed her eyes, she felt the orchard's silent pull, beckoning in ways she couldn't ignore.

A chill ran through her when she finally rose from bed and got dressed. She pressed a palm to the window, feeling the glass vibrate slightly in the night breeze. Beyond the cottage walls, the orchard glowed under a pale moon, branches swaying as though they called her name.

She chewed her bottom lip, debating if she should risk stepping out by herself. Yet the restlessness in her bones was too strong to bear. She wasn't going to sleep tonight unless she confronted whatever tugged at her senses.

She slid open the window, letting the orchard's nocturnal air wash into her room. The freshness smelled of damp leaves and distant salt, a combination that made her heart skip. With quiet determination, Emma climbed onto the sill and swung her legs over the edge, pausing only to make sure her foot found steady purchase on the low ledge below.

She glanced around for the fox that sometimes roamed around Sadie's property, but the yard was empty. Her breath wavered in her throat as she dropped softly to the ground, brushing grass and dirt off her hands.

No lantern was lit outside, but the moon was bright enough for Emma to navigate the winding path that separated the cottage from the orchard's entrance. Silver light spilled across the edges of drooping apple boughs, illuminating each twist in the trunk. She tugged her sweater closer, remembering Sadie's many warnings.

The orchard might provide sanctuary for those who knew how to listen, but illusions could lurk here as well, especially if a powerful witch or warlock wanted to manipulate the shadows. Emma felt a distinct awareness beneath her feet, as though the orchard recognized her presence and rose to greet her.

She slipped into the grove, letting the row of trees guide her deeper toward the heart of the property. Weeds and wildflowers brushed against her ankles. Every now and then, a night bird called from somewhere above, but the orchard was mostly quiet.

Her fingers lightly touched the trunk of a nearby tree, seeking comfort in the rough bark. A faint warmth broke through her anxiety, reminding her that she refused to cower from magic that could be harnessed for good. Sadie had said that if Emma trusted her instincts, the orchard would reciprocate.

She followed an unspoken sense of direction, turning past clusters of apple branches into a small clearing. There, half-hidden by the curved trunk of a venerable oak, she spotted a familiar figure.

Ian leaned against the bark; one hand curled loose at his side. His dark hair caught thin streaks of moonlight. His jacket was slightly rumpled as though he hadn't planned on sleeping either. At first, Emma tensed, uncertain if he wanted her company in a place that felt so private.

Then she remembered the conversations they had shared, the mutual worry that kept them both on edge. Part of her suspected he might be relieved she found him.

Emma's soft footstep on the thick grass made him glance up. Their eyes met, and the tension in his shoulders eased. He made no effort to hide a small, grateful tilt of his lips. She stepped closer, drawn by the quiet magnetism she felt every time they stood in the orchard's hush together.

"I didn't think anyone else would be awake," Emma said, keeping her voice low. The night pressed around them, muffling every sound. Even the distant rustle of leaves seemed muted, as though nature herself held her breath.

Ian exhaled a shaky laugh. "I could say the same. Though I can't remember the last time I slept without nightmares." He looked away, his gaze fixed on the moonlit clearing as if searching for answers he had yet to find. "Something told me I might find peace here."

Emma nodded, a lump forming in her throat. She had heard him mention nighttime restlessness before, hints that illusions haunted him more severely than he admitted. She recalled Sadie's cautions against ignoring the signs of an overburdened warlock. Yet Emma couldn't help feeling a fierce sense of empathy whenever she saw the flickers of exhaustion in his eyes.

She shuffled closer, arms folded for warmth. "The orchard soothes me, too," she confessed. "I keep hoping it will calm the worst of my doubts, but lately I can hardly tell if the orchard is offering guidance or simply letting me wander."

He studied her in bluish gloom. "Maybe you're the one guiding it. Sadie told me once that land containing old magic learns to reflect the witch who walks it."

A swift ache of memory burned in Emma's chest. She hadn't realized Sadie ever spoke with Ian at enough length to offer orchard secrets. Yet something about that made sense: Sadie was protective of Emma, but she also recognized anyone wounded by illusions deserved a chance at healing. Maybe Sadie had seen the same pain in Ian that Emma saw now.

She gave him a faint, uncertain smile. "Did my grandmother mention anything else?" The question came out timid, as though she wasn't entirely sure she wanted the answer.

He hesitated, the tense line of his jaw hinting at the

weight of unspoken truths. "She warned me to tread carefully around illusions, yes, but she also said I shouldn't bury my need for connection out of fear."

His tone thinned, as though embarrassed by the candid admission. "Part of me thinks she caught me once, rummaging in the orchard, hoping to glean a protective object from one of the oaks. I told her I was hungry for any small relief. She gave me one of her hand-crafted wards, but it never seemed as strong as when she cast it."

Emma's mind returned to the wards Sadie used over the cottage. The protective runes had always glowed faintly whenever Emma or Sadie felt a spike of dark energy. If Ian had tried to replicate those wards alone, she understood how that might have fallen short.

Sadie's magic was complex, shaped by generations of Turner lineage. Emma wondered if her own blossoming power could help him more than he realized. The thought was both comforting and terrifying. She patted the tree behind her, nervously sliding her fingers across curling bark.

"Sadie's wards are rooted in our bloodline," Emma said. "She tried to teach me some of her incantations, but I'm still learning. I worry I will do more harm than good if I try to help you. This is all so new." She realized how vulnerable her words sounded, but the orchard's aura made pretense feel pointless.

A soft glimmer of understanding crossed his face. "I know. If it helps, your presence alone dulls the edges of my nightmares. Whenever you appear, I feel... steadier." He swallowed, his gaze dropping to the ground. "That probably sounds desperate."

Emma's heart gave a sharp tug, some combination of compassion and a spark of bittersweet longing. She remembered their brief, charged moments in the library corners and how her pulse had pounded with the sense that they were dancing near a cliff. "Then we can be desperate together," she finally managed, voice almost breaking. "I don't exactly have a perfect handle on illusions or curses. And the more I learn, the more I realize how reckless it is to charge ahead. Sometimes I question if I should trust magic at all… or trust my heart over reason."

"It feels like something bigger than either of us," he said quietly, letting the orchard's quiet swallow the space between them. The wind picked up, stirring his dark hair away from his forehead. He still looked exhausted, but in the moonlight, Emma caught a gentleness in his expression that made her throat tighten.

She remembered Sadie telling her not to run from powerful connections, even if those bonds seemed fraught with risk. Emma also remembered every rumor that warned her about warlocks with illusions in their blood. She stood at a precarious crossroad: either she reached out, or she walled herself off before the orchard's magic could entwine them further. Her heart hammered with the thought of stepping closer.

When she shifted her weight a fraction, her boot scuffed a patch of dirt. Ian lifted his head. For a moment, they simply stared at each other, the orchard's quiet giving shape to unspoken confessions.

Emma's mind spun with questions she lacked the courage to ask. She wondered how many times he had come here alone, hoping to outrun illusions that twisted his sleep. She wondered if her own presence could truly offer him a brief reprieve.

In silence, she stepped forward. Night air pressed warm against her cheeks, or perhaps that was just the heat flooding her veins. They were not quite shoulder to shoulder, but close enough that she could catch the steady cadence of his breathing. His jacket smelled faintly of pine and something else, a lingering trace of salt from the nearby sea.

She swallowed. "Ian?"

In the shadows of the orchard, his eyes appeared more luminous than usual, flecks of gold hinting at the energy that so often wrestled inside him. "Yes?"

Emma felt her pulse rattle as she gathered the nerve to speak. "I don't want you to be alone with your nightmares, but I'm also afraid I can't protect everyone. I don't even know if I can protect myself from illusions that might be lurking in Crestwood."

His voice was gentle. "Maybe protecting me is not your burden alone. Maybe what we need is a chance to figure this out together." He paused, letting the breeze dust leaves across the clearing. "I realize that might come across as naive, given all the caution your grandmother has offered you. I just—" He pressed his lips into a firm line. "I can't spend every night fighting illusions single-handedly."

Emma's chest constricted. She thought of the library's

dim corners, where they had whispered about half-researched spells and haunted memories. She remembered physically trembling at the slightest hint of Catherine's footsteps. Yet amid all that, she had felt safer with Ian than she ever expected.

She lowered her gaze to the ground, noticing a trail of fallen leaves scattered like silver coins in the moonlight. "I understand," she murmured. "I don't have many solutions, but I know I can't let fear drive me away from you. It is sickening, sometimes, how confusion and yearning get tangled up in my head."

Her confession made her cheeks burn, but she forced herself to hold his gaze again. "Sadie once said that the orchard listens for the truth in our hearts. Maybe tonight it will listen to yours... or mine."

Ian took a quiet step forward, the grass under his feet seeming louder than any thunder could have been in that moment. A subtle tension radiated from him, not hostility but something coiled with emotion. Emma felt her heartbeat quicken, uncertain if she wanted to pull back or close the distance between them. She stayed put, letting her nerves unravel in the orchard's silent watch.

He held her gaze. "Your grandmother told you that you have a knack for focusing magic without fully realizing it. You bring clarity just by being near. I have never had that clarity before. It feels like a luxury to stand here, not drowning in illusions."

Emma wondered if he felt the same crackle that wove through her, as though the orchard's energy pulsed under their feet, bridging invisible lines between their uncertain hearts. She couldn't deny that something about Ian's presence gave her a sense of completeness, a notion that baffled her rational mind. They had barely known each other for more than a handful of encounters, yet a lifetime of secrets seemed to bind them.

She looked down, trying to quiet the trembling in her hands. The orchard glimmered under the moon, branches twisted overhead in a canopy that felt both protective and ominous. Tendrils of vine curled around the nearest trunk, and Emma sensed a heartbeat in the ground, if only in her imagination.

"You asked if you should trust magic or your heart," Ian said softly. "Maybe they are not separate. Maybe your heart is just telling you where your magic wants you to step."

Emma's lips curled into a delicate smile, the orchard listening in on their conversation like a silent third presence. The moment was so unexpectedly intimate that she had to coax herself to take a steady breath.

She recalled how earlier that evening, she had wrestled with the question of whether this unsettled feeling in her chest was excitement or fear. Now, it didn't seem to matter. Both emotions filled her with equal measure.

She lifted her eyes and found his expression mirroring her own. A slight tension lingered in the quick movements of his hands, as if he was counting the reasons to hold back but lacked the will to do so. Moonlight carved the angles of his face, highlighting the worry that lingered just beneath his calm.

Without warning, a wind swept through the orchard,

lifting stray leaves into a gentle dance around them. The hush that followed felt charged. Emma had the sudden urge to bridge the final gap between them, to touch him in a way that might reassure them both they were not alone in this labyrinth of illusions and curses.

She took one last breath for courage. Then she closed the space between them, heart pounding so loudly she was certain he could hear it. Her voice trembled as she spoke. "You once said my presence blunted your nightmares. Let me try."

His eyes darkened with emotion, and for an instant, Emma wondered if she had overstepped. But he didn't move away. Instead, he swallowed hard, lips parting with words that didn't fully form. Their proximity sent a warm hum along Emma's skin, the orchard's hush intensifying as though each branch, each leaf, waited for her to speak again.

She didn't speak. Instead, she lifted her hand, hesitant fingers hovering near his arm. Part of her mind clambered for an escape in case he recoiled. But he didn't. A flicker of hope lit his features, and that was all the encouragement she needed.

By the time Emma tentatively placed her hand on Ian's arm, they were closer than they had ever been—bonded by uncertainty, yearning, and the promise that all roads ahead would be as dangerous as they would be intoxicating.

TWO

Moonlight bathed the orchard in pale silver, turning every leaf and twisted branch into a haze of glimmering shapes. Emma stood close to Ian, her heartbeat racing as his hand angled her chin upward. While the rest of the world seemed to wait in tense silence, she allowed herself to focus on the warmth of his skin against hers. She felt the night's cool air swirling across the back of her neck, prickling her senses. The orchard felt very much awake, as if it had paused its slow breathing just for them.

She looked into Ian's eyes, gold flecks barely visible in the low light, but present enough to stir a keen awareness in her. He was still so much a mystery, a warlock carrying burdens that his slender frame and gentle expression belied. Yet her heart softened whenever she saw the flicker of vulnerability he tried so hard to hide. She could almost believe the rustling leaves had gone still on purpose, granting them a moment free of illusions and old curses.

His voice, quiet and tentative, reached her amid the steady drum of her pulse. "Emma?"

She angled her head, the blade of moonlight brushing her hair so it gleamed at the edges. "Yes?" she replied softly.

A trembling breath passed his lips. His fingers grazed her cheek, sending a jolt of surprise and heat through her. They had shared glances and half-steps of closeness before, but this readiness, this boldness—felt new and thrilling. As his fingers trailed upward, she realized she wanted that gentle contact every bit as much as he seemed to need it. A swirl of nervous excitement churned in her stomach.

She parted her lips to speak, but words failed her; all her thoughts tangled in the electricity in the air. Ian leaned in, and his breath fanned over her face, mingling wind-scent and something deeper, maybe the faint spice he always carried.

The orchard, for once, didn't intrude with flickers of illusions. No strange rustles or half-shaped silhouettes. Just quiet, moonlit acceptance, as if the orchard itself had decided to give them this fragile peace.

She shut her eyes, surrendering, and felt his mouth brush hers. That first featherlight press of his lips ignited her senses, a sweet jolt snapping through her like a spark. Her entire body responded, shoulders going taut with surprise, then melting as she eased into the kiss.

The orchard's magic seemed to flare beneath the surface of her skin, as if it recognized this union of energies. She tasted a hint of salt, the remnant of his earlier anxiety, and something warm that reminded her she wasn't alone in her heartbreaks or fears.

Emma felt the jolt of it deep in her bones, her body lighting up at the sensation of his mouth on hers. Warm, firm, careful. Her fingers caught the edge of his sleeve, a silent plea, and that was all it took.

Ian let out a shaky breath, and then he kissed her again—deeper this time, more certain, more there. His hands framed her face now, thumbs skimming over her cheekbones, tilting her head just the way he wanted. Heat flared low in her stomach as he angled his body closer, pressing just enough for her to feel the warmth of him against the night's chill.

Emma melted into it, into him.

One of her hands slid up, fingers threading into the dark strands of his hair, tugging just slightly, just enough to make him exhale sharply against her lips. The sound sent a shiver straight down her spine. His grip on her tightened in response, one hand slipping down to her waist, fingers splaying over the curve of her hip as if anchoring himself to her.

He kissed her like she was something he had been starving for, something forbidden but irresistible.

The world blurred. Nothing else existed—not the orchard, not the warnings echoing in the back of her mind, not the dangers waiting for them beyond this moment. Just the heat of Ian's mouth, the way he tasted like salt and something sweetly intoxicating, the way he sighed against her when she bit lightly at his lower lip.

The orchard pulsed around them, responding to the surge of energy between them.

The kiss deepened, slow and unhurried but devastatingly thorough. Ian took his time, as if trying to memorize every inch of her mouth, as if he didn't trust himself to stop once he started. Emma's body pressed against his without thinking, without hesitation. She felt the sharp inhale he took when she curled her fingers against the back of his neck, dragging him impossibly closer.

His restraint was unraveling.

And gods, she wanted him to lose it completely.

Emma tilted her head, letting him take what he wanted, letting herself take what she wanted. His lips parted against hers, his tongue tracing the seam of her mouth before she let him in. A slow, languid slide of heat that sent a rush of electricity through her veins.

His hand slipped under the hem of her sweater, fingers trailing fire over the bare skin at her waist. Emma gasped into the kiss, and Ian groaned softly, like he was barely holding himself together.

He pulled back just enough to rest his forehead against hers, their breaths mingling in the cool air. His fingers still pressed against her skin, his body still taut with tension.

They stood there, wrapped in the lingering heat of the kiss, the orchard watching with silent approval.

When the kiss broke, leaving her heart punching against her ribs, Emma unraveled from intimacy with a quivering inhale. She let her gaze drift from the subtle curve of Ian's bottom lip to the faint lines of worry etched around his eyes.

His expression brimmed with a disbelief she felt in herself. "That was probably—" He struggled to find words and exhaled. "I have wanted to do that for... longer than I should admit."

She managed to smile. "I'm glad you did."

They stood there, exchanging breaths. A shiver raced through Emma's limbs, but it had nothing to do with the night's chill and everything to do with the sudden closeness.

She could sense Ian's hesitation. The wariness he never fully shed flickered across his features, reminding her that deep fears likely still tugged at him. Yet in the afterglow of that kiss, she felt him trying to believe it was all right to share these soft, dangerous moments.

He glanced away, nudging a fallen apple with his toe. "I hope," he began, "I hope this isn't another thing I have to run from."

Her chest tightened. She recalled the night she first saw him in the woods. "You don't have to run from me," she said gently.

Ian swallowed, his gaze sweeping the length of her throat before fixing on her eyes. "I'm not used to... closeness," he admitted. "Not when nightmares might strike without warning."

Soft wind curled over them, setting the leaves overhead trembling. Emma raised a hand, letting her fingertips brush the side of his face. "We can figure it out," she said, voice low. "Nightmares, illusions, the rest of this tangled mess. For now, it's just us."

He let out a quiet laugh that sounded almost disbelieving. "You make it sound simple."

"I wish it was." She settled her palm over his shoulder, feeling the tension in the line of his muscles. The orchard's thick smell of loamy soil and moss swirled around them. "But... I don't want to push you away. I'm tired of letting fear decide everything."

Ian's dark lashes lowered. For an instant, his wariness cracked, revealing a raw mixture of hope and vulnerability that rippled through him. She felt his arm slide around her waist, slowly enough to give her time to pull away if she wanted. She didn't. Instead, she leaned against him, inhaling his warmth.

They stayed pressed close in that quiet embrace, broken only by the whisper of nocturnal insects. A single star flickered overhead, peeking through the canopy as if bearing silent witness.

Emma tried to store the sensation of his arms around her for safekeeping. These fleeting moments of comfort had felt impossible weeks ago, when her mind reeled with distrust and confusion. Now, she realized that letting her heart open took more strength than any incantation she had cast.

His chin rested gently at the top of her head. After a moment, he spoke against her hair. "Do you think... do you think the orchard approves?" His voice carried a nervous grin. "Feels like it's watching us."

She tilted her head to catch his eyes, an amused twitch at her lips. "If it didn't approve," she teased, "we'd probably sense the branches swaying in protest. But I don't feel anything ominous."

She risked a glance at the nearest apple bough, which hung heavy with fruit despite the late hour. Nothing stirred. The trees wore an almost protective aura, as though they guarded this fragile unity between them.

He eased back slightly, though he kept her within the circle of his arms. A question formed in his expression. "Emma, do you regret it?" he asked softly. "Kissing me?"

Her response came before she could overthink. "No." Warmth rushed along her cheeks. She clutched his shirt, the fabric brushing her knuckles. "I don't regret it."

His relief was evident, and he closed his eyes for a fraction of a second, as if releasing a tension that had coiled too tightly in him. Emma's heart squeezed at the thought that perhaps no one had ever told him it was all right to be close, that his magic or his curse didn't have to overshadow every sincere moment. She might not be able to solve all his worries, but she could stand beside him without flinching.

A faint hum prickled at the back of her mind, and for a moment, she stiffened. Magic sometimes stirred unpredictably when her emotions ran high. She cast a furtive glance around the orchard, expecting a swirl of illusions or flicker of unnatural light. However, she saw only the thick trunk of the closest oak and a shimmer of moonbeams caught in the tall grass. The orchard's wards, at least for now, appeared stable.

She stepped out of Ian's embrace, though not too far, and smoothed her sweater's rumpled edge. "I can't give you every answer," Emma said. "I've barely learned to control my own power, and... there's so much we don't know."

He tilted his head in acknowledgment, lines of seriousness returning to his brow. "I know."

"But I want to be here," she continued firmly, voice quivering only slightly. "If illusions come for you again, or if worry gnaws at you..." We can protect ourselves. Together."

Ian's lips quirked with what looked like gratitude. He trailed a thumb across her cheek. "That together part means more to me than you realize."

Perhaps it had always been nudging them toward this shared resolve. Emma's breath caught at the thought that her grandmother, in her own quiet way, might have hoped for this alliance. Even so, Emma pushed that rush of sentiment aside, focusing on the present. She couldn't wade too deeply into regrets or the illusions that might lurk beyond. Tonight should be about trust. If only for this slender, starlit hour.

Ian's arm drifted to her elbow, a gentle nudge drawing her attention back to him. "Thank you," he whispered.

She offered a small, wry laugh. "Don't thank me for kissing you," she said, cheeks warming again. "I wanted that, too."

He chuckled, more ease in his eyes than she had seen before. "Not just for that. For not treating me like I'm one step away from unleashing something terrible." He hesitated. "I still fear I might, but... you make me believe in another path."

Emma understood that fear. She let her hand glide along his forearm, feeling the subtle tension in the corded muscle, the faint hum of his warlock energy. "I've seen how some things aren't exactly as they seem," she said softly. "But I also see that you're you." Her breath caught for half a second. Opening herself like this felt terrifying. "If it ever becomes too much, we'll handle it. That's all I can promise. We won't let illusions define us."

He curved a hand around her waist, pulling her nearer. She sensed that longing again, a pull that made her pulse pound. This time, she rose onto her toes first. The second kiss was deeper, warmed by the promise they had just given each other.

It reached something in her that ached for safety and acceptance. Her head spun as their lips met, and an upswell of energy sparked in her core. She half expected the orchard to respond with glimmers of light or swirling leaves, but the grove stayed subdued, allowing them this quiet intimacy.

When the kiss broke once more, she found her body felt both weightless and anchored, as if their connection had grounded her. She couldn't have stepped away if the trees caught fire. Yet she managed to draw back an inch, enough to meet his trembling gaze.

He tucked a stray strand of her hair behind her ear. "I'm sorry I'm not calmer," he murmured, voice thick with emotion. "Part of me worries that any strong feeling I have might wake illusions in my mind."

Her heart panged with sympathy. "I know," she said. "But you don't have to apologize for caring," she swallowed. "Just... don't vanish. Not unless it's really what you want."

He traced the curve of her jaw, a ghost of a smile touching his lips. "I don't want to vanish. Not from you."

Soft comfort emanated from the forest floor beneath her boots. A raccoon scurried in the distance, rustling leaves, but the creature kept its distance. She touched the center of Ian's chest, feeling the slight hammer of his heartbeat as it matched her own unsteady rhythm.

She found her voice amid the swirl of sensations. "How do you feel?"

He drew a trembling breath. "I feel awake." He let out a hesitant laugh. "That might sound strange, but it's like... everything inside me is still fragile, but it's not as dark. Your presence helps me chase the shadows back."

Her heart swelled at the thought. "Good," she whispered. "You do the same for me, you know. Whenever I start doubting myself, you remind me that it's okay to try. That I'm not alone."

He lowered his forehead to hers, and for a moment, they simply breathed in unison. Emma studied the line of his face, memorizing the angle of his cheekbones and the slight furrow that had eased at the corners of his eyes. She never imagined she could feel so vulnerable and so safe at once.

A gentle breeze stirred through the trees. The branches overhead quivered, letting thin beams of moonlight shift between them. The hush of night insects continued.

Emma caught the faint perfume of crushed grass underfoot, mingling with the natural musk of Ian's jacket.

Her awareness of the orchard sharpened, as though her senses had expanded from the rush of contact between them.

She rested her cheek on his chest, letting the quiet settle over them like a soft blanket. Time felt slow, measured only by the pattern of his breaths and the intermittent chirp of crickets. She didn't know how long they stood like that, but eventually, she felt a subtle shift. The air seemed to press in with unspoken curiosity, or maybe the orchard recognized that humans couldn't remain in suspended bliss forever.

She stepped back, gliding her hands from his shoulders to his wrists. Heat lingered in her veins, making her skin tingle. Her lips still felt warm from the kisses they shared. He watched her, eyes shining with a mixture of hope and caution.

She tried to find the right words, but nothing came. Ian's expression conveyed that he, too, wrestled with the rawness of what had passed between them. Their bond, delicate yet compelling, was no longer just an idea. It was a real thread that bound them more tightly than any incantation could.

She squeezed his fingers, gently letting them go. "We should... breathe," she said softly. Her heart still pounded, and she couldn't stop smiling. "That was... a lot."

He nodded, stepping back in unison. The space between them felt as charged as the moment they first kissed, but this time, a calm acceptance replaced the desperate thrum of adrenaline.

They exchanged a long look, a mixture of relief and

lingering tension. Emma drew in the cool night air. She felt an undeniable closeness to Ian, as though they had waded into deeper waters together.

Slowly, she trailed her gaze around the ring of trees. The night was full of potential, but it was also late, and she was certain the cottage lamp had been left glowing. Her stomach fluttered at the thought of walking back alone, her mind reckless with the feel of Ian's kiss. Yet she couldn't bring herself to regret any of it.

He dipped his head, murmuring her name in a voice rough with emotion. "Emma?"

She stepped forward—not to close the distance entirely, but to keep the bond unbroken. "I'm ready," she said, even though she couldn't define exactly what she was ready for. Possibly everything. Possibly just learning how to hold onto these warm sparks in the darkness.

He swallowed hard. She noticed the pulse at his throat jump. He ran a hand through his hair, exhaling. Then they both eased away. Footsteps brushed the soft grass, dew clinging to their ankles.

They hardly spoke while they withdrew from that intimate circle of the orchard, but neither of them looked away. Every movement felt deliberate, as if balancing on the cusp of a promise neither wanted to break.

They reached a clearing bordered by a group of ancient oaks, their thick trunks forming a quiet boundary. Emma's cheeks still burned. Ian's eyes, however, were steady on her. It wasn't the hungry apparition of illusions but a genuine gaze, full of unspoken emotion.

She let out a final shuddery breath. Slowly, she and Ian

came to stand face-to-face in the moonlit glow, leaving only a half-step between them. Heartbeats pounded in that thread of space. She noticed how his hand hovered near her elbow, tempted to close the distance again, but holding back out of respect for the clarity they both needed.

Emma's voice was no more than a hush. "Whatever comes next," she said, "we'll face it."

He dipped his head, a fleeting smile crossing his lips. "We will," he answered softly.

They each took one small step back, easing the intensity of their closeness, yet maintaining the fragile thread of connection. The quiet carried their steady exhales, and the moonlight caught the warmth in each other's eyes, bearing witness as they stood facing one another in that ring of ancient trees, alone and together in equal measure.

THREE

Emma awoke to a glow of warmth that made her heart skip. Her cheeks still flushed as she recalled the stolen moment with Ian from last night. The memory of his lips against hers lingered in her thoughts, refusing to be dismissed by the morning light. Even at dawn, with sunlight stretching across her bedroom's small window, her entire body felt alight with both anticipation and guilt. She sat upright in bed, fingers pressing over her lips as though the gentle pressure might pull her back into that charged instant.

She forced a steady breath. She knew that Sadie would caution her not to surrender to raw emotion. Magic fed on feeling, and letting it spark to life without control could be dangerous. Yet Emma couldn't ignore the deep thrum in her chest that pulsed every time her mind returned to Ian. She closed her eyes, recalling the moonlit shadows, the faint rustle of leaves under her boots, and the eager tilt of his head when he drew her closer. The thought brought a rush of warmth that made her head spin all over again.

Eventually, she peeled away her bed sheets and stood. The hardwood floor felt cool against her bare feet. She slipped on a light sweater to ward off the early breeze, then made her way to the small mirror resting on a dresser. Dark rings under her eyes revealed how poorly she had slept. Her mind had buzzed through the night, refusing to settle even after she crawled under her quilt. At one point, she thought she heard the distant call of an owl, though the memory might have drifted between waking and dreaming. She pushed away a stray lock of hair, exhaling softly.

She padded along the cottage's creaking floors, inhaling the blend of herbal fragrance and faint salt that always seemed to cling to Sadie's home. She heard a soft hum from the kitchen, the sound of Sadie preparing tea. Emma paused in the hallway, uncertain if she wanted to face her grandmother's keen gaze just yet. Sadie's perception rarely missed anything, and Emma's face felt too warm to hide her swirling emotions.

"Sleeping well?" Sadie called in a gentle tone, her voice carrying into the hallway. There was kindness in the question, but also a hint of amusement. Emma doubted Sadie truly believed she had slept soundly.

Emma cleared her throat. "Well enough," she said when she stepped into the kitchen. She kept her hands folded behind her back. "I woke up early. I... might have a little practice session this morning on the porch, if that's all right."

Sadie offered a knowing smile, stirring the tea. She was dressed in a loose cardigan and worn slippers, silver-streaked hair gathered into a low bun. "You look restless." She set the wooden spoon aside. "Something on your mind?"

Emma felt her cheeks betray her with a slight flush. She wanted to mention the current that stoked her entire body whenever she pictured Ian's face. Instead, she slid onto a nearby chair, feigning a casual shrug. "I'm fine. Maybe I just need to burn some energy with a spell or two."

Sadie arched an eyebrow, though her smile remained gentle. "Then you should. Just remember to stay focused. Letting your mind wander might unravel the incantation."

Emma nodded, biting her lip against too vivid a recollection of Ian's quiet voice under moonlight. Her grandmother's words carried a warning that was more than simple advice. Emma felt the reminder: illusions, curses, and deeper threats were never far behind. She released a shaky breath and rose from the table. "I'll be careful," she said. "I promise."

Outside, the morning air was crisp and cool. The orchard stretched some distance behind the cottage, leaves drifting in gentle motion. The porch creaked when she stepped onto its wooden boards, and she lifted her gaze toward the sky. Thin clouds glowed with traces of pale gold. Her pulse quickened as she placed both feet firmly, bracing herself for a simple summoning spell Sadie once demonstrated.

She closed her eyes and recited the words from

memory. Her breath fanned out in slow beats, and her fingertips tingled as she coaxed a thin strand of magic from her core. She used to dread spells like this, worried they might reveal more than she could control. Yet now, the orchard's subtle energy felt familiar, like a second heartbeat.

She began chanting softly, letting the incantation roll across her tongue:

"Let wind and leaf converge in light,

Awaken now to gifted sight..."

The air stirred, swirling around her ankles. A faint glow shimmered in front of her outstretched hand. Emma kept her mind on the technique Sadie had taught her, shaping the invisible forces into a small flutter of energy. She pictured a gentle spiral of wind rising over the cottage steps.

But then she remembered the brush of Ian's hand against hers, how effortlessly he had melted her anxieties in that charged moment. A sudden wave of longing surged into her thoughts, and her control faltered. The glow intensified and flared. The swirl of wind came alive with abrupt force, kicking up leaves and rattling the overhead branches.

Alarmed, Emma opened her eyes. She tried to pull back, heart pounding, but the magic refused to obey her fractured focus. The gust exploded in a wild burst, shaking the porch rails and cracking a flowerpot against the side of the cottage. Bits of pottery clattered down the steps.

Before Emma could react, Sadie rushed onto the porch. Her grandmother's voice cut through the air in a brisk incantation that Emma recognized from old diaries. A soothing calm blanketed the rogue energy, steadying it until the wind settled. Broken bits of pottery tumbled to a rest against the porch rail.

Emma stood there; face flushed with embarrassment. Sadie lowered her hands and gave Emma a gentle look. "Are you injured?"

Emma shook her head, eyes still brimming with regret. "No... I'm so sorry. I lost concentration. I didn't mean to—"

Sadie silenced her with a soft wave of her hand. "No harm done. But you must be more mindful." Her tone softened even further. "Magic is shaped by emotions, Emma. All it takes is a burst of excitement or fear to reshape a single incantation into something else."

Emma swallowed. She could still feel her heart hammering. "Did I damage anything besides the flowerpot?"

Sadie's eyes landed momentarily on the scattered pottery fragments, then returned to Emma. "Only the pot, which can be replaced. You, on the other hand, can't be." She paused; kindness laced in every syllable. "I know your mind is elsewhere. You don't have to tell me why, but I suspect I already know. Just be cautious."

Emma nodded sheepishly. Sadie smiled and handed her a small broom propped against the porch wall. Emma took it, her body still buzzing with leftover adrenaline. While she swept the broken pieces into a neat pile, Sadie used a few whispered words to calm the lingering magic. The orchard's rustling quieted, as though the land itself recognized that all was well again.

When they finished tidying, Sadie laid a comforting hand on Emma's shoulder. "Take the day to center yourself," she suggested. "Organize your mind and your heart before you attempt further spells."

Emma nodded, grateful for her grandmother's understanding. The swirl of shame receded, though the memory of Ian's face still simmered in her chest, fueling the distraction that had nearly flung magic out of control.

She spent the next hour dusting the cottage windowsills, one of many chores she had skillfully avoided until now. Each sweep of the rag felt mechanical, an effort to keep her thoughts from drifting to last night. Eventually, she paused by the window, letting her gaze wander across the orchard's entrance. The sunlight highlighted green leaves and the occasional glimmer of red apples deeper inside. Her heart squeezed with the memory of how she had ventured there at night, footsteps uncertain until she spotted Ian's silhouette among the trees.

Every time she let her guard down, the memory of that kiss flickered into her awareness. She could almost taste the salt of the wind lingering on his lips. The thought left her throat dry, so she pushed it away by returning to her dusting. With a determined inhale, she straightened the row of small ceramic trinkets Sadie used for mixing dried herbs, each shaped like animals. She was grateful for any distraction. She moved from the living room to the small den, adjusting a pile of old books that chronicled local folklore. The covers felt worn under her fingertips, and she remembered the many nights she had pored over them in search of magical knowledge.

She couldn't keep wandering the house forever. Eventually, she grabbed a cloth and ventured outside to check on a few paths that Sadie wanted cleared of fallen branches. The gentle sunlight brushed her skin as she followed the winding path through the trees swaying in a mild breeze. She paused at a juncture where one old apple tree arched over a small patch of wildflowers. The flowers danced, their petals nodding in color. She bent to pick up stray twigs from the ground, occasionally glancing around to see if a fox or a wandering doe might appear.

Sadie had often reminded her that the orchard's magic was living, sensitive to emotions. Still, an undercurrent of nervous energy slipped through her spine. She set her jaw and kept working, hoping manual labor might be enough to steady the flutter in her stomach.

By late afternoon, she had finished storing the broken twigs near the compost area behind the cottage. Her legs felt tired, and her skin glowed with the warmth of mild exertion. She wiped her forehead, glancing back at the orchard's rows. The day had passed without any reappearance of uncontrollable magic, and for that, she was relieved. Yet the ache of longing for Ian's presence hadn't lessened.

She wandered inside, where Sadie was tinkering with a small pot of herbs on the stove. The aroma of rosemary drifted through the air. Emma set a teapot on the counter and offered a shy smile. "Need help?"

Sadie shook her head, stirring the mixture. "Not at the

moment. Why not take a seat? You look like you have been out in the heat for hours."

Emma sighed. She settled at the small kitchen table, eyes fixed on the curling steam rising from Sadie's pot. "I tried to keep busy," she admitted. "I thought it might help me forget certain... distractions."

Sadie gave a thoughtful hum but didn't press. Emma adored that about her grandmother: she offered space rather than prodding for details. Emma found herself drumming her fingers on the tabletop, lost in a swirl of recollections about Ian's gaze or the comforting breeze that had wrapped around them both.

She forced herself to stand and took a glass from the cupboard, filling it with water. A fleeting moment of silence passed, broken only by the soft crackle of whatever Sadie brewed. Emma lifted the cup to her lips, letting the cool water anchor her. She started thinking of ways to release the tension that had tied itself in knots at the base of her spine. Maybe a bath with a pinch of lavender oil would help, or a quiet reading session with her mother's old marine biology texts. She needed any method to quell the rush of swirling emotion that threatened her magical focus.

As the sunlight dimmed beyond the windows, Emma busied herself with dinner. She prepared a simple meal of vegetable soup and bread, hoping the simple motions of chopping and stirring would keep her mind grounded. Sadie stayed close, occasionally tasting the broth and offering a comment. The mild chatter about dusty cookbooks and half-forgotten recipes only partially masked Emma's thoughts, but she appreciated the reprieve.

When they finally ate, the small dining area felt cozy and calm. Sadie told her a brief story about an old family recipe for spiced cider, describing how the orchard's apples had refused to spoil one autumn long ago. Emma nodded at each twist, but her mind slipped repeatedly back to Ian. She wondered if he felt the same longing today, if he too had struggled to focus on spells or chores.

Sadie's voice cut softly through Emma's musings. "You seem a thousand miles away. If you need rest, don't push it too hard."

Emma blinked. Her spoon hovered just above her bowl. The soup's steam curled in lazy spirals. "Yes," she said quietly. "Maybe I'll turn in early."

She cleared the dishes soon after, ignoring Sadie's suggestion that she at least finish her bread. Her stomach felt twisted in anticipation of something she couldn't name, so she retreated to the quiet of her bedroom. Her walls were lined with small trinkets and the sounds of the ocean seeped through the open window. She ran her hand over the windowsill, recalling how she had slipped out in the middle of the night to meet Ian among the trees.

She prepared for bed, brushing her hair with slow strokes, then stepped into a soft nightgown that felt comforting against her skin. The evening air brought a delicate chill, so she wrapped herself in a light blanket and sat on the edge of her bed.

Her heart pounded at the memory of Ian's final words to her before they had parted. She remembered the way he had inhaled, as though savoring the moment. Even now, she could see his gaze in her mind's eye, the subtle flecks of gold that hinted at marvelous secrets.

The day had been a blur of distractions, chores, and suppressed emotions. Now, in the privacy of her dim room, she confronted the truth: she wanted to be near him again. The thought made her insides flutter with a mix of eagerness and fear. Sadie was right that raw emotion could unravel spells, but how could Emma shut down the tug in her chest that called her to him?

She slid under the covers, curling on her side. The faint creak of the old cottage lulled her, and she exhaled softly, letting her eyes drift shut. She recited a small chant in her head, hoping it might slow the tender ache that pulsed through her thoughts. Burke, a friendly cat that sometimes roamed outside, mewed faintly at the wall. She half-wished the fox would appear just to offer a curious distraction.

Yet no fox, no cat, no owl dared interrupt. Emma closed her eyes tighter, her mind filling with the imagery of last night's orchard path. She pictured Ian leaning against that twisted trunk, breath purling into the rest of the orchard. She recalled how her own chest felt tight, how her fingers trembled until she placed her hand on his arm. Her lips tingled at the memory. Even hours later, a single breath was enough to bring that taste of moonlit enchantment back to life.

She sank deeper into her pillow and released a quiet shiver. She didn't know if she should yearn for him again or erect walls to keep herself safe. Her heart told her to trust the warmth between them, but caution lurked at the edges, reminding her that illusions and curses prowled Crestwood. She swallowed, unsure which urge was stronger.

Her tired limbs finally began to relax. Her breathing slowed. Sleep teased at the corners of her consciousness, whispering that tomorrow would bring its own challenges. As she felt her mind slip away, the ache in her chest pulsed one final time.

She fell asleep that night still aching for the spark of Ian's presence, torn between curiosity, longing, and the certain knowledge that true danger lurked nearer every time she dropped her guard.

CHAPTER

FOUR

Emma shivered against the cool wind that swept in from the sea. The late-morning sky hung over Crestwood in heavy, gray clouds, threatening a storm that had yet to break. She clutched the sleeves of her sweater as she followed the winding path along the cliffs. The ocean's crashing roar reverberated in her chest, each wave slamming the shore below and stirring a fresh gust of salt air. She felt on edge, almost as though the sea's unrest reflected the turmoil spinning inside her mind.

She spotted Ian standing near an outcropping of tall grass. His posture was rigid, arms crossed protectively over his chest, and even from a distance, she recognized the tension in his shoulders. Shadows circled his eyes, so dark they looked like smears of ash. His sleepless nights had taken a toll. Emma slowed her approach, swallowing the hollow feeling in her throat. Each step brought her closer until she saw the tightness in his jaw, the way his fingers dug into the worn fabric of his jacket.

She cleared her throat softly. "Ian," she said, hoping he could find some comfort simply in her presence. The wind gusted against her words, scattering them over the cliffs.

He turned and let his arms fall to his sides. His eyes held a familiar warmth, but they were laced with exhaustion that made her chest tighten. He forced a small smile that betrayed the weariness he fought to hide. "I hoped you would find me," he murmured. His voice sounded raw and scratchy, as though he had spent the night wrestling nightmares rather than sleeping.

She drew closer, the wind ruffling her hair around her face. Below, the surf crashed in a thunderous rhythm. "I'm glad you're here," she replied. "I was worried when I got your message." She had awakened earlier to find a short note wedged between the pages of an old orchard ledger, telling her to meet him on the coastline path. He seldom asked for help openly. That alone was cause enough for concern.

He exhaled slowly, gazing out over the water. "I had another one last night," he said, his voice barely above a whisper. "A nightmare so vivid that I woke up screaming. It felt... real. Like the illusions had torn a hole in my mind."

Emma stepped forward until she stood at his side. The damp grass brushed her ankles. She looked at his profile, taking in the rigid line of his jaw and the shallow lines etched at the corners of his eyes. "What did you see?" she asked gently.

He swallowed, his Adam's apple bobbing in his throat. Then he closed his eyes as though bracing himself. "Spectral shapes. They walked right out of the shadows in my room. They whispered in voices I recognized, but I'm too shaken to recall exactly whose. I think they were illusions that Catherine created before, shapes she used to torment me, but each time they appear, they feel stronger."

Emma's heart lurched at the mention of Catherine, the librarian who, for some reason, made her hair stand on end. Emma couldn't shake the memory of how Catherine had singled out Ian's vulnerabilities to manipulate his dreams. "Are they threatening you?" she asked. "Or me?" Fear twisted inside her at the thought that Catherine might have discovered new ways to reach him.

He opened his eyes and met her gaze. Their dark gold color flickered in the gray light. "They stood over me, whispering my name. Then they said it would soon be your turn." His voice shook slightly. "I can't tell whether they spoke the truth or if it was just another twisted illusion. Either way, the nightmares seemed to feed off my terror. Every moment I tried to fight back, the shapes drew closer."

Emma laid a hand on his arm, feeling how tightly he gripped his jacket sleeve. "I won't let them drag you under," she said, injecting as much resolve as she could into her words. She could still remember the night in the orchard, where they had stolen kisses under the moonlight. Those gentle moments felt worlds away now, overshadowed by the creeping darkness that haunted his rest.

He closed his eyes at her touch, as though grounding himself in that small gesture. "I'm afraid, Emma," he admitted. "Afraid this curse in my blood, the illusions, all of it... will infect you, too. There's a story passed down on my father's side—my great-uncle's fiancée fell victim to matching nightmares. Supposedly, the illusions destroyed her mind, and he fled Crestwood to spare her more pain. The family never saw him again."

She hadn't known that detail. Sadie had mentioned that the Williams family had a dark tangle of tragedies in its past, but hearing this reminded her how deeply fear ran in Ian's lineage. She squeezed his arm, then carefully laced her fingers through his. "I can't promise everything is going to be easy," she said quietly. "But I do know that my grandmother has methods to tame restless spirits, illusions, or anything that hunts us in our sleep. She taught me a few techniques to calm the mind so illusions can't latch on as easily. We can try them, if you're willing."

He let out a slow breath, enveloping her smaller hand in his. A gust of wind swept across them, carrying the tang of salt and the faint crackle of distant thunder. "I'm willing," he whispered, as though the confession cost him more energy than he had to spare. "I just don't know if it will be enough."

They turned as one and began walking up the narrow path that curved closer to a rocky ledge. The sea churned below them, sending up a haze of brine that settled on Emma's cheeks. She felt the tension in Ian's grip and tried to match her pace to his. "Come," she said, "let's find a spot to sit. We can at least go through the first calming step Sadie taught me."

He nodded, the faint lines of worry etched in his face. Together, they moved to a flat outcropping that overlooked the waves. The wind whipped the grass around their ankles. Emma guided him to sit on a patch of smooth stone, and she settled beside him, legs crossing beneath her. They faced the open water. The horizon was streaked with dark purple clouds. Lightning flickered in the distance, but the storm held off, rumbling as if it were waiting for them to speak.

Emma inhaled to steady herself. She recalled how Sadie would place her hands around a trembling animal to calm it, gently weaving a chant that bridged the gap between fear and peace. She had less confidence in her ability to do this for Ian, whose nightmares sprang from a centuries-old family curse, but she had to try. "Do you remember the orchard?" she asked softly. "The night we... we found quiet among the apple trees?"

A faint smile ghosted across his lips. "I do," he murmured. "It felt safe, somehow. Even with all the tension crackling between us, there was this calm that made it hard to think about anything but... well... you."

Heat warmed her cheeks at the memory. "I want you to try holding onto that feeling," she said. "That calm. Think of the orchard, its leaves rustling at night, your breath steady. Imagine the illusions dissolving in that moonlit quiet, replaced by the orchard's acceptance." She paused to recall the chant Sadie had once demonstrated. The words felt rusty on her tongue, but she trusted the intention behind them.

Placing her free hand on top of their joined fingers, she began in a gentle, low tone.

"In gentle sway of orchard deep
Hush the mind and cradle sleep.
By sea and leaf, release my sight,
Let nightmares yield to peaceful night."

Ian's posture eased fractionally. He closed his eyes and exhaled shakily. Emma watched him, noticing how his face relaxed at the edges. His shoulders no longer pressed so tensely against his collarbones. She continued speaking, letting the words roll through the space between them.

"By brine and root, by calm of air,
Let illusions fade into humble prayer.
In orchard's hush and dawn so bright,
Cradle this heart through darkest fright."

He didn't speak, but his breathing grew more even, and Emma could faintly sense a warmth in her chest, similar to the rush she felt whenever her emotions allowed her magic to twist outward. A small part of her mind knew this was only a first step. Sadie's instructions were always thorough, urging repeated sessions and layered wards for deeper healing. Still, she hoped offering Ian this flicker of solace might steady him for a time.

When she finished, the silence lingered, laced with the

distant thunder and the crash of waves below. Ian slowly opened his eyes, a moisture shining in them that wasn't quite tears. He squeezed her hand, gazing at her with raw gratitude. "I can still feel them," he said, voice wavering only slightly, "like shadows at the edge of my mind. But your chant... it's keeping them from lunging forward."

She smiled, relief mingling with caution. "That's how Sadie's spells often work," she replied. "They're about coaxing illusions back into the darkness; never forcing them out with brute strength. They feed on fear, so if we can replace a bit of that fear with calm, they lose some of their hold."

He bowed his head, as though the responsibility of a centuries-old curse weighed more heavily in the face of her kindness. "I wish I could scrub them out entirely," he rasped. "Sometimes, I'm terrified that one night, they'll show me something so horrifying that I break, and I'll wake hurting someone I love."

Emma's stomach knotted at the starkness of his words. Deep inside, she feared how her growing feelings for Ian might twist her own weakness. "I trust you," she said gently, lifting his hand to her chest so he could feel her heartbeat. "And I believe you won't let fear control you."

His breath caught at her gesture, and for a fragile moment, she sensed the same electric pull that first sparked between them in the orchard. The memory of his kiss hung in her mind, an echo that stirred warmth in her ribs. The wind ruffled his hair, and she thought she saw a fleeting softness in his eyes. It reminded her that, beyond curses and illusions, something powerful had blossomed between them.

He parted his lips as though to speak, then frowned at something in the distance. Out at sea, a fork of lightning sliced through the sky, followed by a low rumble that vibrated the stone beneath them. The storm was drawing nearer. Emma glanced over her shoulder, noticing how the coast beyond Crestwood seemed lost in a curtain of dark rain. The day felt poised in suspension, as if waiting for one final push that might rearrange every piece of their fragile calm.

"We should find shelter," she said softly. "That rain is going to be on top of us soon, and I don't fancy getting caught in it." She released his hand reluctantly and pushed to her feet. Though the air was humid, the impending storm brought a chill that reminded Emma how precarious their peace truly was.

Ian stood, sliding both hands into his jacket pockets. For a moment, he kept his gaze fixed on the tumultuous ocean, then he turned to her. "Emma," he said, voice subdued. "Thank you... for this. For showing me that chant, for being here. I don't know what I'd do if I had to face all of this alone."

She touched his arm again, letting her fingers linger against the worn fabric of his sleeve. "You're not alone," she promised. "As long as I can stand with you, I will. I only wish I was certain my new spells could truly stop the nightmares. We're only starting to understand them."

He nodded, swallowing. "I know. We may not have a

guarantee, but you've given me some hope. It's more than I had this morning." His lips curved into a ghost of a smile. "You make it seem possible that we might outrun these dreams—or at least face them head-on."

Ian had never felt so much warmth as Emma's presence beside him, the quiet steadiness she offered as she laced her fingers through his. Emma squeezed his hand, grounding him, her touch, a lifeline. "Tell me about yourself, about your family?" she asked.

"Not much to say when it comes to family," he choked telling her as much as he knew. Although he was only 20 years old, he had been on his own for as long as he could remember, being cared for by his much older brother James who had moved to London three years ago. James had provided him with shelter and plenty of funds but not much in the way of nurturing or even teaching him the ways of a warlock. Before leaving, James told Ian of the "Williams curse," that had affected generations before them so "better to lay off the magic to be on the safe side." Ian had always known that his mother had died a few days after his birth. But he had never really known what happened to his father. James had said that he just went a little nuts, with the curse and all, and up and left one day when Ian was about six.

"So, you're basically an orphan, just like me," Emma said with a tear in her eye. "That explains a lot. What about your brother, James, do you stay in touch?"

"I hear from him every so often when he sends an accounting statement since he manages my inheritance," Ian winced. "Apparently, I'm rather rich."

"Well, that's not like me, in terms of money," Emma laughed. "But I was rich in love. I'm so sorry you didn't have that, Ian."

She had given him words of comfort, spoken in that soft voice that always managed to slip through the cracks in his defenses. And he had tried—tried so hard—to hold himself together, to keep his fears and nightmares locked away where they couldn't touch her.

But it was too much.

Ian's breath hitched. The weight of everything, the loneliness, the illusions, the fear, the nights spent gasping awake with the taste of terror in his mouth—pressed into his chest all at once. He bowed his head, swallowing against the tightness in his throat. It felt like his body was betraying him, his emotions clawing their way up, no matter how much he tried to shove them down.

"I don't..." His voice broke. He clenched his jaw, shaking his head. "I don't know how to do this, Emma."

She didn't pull away. She didn't press him for more. She simply shifted, closing the space between them, until her forehead rested against his. Her breath was warm, her scent wrapped around him—apples and earth and something undeniably her.

"You don't have to do it alone," she murmured.

Ian exhaled sharply, his fingers tightening around hers. He wanted to believe her. Wanted to believe that he wasn't too far gone, that the darkness twisting through his mind hadn't already taken too much of him. But when he opened his mouth, the words tangled in his chest, trapped beneath the rising wave of emotion.

Emma must have felt the way his breath came too fast, too unsteady—because she reached up, her palm pressing gently over his heart. "Ian," she whispered. Just his name, like it was something sacred.

And that was it. That was all it took for the dam to break.

A shudder ran through him as he exhaled, a ragged, uneven sound. His hands found her face, thumbs brushing lightly over her cheeks, as if he needed to convince himself she was real. His fingers trembled as he cradled her, his forehead still resting against hers.

"I don't deserve this," he rasped.

Emma didn't hesitate. "You do."

She kissed him before he could argue, before he could drown in his own doubt.

The first brush of her lips was soft, careful—like she was afraid he might pull away. But Ian didn't. He couldn't. He leaned in, letting himself sink into her, letting himself believe in the warmth of her mouth, the way her breath mingled with his.

Emma sighed against him, and the sound sent a shiver straight through him. He deepened the kiss, his hands sliding into her hair, gripping just tight enough to make her gasp softly against his lips. His heart pounded, not with fear, but with something else entirely, something hot and aching and desperate.

Her fingers curled into the fabric of his jacket, pulling him closer. Closer.

Ian didn't fight it. He let himself get lost in her, in the way she tasted—sweet and warm, tinged with salt from the sea air. He kissed her like he was afraid this moment might slip through his fingers, like he needed to memorize every second, every sensation. The way she melted into him. The way her fingers tangled in his hair, tugging lightly, drawing a quiet groan from his throat.

The world faded.

The storm, the illusions, the fear—they didn't matter.

There was only this. Only her.

When they finally broke apart, Ian was breathing hard, his forehead still pressed to hers. Emma's lips were slightly parted, her cheeks flushed, but she didn't move away. She just held him there, letting him have this moment.

Ian exhaled, his chest rising and falling in uneven beats. "I don't know how to be the kind of person who deserves this," he admitted, his voice hoarse.

Emma reached up, her thumb tracing the line of his jaw, her touch featherlight. "You already are."

He swallowed hard, a flicker of something like disbelief passing through his expression. But Emma had never been one to let him retreat into his doubts. She kissed him again—slower this time, softer. A quiet promise against his lips.

Ian trembled beneath her touch, overwhelmed by the depth of it, by the realization that he wasn't alone in this. That maybe, just maybe, he could hold onto this feeling, this warmth, without it slipping away.

He let out a shaky laugh, something raw threading through the sound. "I'm terrified," he admitted. "But I don't want to lose this."

Emma smiled, brushing another kiss to the corner of his mouth. "Then don't."

Lightning flashed again, briefly illuminating the path that twisted back toward town. Emma turned, heart pounding, uncertain of her feelings for Ian. She needed to keep practicing exercises Sadie had documented, but doubts swirled inside her. Even Sadie's defensive wards had their limits, and Catherine's illusions—or the curse nestled in Ian's bloodline—might find new ways to rip open the protective net they tried to stitch.

They started walking. Each footstep crunched through loose gravel. Thunder boomed louder, as if urging them to hurry. Emma kept hold of his arm, guiding him around a jagged rock outcropping. If the storm broke overhead before they found a safe place, they would be in for a soaking. She hoped the orchard wasn't trouble waiting to spring from the trees, but she pushed the worry back for now. The orchard had become both an ally and a silent witness to their unfolding story, so she believed it might at least shelter them if needed.

Ian's shoulders relaxed slightly as they followed the final bend in the coastline trail. Despite the brine stinging her lips, Emma felt an unexpected surge of protectiveness swell in her chest. She wanted to corner every stray illusion that plagued his nights, dispel them one by one using every incantation Sadie had taught her. She wanted to prove that the orchard's strength—and the connection she shared with Ian—could overcome even the darkest shapes haunting his dreams.

Yet as they halted at a grassy patch overlooking a sheer

drop, thunder rolled overhead, echoing in the hollows of Emma's bones. She heard the trembling in Ian's inhalation and wondered if the illusions were stirring again, just out of reach of her newly learned chant. An anxious hush fell. She realized he must be thinking of his great-uncle's fiancée, of that painful cautionary tale. Emma's pulse throbbed, and her thoughts fluttered with fear at the idea that the nightmares might latch onto her mind the way they had latched onto him.

He pressed his lips together, struggling to find words. She waited, offering a reassuring squeeze to his arm because her own voice felt trapped. In that moment, the world seemed poised on the cusp of a storm, winds scouring the cliffs, skies flickering with far-off lightning. Her heart braced for the question: Could they truly hold off a centuries-old curse, or were they naïve to believe the orchard's magic and their own fragile bond might suffice?

They stood uncertain of what came next. She opened her mouth to speak, but no sound emerged. A heavy rumble of thunder rolled in from the horizon, shaking the rocky ground beneath their feet. Quiet closed in around them, and some part of her recognized that this stillness was fragile. Neither one of them knew if the nightmares could truly be quenched or if everything between them would unravel under the strain.

She breathed in, longing for words of confidence she didn't fully possess. Instead, she settled for sliding her hand firmly into his and letting him decide whether to cling back. His trembling fingers wove into hers. The silence that followed felt brittle, broken only by the tide pounding the cliffs below.

Thunder rumbled again, and the day darkened. Silence thickened around them, echoing with unspoken questions they were too afraid to voice. Neither one knew if these nightmares could be quelled or if their growing bond would only deepen the threat.

FIVE

Emma woke to the pale light of day slipping through her bedroom curtains. Tension clung to her mind, an echo of the restless hours she had spent imagining worst-case scenarios for Ian. She rose and stretched, quietly resolving that she would no longer remain a mere observer of the conflicts swirling around her life. She pulled on warm clothes, mindful of the morning chill that usually hovered over Sadie's cottage.

As she walked down the hallway, Emma found Sadie in the kitchen. The older woman looked visibly drained, half-sitting on a stool while stirring a plain cup of tea. Sadie lifted her gaze, her face etched with fine lines of exhaustion. It was impossible to overlook the lingering fatigue that weighed on her. Emma knew Sadie had spent most of last night reinforcing fresh wards around the cottage's perimeter, prompted by a menacing hint of Catherine's aura that Sadie had sensed in the orchard's shadows. Now, jagged flecks of worry could be seen in Sadie's eyes.

Emma cleared her throat. "Sadie, I need to ask something important." She forced herself to speak calmly, though her pulse thudded with nervous energy. In her mind, she pictured Ian's weary face, the dark circles that had deepened around his eyes after his most recent nightmares.

Sadie nodded, setting aside her tea with a trembling hand. "Speak, child," she said gently, though her brow knitted in concern.

Taking a breath, Emma began. "What are you afraid of?"

"Well, I didn't want to worry you but since you mentioned that you had strange feelings when you met Catherine in the library, I should tell you that not all witches are good, like me. There are some that use their magical power to spread darkness and chaos. Catherine is that kind of witch. She's been up to no good for years in Crestwood casting malevolent spells that I try to counterbalance for the good of the community. Some people here are suspicious of witches in general but most people here suspect that she's bad and I'm good but they keep their distance from both of us just in case."

"What sort of things does Catherine do?" Emma asked.

"Let's see. She's been fairly quiet for years but lately she's been up to no good again. She casts out illusions that make people see things that aren't there and even cause nightmares. She can call up the wind and rain to wreck storms on the town. She hides knowledge that people are actively seeking in the library. I think you've had a brush with that one."

"Yes, I have, like she was reading my mind, or something," confessed Emma. "It's creepy how she stared at me."

"She basically feeds off of other's fears and insecurities and spreads general chaos. "She knows you're a Turner so she probably felt your growing power. I've spotted her lurking around the orchard lately so that's why I've been fortifying the cottage's wards.".

"Should I be scared of her, Sadie?" asked Emma.

"You should always be wary of her, stay away from her as much as you can."

Well, we can't keep patching the situation with small spells and half-measures. I want to protect Ian from the illusions that keep tormenting him. Whatever training you can give me to strengthen wards or handle bigger spells—" She paused, searching for the right words. "I want you to teach me. Intensely. No more tiptoeing around."

Sadie sighed, her shoulders slumping. She looked older at that moment, as though each word Emma spoke placed another weight upon her. "You know my power is not limitless, child," she said. "I have to be careful with advanced instruction, especially because you're still learning to harness raw emotional energy."

"But you just told me you saw Catherine prowling again," Emma insisted. She folded her arms, feeling a swirl of desperation. "I can't let you or Ian stand alone. I can't keep waiting for illusions to ambush us. If you don't teach me, who will?"

Quiet tension filled the kitchen. The teakettle's gentle whistle remained the only sound for a moment. Then Sadie inhaled slowly and gave a slight nod. "All right. We'll try," she said, voice subdued and faintly resigned. "You must promise me, Emma, that you'll remain calm and follow my instructions with utmost care. Harnessing powerful spells too quickly could be dangerous, especially if you let your emotions run untethered."

Emma felt a surge of relief. She crossed the small kitchen and placed her hand lightly over Sadie's. "I promise," she whispered, though her heart pounded in anticipation. She knew that her emotions, particularly the fierce swirl of worry and affection she felt whenever she thought of Ian—could easily overwhelm her.

Soon after, they moved outside to begin. Sadie led her through the orchard, guiding her to a patch of grass where smooth, round stones and bits of chalk lay arranged in a circle. Morning wind carried the scent of damp leaves, and faint birdsong drifted from deep within the rows of apple trees. The orchard rustled as if waking to their presence. Though patches of sunlight scored the path, Emma shivered at the crisp air nipping at her cheeks.

"Here," said Sadie, lowering herself onto one knee to pick up the chalk. "I want you to draw the shape I have shown you before—an outer ring, then a star inside that ring. The star's points will anchor your defensive wards."

Emma knelt and began sketching on the grass, pressing the chalk against a flat stone so the symbol would stand out. Her pulse quickened when she remembered the stifling sense of failure she had felt the last time she tried a complex incantation. Still, she forced her mind to remain steady, repeating Sadie's instructions in her head.

"Good," Sadie said quietly, once Emma finished the star. "We shall place a wooden figure at the center. Then you'll attempt to conjure a protective vortex around it. This vortex should keep anything harmful from reaching the figure."

Emma nodded. She picked up a small carved figurine shaped like a crouching fox—a creation Sadie had once shown her as a practice object. Placing it gently at the diagram's center, she stepped back and exhaled. Her fingers tingled with a mounting current of energy. "I'm ready," she said.

Sadie slipped a piece of driftwood into Emma's hand. "Channel through this," she advised. "It steadies the flow if your emotions spike."

Emma shut her eyes. She began chanting softly—an incantation she had memorized from Sadie's diaries:

"Circle stand and star take form,
Shield this shape from threats so worn.
Gather winds in focused reach,
Let no harm this figure breach."

Her voice felt steady at first. She visualized the spiraling air forming a gentle barrier. But an image of Ian's haunted expression flickered in her mind—a reminder of how much she wanted to succeed. The longing to protect him from every lurking illusion flared so fiercely that it ignited a rush of magic.

Emma sensed the sudden spark of raw power snapping at her fingertips. Her shoulders seized. The incantation's tight pattern shattered. Instead of a controlled swirl, she felt a chaotic blast rippling outward. She opened her eyes, just in time to see the vortex form wildly around the carved fox and lash at the nearest branches overhead.

"Emma!" Sadie shouted. Emma felt her grandmother's warning like a jolt. She tried to pull back, but the swirl had gained a life of its own, whipped by her untamed emotions.

A cracking sound echoed. A thick apple tree branch snapped loose and hurtled toward them, leaves scattering in the sudden gust. Emma's pulse thundered. She braced herself for impact, but in a flash of practiced grace, Sadie spoke a brief counter-spell and lifted her hand. A shimmering wave of magic deflected the flying branch, sending wood and twigs clattering harmlessly onto the grass.

Gasping, Emma pressed her hand to her chest, knees trembling. She watched the broken limb roll to a stop a few feet away. Needles of embarrassment prickled through her skin.

Sadie exhaled, stepping forward gingerly until she stood face to face with Emma. Though the older woman's voice remained calm, the worry plain in her eyes cut deeper than any scolding. "You let your emotion override the control we have been building," she said gently. She placed a hand on Emma's shoulder. "That is exactly the risk I warned you about."

Emma bent her head, hot shame rising in her chest. "I'm so sorry," she murmured. "I lost sight of the tethering chants. I thought if I just threw more power at it, it would hold."

"You can't rush this," Sadie cautioned. She lowered her hand. "Power does not compensate for control. Each day you must prepare your mind. If you let your desire or your fear seep too strongly into a single spell, it can shift the entire incantation."

"I know," Emma whispered, voice thick. Her throat felt tight with the sting of frustration. In her yearning to master these wards, she was forgetting the most basic steps. "Let me try again," she offered, swallowing hard and wiping sweaty palms on her coat sleeves.

Sadie, however, shook her head. "That is enough for now," she said. "We'll continue later. My reserves are not as strong today, and your magic will only turn more erratic if you attempt it again without centering yourself. Gather in what we have learned."

"But I need—" Emma started, her frustration surging, then halted. She realized that pressing Sadie further wouldn't do anything but wring more tension into the air. "All right," she muttered instead, biting her lip. She stared at the ruined branch on the grass, heart pounding with guilt. If that had struck Sadie, Emma would never have forgiven herself.

Sadie's tone softened. "I understand you want to protect him," she said gently, understanding flickering in her eyes. "But training is earned through steps, not leaps. Eventually your emotional bond with him might help you cast powerful wards, but only once you know how to guide that energy instead of letting it run wild."

Emma nodded. Her cheeks burned, and sadness squeezed her heart. She bowed her head to gather the scattered twigs, hoping to rid herself of at least one reminder of her failure. In the distance, crows let out a series of caws, as though unsettled by the commotion. Sadie murmured a few quiet words, restoring calm to the orchard. Gradually, the swirl of magic around them returned to a gentle hush.

By early evening, the sky had taken on a cloudy haze, and Sadie retired early after dinner to soothe the weariness that Emma's mishap had pressed on her. Emma helped put away the chalks and the wooden figure, carefully returning them to a small wooden box. The orchard's breeze still felt cool against her skin, brushing away the lingering sense of defeat.

She slipped back into the cottage and found herself pacing the narrow hallway leading to her bedroom. Over and over, her mind replayed that moment of losing control. She remembered how fiercely she had wanted the magic to succeed, how the surge of raw power felt both exhilarating and terrifying. She had thought love and fear might blend into a protective strength, but all they had done was send a branch hurtling across the orchard.

Sighing, she pushed open her bedroom door. The space was lit by the soft amber glow of a lamp on her bedside table. She sank onto the edge of her bed, dropping her head into her hands.

In the quiet, she pulled her grandmother's instruction back to the forefront of her thoughts. Sadie had said that each day's training must be measured, that raw emotion could twist a spell's purpose if the caster lacked balance. Emma conceded that her wish to protect Ian was no small feeling. It roared inside her like a storm, refusing to fade into polite calm. She wanted him safe from every lurking horror that Catherine's illusions might spawn. Still, she couldn't ignore her grandmother's lesson. Rage, fear, or even love—any of these emotions could turn a spell into something far more dangerous.

She lifted her head, gazing into the lamplight. She wondered if love itself could be shaped into a ward, or if her fierce devotion would forever teeter between salvation and cataclysm. What if the power of her feelings proved too strong to handle? Could she ever gather enough control to channel it well?

Her heart pounded at the thought of Ian's haunted eyes. She longed to shield him from the illusions that gnawed at his mind. But the demonstration that afternoon reminded her that magic was never just a matter of wishing. It demanded discipline. It demanded calm.

She reached for a small notebook she kept on the bedside table and scribbled a few lines of Sadie's incantations. She paused, then added a short reflection: "Love is strength, but untempered, it can break me. I can't protect him if I can't control myself."

Closing the notebook, Emma silently hoped tomorrow's lessons would go better. She let the calm of the cottage wrap around her, the old walls hinting at a silent promise that she would grow stronger in time. Footsteps rustled in the hallway, and she guessed Sadie was settling in for the night. Emma would let her grandmother rest, and she would face the next day's lessons with renewed determination.

For a while, she thought of Ian's face once again, felt her pulse tighten, then whispered, "Let me figure out how to use this heart, this feeling, without losing the magic we both need."

Emma exhaled, sinking back onto the bed to surrender to whatever uneasy dreams would claim her. Even the orchard felt far away now, murmuring its subdued hope in the wind outside. She closed her eyes with a final wish: her next attempt would fuse her emotions and her power in harmony, rather than letting one devour the other.

SIX

Emma hovered near the kitchen window, eyes tracing the pattern of raindrops as they dribbled across the glass. Each drop clung stubbornly before sliding downward, like tiny messengers urging her to face the night's uncertainties. The cottage felt unnervingly quiet outside of the steady drip of water from the eaves. A single gas lamp glowed in the hallway behind her, painting shadows that elongated across the worn wooden floorboards. She inhaled slowly, attempting to wrangle her anxious heart.

She had known he might come tonight, though they had made no explicit plans. All day, she had sensed tension. Sadie had called it a "storm in the veins," a phrase that once confounded Emma but now felt unsettlingly apt. Sometimes, Crestwood's magic seemed to whisper in warning. Now, with the evening descended into cool, unrelenting rain, Emma's anticipation outweighed her dread. He would need a haven if the illusions tormented him again.

A knock broke the silence. It was soft, uneasy. She moved quickly, unbolting the back door and clasping the handle with damp palms. As soon as she opened it, Ian stood in the weak light, his hair plastered to his forehead. Water trickled down the collar of his jacket onto the threshold. He looked exhausted, as though he had run through the orchard rather than taking a simple walk. Their eyes met, and for a moment, neither spoke. She only noticed how his breaths rasped in the moist air, his clothes dripping onto the porch floor.

Emma stepped aside to allow him in. "You're soaked," she murmured, her voice catching at the sight of him. The tension in his shoulders betrayed a deeper turmoil than just the rain. She shut the door behind him, sealing out the chill of the night. Then, she gestured for him to follow her toward the kitchen, where she had left the kettle warming on a low flame. The cottage was dark, save for that luminous lamp in the hall and the small lamp on the kitchen table. Shadows slipped around them, cast into restless shapes by the flicker of the flame.

"I couldn't stay away," Ian said quietly, as though apologizing. He stripped off his damp jacket, draping it over a chair. His hair clung to the nape of his neck. Emma fetched a towel from a cupboard and handed it to him, offering a fleeting smile. She couldn't ignore the tremor in his hands when he reached out.

"It's alright. I... had a feeling you might come," she admitted, drawing her lower lip between her teeth. She tried not to stare at his drawn features. The space between them felt charged, laced with unspoken fears. Only a few days had passed since they last spoke along the coastline path, yet something about his mounting anxieties had twisted his expression into a haunted mask.

She turned to the stove, ladling warm herbal tea into two mugs. The steam curled upward, carrying the faint tang of rosemary and lavender—Sadie's blend for soothing frayed nerves. Emma had grown accustomed to steeping this recipe in the late evening, half-hoping it would calm her own swirling worries about illusions and curses. Now, she offered it to him, resisting the urge to wrap her hands around his for reassurance. His eyes flicked up to hers, gratitude flickering across his features. He accepted the mug, fingers still trembling.

They moved out of the kitchen together, footsteps echoing in the narrow hallway. The single lamp at the far end revealed a modest stretch of wall lined with old photographs, some featuring Emma's parents in happier times. She tried not to dwell on the hollow pang that always followed these glimpses of her old life. Instead, she focused on Ian's uneven breathing. Guilt coiled in her stomach, wondering if her attempt to ease his fears might only draw them both deeper into danger.

She settled on a low wooden bench by the wall, and he sank down beside her. The lamp's glow danced across his face now, illuminating new shadows beneath his eyes. The hallway walls felt close, but also strangely comforting, like a small sanctuary within the cottage. Emma draped another towel over his shoulders, silently urging him to dry off, but he merely held his mug between his hands.

Soon, the quiet overwhelmed them, pressing in until Ian cleared his throat. "I need you to know something," he said softly, refusing to meet her gaze at first. The tension in his voice tugged at her chest. With a slight turn of his head, he risked looking at her. Light traced the line of his jaw, and she noticed the subtle bruise-like circles under his eyes of lost sleep.

"Tell me," Emma murmured. She placed one hand palm down against the bench, resisting the urge to reach for him before he was ready. She could feel the faint vibrations of her own magic stirring in her fingertips, a nervous hum that threatened to trigger a stray spark if she didn't keep it contained.

He let out a shaky breath that sounded too close to a sob. "I keep seeing you in my nightmares. Your eyes, your face... twisted by the illusions." His free hand clenched, knuckles whitening. "Every time I fall asleep, they show me an image of you, frightened or hurt. It's like my mind can't separate my own terror from what the illusions force me to see. And I can't... I can't watch you suffer. Even in a dream, it crushes me."

Emma's heart pounded, a swell of fierce emotion knotting in her throat. She inhaled, trying to remain steady, because the anguish in his voice demanded that she be calm. She let a few seconds pass, unsure how to respond. Steam curled from her mug, drifting into the quiet.

Gently, she touched his arm, feeling the damp sleeve of his shirt. "Ian," she said, voice barely above a whisper, "you aren't alone in this. I'd rather face any nightmare you have—real or imagined—than let you bear it by yourself." The words felt bold, but she meant every syllable. She couldn't stand the idea of him battling those apparitions in solitude, especially if they had started conjuring images of her.

His gaze flickered, and a tear escaped the corner of one eye, trailing down his cheek. He set the tea aside on the bench, letting it clink softly against the wood. The next moment, she reached up, her fingertips brushing that single tear away. Her touch hesitated against his jaw, feeling the slight rasp of stubble. For an instant, an unspoken question passed between them: would nurturing this closeness invite more heartbreak?

He lowered his forehead until it rested against hers, the narrow space between them charged with sorrow and something else—hope, perhaps. Emma felt his breath feather against her lips. The lamplight flickered, painting his face in shifting gold, and she realized how heavily he carried every ounce of guilt for the illusions haunting him. She closed her eyes, letting the gentle rhythm of his breathing guide her own.

"If the nightmares ever reach for you," he whispered, voice slightly hoarse, "I'll never forgive myself. My bloodline is cursed. We both know it. What if these illusions latch onto you? I've read about curses that spread to the people closest to the afflicted... I won't let that happen."

A protective spark flared in Emma's gut, as instantly as if she had cast a ward. She pulled back just enough to meet his eyes. "Don't push me away," she pleaded softly.

"We can find a way to fight this together. I've been working with Sadie on controlling illusions or at least learning to dampen their impact. We are making progress, even if it feels slow." She swallowed, remembering how some of her attempts to conjure protective fields had gone awry, but she held onto the flicker of success she had glimpsed when she practiced Sadie's chants. "I'm stronger than you think, Ian. And we can be stronger together."

His hand found hers, his grip uncertain, as though he worried one wrong move might break her resolve. The contact eased a fraction of the tension in her chest. "I believe you," he admitted after a moment, but his words sounded laced with doubt. "I just... I remember the stories my brother James told me. Relatives who lost loved ones because they tried to join them in fighting illusions. Some ended up half-crazed, others, like my father, disappeared from Crestwood entirely. Shame drove them away, or maybe the illusions did. I don't know. But it's a dark legacy."

Emma's heart tightened. She was learning bits and pieces of Ian's family history through old diaries, but hearing the distress in his voice was different than reading about it in dusty pages. She could feel how that legacy chipped away at his self-worth, an unrelenting whisper telling him he was destined to hurt anyone who cared for him. She squeezed his hand. "We are not your ancestors. You aren't repeating their mistakes. And I'm not helpless."

He let out a shaky laugh that died quickly in his throat. "Everything about you defies my assumptions. You see how I'm trembling, and you don't flinch. You learn about illusions, and your first instinct is to stand beside me. Even when I swore to steer clear of you, I ended up here. It's as if Crestwood's orchard itself is guiding me back."

She couldn't deny that something about the orchard's quiet magic seemed to bind them, offering small pockets of serenity when everything else felt dangerous. She wondered if the orchard sensed how deeply they needed each other. A faint memory surfaced of how the orchard's branches often rustled when they drew near, as if granting them tacit permission to share burdens. She almost voiced the thought out loud but decided not to break this fragile moment. Instead, she let her hand trace the top of his, following the curve of his knuckles.

Rain pelted the windowpanes, mingling with the hush of the cottage's settled floorboards. Shadows danced again as the lamplight flickered, illuminating the worry etched around Ian's eyes. She imagined him wandering the orchard's edge before coming here, or standing in the open fields of low grass, letting the sky's tears mix with his own. Her chest constricted at the thought of him, drenched and tormented, deciding whether to knock on her door.

She reached out and tucked a damp strand of his hair behind his ear. "Drink your tea. It should help calm you a little." Her voice was gentle but firm. She needed him to know that some small comforts still existed—warm tea, a caring touch, a quiet hallway in which to breathe. These were the things that kept nightmares at bay, if only for a few precious moments.

With obvious effort, he lifted the mug and took a sip.

Emma noticed how his hands were still unsteady, but at least he managed a measured breath as the herbal fragrance curled around them. Silence stretched, though it felt more like a tentative refuge than an awkward gap. Outside, thunder cracked faintly in the distance, as though the storm might gather again.

After swallowing another mouthful of tea, Ian cleared his throat. "Thank you," he murmured. "I don't deserve this kindness, but I'm too weak to turn it away tonight."

Emma's fingers twitched against the ceramic of her own cup. She almost wanted to scold him, to push back against the self-inflicted guilt weighing down his words, but instead, she did something simpler. Something more honest. She reached out, trailing her fingertips across his palm before letting her smaller hand settle against his. The warmth of his skin sent a delicate shiver through her.

"I'm not offering kindness out of pity," she said softly. "It's because I care about you. Your nightmares... they don't scare me enough to run."

She felt the weight of the moment settle between them, heavy and expectant. The space between their hands felt fragile, charged. He could pull away, she thought. He could let his fear win, let the walls he always seemed to rebuild around himself push her out again.

Instead, he turned his hand over, curling his fingers around hers.

Her cheeks warmed, but she refused to look away. Refused to pretend this didn't matter.

A beat passed before Ian exhaled, slow and unsteady, and she sensed his restraint crumbling at the edges. His body remained tense, a thread pulled too tight, but he didn't retreat. "I tried to stay away," he admitted, the words barely a whisper. "But every time I close my eyes, it's your face. Part of the illusions, part of my own mind... sometimes it's comfort, sometimes it's fear. It's all tangled. Perhaps that is how curses work. They prey on what we love most."

Emma's breath caught.

Her throat tightened at the raw honesty in his voice, at the unguarded way he looked at her. No illusions now, no shadows twisting his features—just Ian, exposed and vulnerable.

"I'm sorry it haunts you," she whispered. "But please don't blame yourself because the illusions latch onto me. I'm not afraid of them. And I'm not leaving you alone with them."

Something flickered in his eyes—an emotion that looked too much like desperation. "You say that now," he said, his voice low, "but if you ever see what they can truly do, how they can warp a person's mind, you may regret throwing in your lot with me."

Emma's resolve didn't waver.

She slid closer along the bench, letting the length of her arm brush his. The air between them thickened, each breath stretching the moment further, deeper. Her voice dropped, quieter now, meant only for him.

"Then show me how to fight them," she murmured. "Let me share what I've learned from Sadie. Together, our magic might be enough to stand a chance. You don't have to face it alone anymore. Neither of us does."

Ian exhaled sharply, shifting the mug of tea into his other hand. With a slow, hesitant movement, his free arm came around her shoulders, pulling her closer against his side. Emma's breath hitched as her body pressed into the warmth of his, the scent of rain-damp fabric and the faint spice of the orchard wrapping around her senses.

She could feel his heartbeat against her cheek, fast and erratic. A tremor ran through him, his body so tightly wound it was as if he was barely holding himself together. But he didn't let go.

Emma closed her eyes, letting herself sink into the moment. She felt the way he clung to her, the way his fingers curled slightly against her arm, anchoring himself. The mixture of relief and sorrow in his eyes kindled something fierce within her, a need to protect him—not just from the illusions, but from the part of himself that believed he had to bear this alone.

She pressed closer, wrapping an arm around his back, holding him as firmly as he held her. The rain softened against the roof, a steady, rhythmic patter that enclosed them in their own world.

For a long moment, they just breathed.

Emma listened to the rise and fall of his chest, felt the slow unraveling of tension in his muscles. She reminded herself that there was no simple solution to curses centuries in the making, no spell that could erase generations of suffering in a single night. But the quiet determination in her chest told her they could endure.

As long as they chose to face each new horror together.

At last, she lifted her head.

Ian's gaze met hers, his expression unreadable but intense. The shadows under his eyes didn't seem so dark in the lamplight, but there was something else there, something raw and open, something vulnerable.

Emma wasn't sure which of them moved first, but suddenly, the space between them was nothing.

Their foreheads brushed, his breath warm against her lips, and Ian reached up with careful fingers, tucking a strand of hair behind her ear. He hesitated, fingertips lingering at her temple, as if memorizing the shape of her.

His throat worked around a swallow. When he spoke, his voice was barely there. "I feel a spark of hope when I'm near you," he admitted, rough and broken. "Like I could be more than this curse… like we could break it."

Emma's heart ached.

She reached up, cupping his face with steady fingers, letting her thumb trace the sharp edge of his cheekbone. His skin was warm beneath her touch, and she felt the way his breath hitched at the contact.

"Then hold on to it," she whispered. "Hold on to me."

Ian let out a shaky exhale, his body trembling as if he was struggling to hold himself together.

Then he wasn't holding himself together anymore.

His lips brushed against hers—soft at first, hesitant, like he wasn't sure if he was allowed this. Like he was afraid of breaking whatever fragile peace existed between them.

Emma didn't let him pull away.

She tilted her head, pressing into the kiss, deepening it with quiet certainty. Ian inhaled sharply against her mouth, his grip tightening around her as though afraid she might vanish if he let go.

There was desperation in the way he kissed her, but not just hunger. Need.

His fingers wove into her hair, tugging slightly, and Emma let out a soft sound against his lips, something between a sigh and surrender. That seemed to undo him completely.

Ian angled his body closer, his free hand sliding down her spine, pressing her flush against him. The heat of him, the way he shook under her touch—it made her heart pound, made her breath hitch.

She had kissed him before. But never like this.

Never like she was the only thing tethering him to the world.

When they finally broke apart, he didn't let go. His forehead rested against hers, their breaths mingling in the dim lamplight.

Ian's fingers traced lightly along her back, reverent, almost disbelieving. "I'm worried I'm not good enough for you," he admitted, his voice hoarse.

Emma smiled softly, her fingers threading through his damp hair. "You already are."

He let out a breath, and it wasn't quite a laugh, but something close. Something lighter than before.

The weight of his sorrow lessened, replaced by a calmer acceptance of the situation. He leaned in until his forehead met hers again, letting a soft smile curve his lips —though it trembled at the edges. Emma let her eyes drift shut, the tension in her own spine melting away. She sensed every breath he took, each one steadier than the last, each one promising they would stand against the nightmares hand in hand.

And for the first time in days, Emma allowed herself to believe that their shared vulnerabilities could become their greatest strength. She let her fingertips curl around his, feeling the promise of their collective resolve. Whatever darkness came next, they would face it together.

CHAPTER

SEVEN

Morning light crept over the windowsill of Sadie's cottage, touching the aged floorboards with delicate gold. Emma stirred on the living room couch, where she had drifted off after a restless night. Her body felt stiff, as if it had braced for an impact that never came. She blinked at the familiar space: dried herbs hung from the rafters, old books teetered on the worn shelves, and the softly glowing runes on the doorframe suggested Sadie had renewed wards before daybreak. Emma stretched; her mind already snagged by a pang of sadness that lodged itself beneath her ribs.

She could still see Ian's face from the previous night, etched with worry while he sipped tea beside her in the hallway. He had looked so tired, as though an entire world was weighing on his shoulders. Emma stood, the wooden boards protesting under her feet, and rubbed the knot at the back of her neck. She wanted to check whether Ian had dozed off somewhere in the cottage, possibly in the small nook near the kitchen or the orchard outside. The stillness told her otherwise.

A folded parchment lay on the kitchen table, its edges curled and a faint smudge of ink staining one corner. Emma's heart kicked as she lifted it. The scrawl was brief, only one line:

It's safer if I keep away.

Her grip tensed, and she noticed the hesitant loops in the handwriting, as if he had debated every letter. She read it twice, then a third time, searching for reassurance within that single sentence. No greetings, no farewell. Only a scraped-together excuse for why he had left without letting her know. Anger and concern roared together in her mind; a twisted knot impossible to untangle. She set the note down on the table, pulse thudding in her ears.

Sadie entered from the adjacent room, a cup of tea in hand. Her silver hair, loosely pinned back, framed a face lined with tension. "You're up early, child," she said softly. Her gaze flicked to the parchment, and a small sigh escaped her lips.

"He left," Emma said, struggling to keep bitterness from strangling her voice. "I woke up and he was... gone." Her nails pressed crescent marks into her palms. The memory of Ian's fearful eyes burned behind her lids. "He thinks he's protecting me by staying away."

The older woman stepped closer. She brushed a thumb over Emma's clenched hand without speaking, a gentle presence that acknowledged the tumult of Emma's emotions. "He must have had reasons," she ventured, though the subdued tone suggested she didn't fully approve of his choice. "Perhaps a nightmare convinced him."

Emma scoffed through tight lips. "He mentioned them getting worse, but how does running solve a curse? He can't do this alone." Her frustration made her fingers tremble. She wanted to fling the note across the kitchen. Instead, she drew a shaky breath and placed it carefully on the table.

Sadie turned away, exhaling in resignation. She left Emma alone with the hush of the cottage walls, and Emma pressed her palm flat against the tabletop as if it might steady her. The quiet crackle of the fire in the hearth did nothing to soothe the panic crawling up her spine. She yearned to chase Ian through the orchard and force him to talk, but she had no clue where he might have gone after a night of torment.

She glanced down at her reflection in the kitchen window. Dark circles shadowed her eyes, and the corners of her mouth were drawn tight. The memory of setting a comforting hand on Ian's arm still lingered at her fingertips, along with the bitter pang that he had slipped away in the dark. With a burst of restless energy, she grabbed her coat from the hook near the door and marched outside.

Nature greeted her with a swirl of cool morning breeze. Dew clung to grass and tree roots, and a faint apple scent hung in the air. Emma's footsteps carried her to the same spot where she had once practiced shielding spells. The runic carvings in the bark of a nearby apple tree glinted under beams of filtered sunlight. She pressed a hand to the trunk, recalling how Ian had once steadied her when a rogue incantation nearly blasted them both. Now, only empty silence remained.

She turned in a slow circle, searching the orchard for any trace of him, her eyes scanning the darker edges where shadows lingered beneath thick clusters of leaves. Nothing. A ripple of frustration broke over her. "He thinks I can't handle this," she mumbled, voice cracking with anger. "He's wrong."

For the next hour, she paced the orchard's rows, occasionally murmuring incantations Sadie had taught her to locate missing magical signatures. Each syllable felt hollow, as though she lacked the vital spark to complete them. Tiny sparks of light flickered at her fingertips, then fizzled, leaving her heart heavier than before. She sensed no trace of Ian's aura, no subtle echo of his presence in the orchard. It was as though the lingering hush swallowed any clue of his direction.

By the time noon arrived, Emma had circled the orchard so many times that her legs ached. She slumped onto a low stump in the clearing, gazing at the patch of grass where she had tried - and failed - to form a controlled vortex days earlier. The wind rustled overhead in a soft lament, and she wondered if Sadie sensed her frustration. Perhaps that was why her grandmother kept her distance—she knew Emma's anger was raw, a snarl of heartbreak and confusion that sought an outlet.

When she finally returned to the cottage, the after-noon sun warmed the front porch. Sadie was seated in a sturdy wooden chair, darning a tear in a kitchen towel with practiced efficiency. She only looked up briefly as Emma crossed the threshold with leaden steps. Even that fleeting glance carried sympathy Emma felt unprepared to receive, so she ducked her head and retreated to her bedroom.

Minutes blurred into hours as she tried to read her old notes on defensive wards. The pages danced with phrases like *Channeling Calm* and *Emotional Tether*, each line a reminder that magic demanded self-control. Her thoughts refused to settle, skidding back to images of Ian: the sadness in his eyes, the slight tremor in his hand, and the unwavering belief that he alone must bear the curse's weight. By late afternoon, the words on the page blurred together in a meaningless haze, and she slammed the notebook shut.

She considered returning to the orchard for more incantation attempts but felt drained. Instead, she found herself pacing the cottage's hallway, cheeks hot with anger. His note continued to replay in her mind: *It's safer if I keep away*. The intention behind it, however misguided, gnawed at her. Safer for whom? She felt no relief. If anything, his absence stirred a new kind of danger in her chest, a coil of worry so tight she struggled to breathe.

As evening approached, Sadie turned on several lamps inside the cottage, placing them on windowsills and side tables to chase away the early nightfall. Emma offered to help, but her movements were stiff with restlessness. She paused by the living room window, staring out into the gathering darkness. Low clouds smothered the sky, hinting at a storm that might roll in overnight. A surge of determination finally cracked her gloom.

"I'm heading outside," she announced quietly, though Sadie didn't ask questions. She simply nodded, understanding that Emma needed the orchard's space to wrestle her thoughts into some semblance of order. Emma pushed open the back door and stepped onto the porch. Chill night air nipped her cheeks, and the light from the cottage behind her cast a faint glow across the first row of gnarled apple trees.

She tucked her hands into her coat pockets, following a winding path around half-buried roots. The orchard felt strangely watchful, as if every branch kept silent vigil over her roiling emotions. Stars peeked through gaps in the clouds, silver shards flickering in the inky sky. Emma drifted toward the center clearing, where she and Sadie often practiced at twilight. She stooped to retrieve a stray pebble near her foot. Without hesitation, she hurled it into the darkness, a small spark of fury spurring her on.

"Why can't you trust me?" she whispered, picturing Ian's midnight-haired silhouette. She half-expected no answer, but letting those words slip from her lips felt better than keeping them locked inside. Her jaw tightened when the orchard provided only mild rustling in return.

She inhaled, shoulders tense. Her mind strayed to the incantations Sadie had painstakingly shown her: the spells that erected protective walls against illusions, the sequences that harnessed the orchard's quiet strength. Emma settled into a mindful stance, eyes shut, arms rising to shape the first motions of a basic warding spell. Her heart thudded with each breath, but the orchard's magic pulsed gently underfoot.

"Circle form, and quiet keep,
Shield me from illusions deep,
Bind the night, from harm be free,
Steady my soul - so mote it be."

She spoke softly, letting the orchard's magic absorb her voice. A faint swirl of wind traced her fingertips as if responding to the words. For a heartbeat, she sensed a calming wave, a gentle presence that might have been her grandmother's wards merging with her own. Still, the glimmer dissipated quickly, as though her raw frustration blocked the spell's full potential.

"Come on," Emma muttered, flexing her fingers. She tried again, reciting more lines and visualizing how she wanted the orchard's energy to wrap her in safety. Each syllable scraped against her anger, and she couldn't anchor enough solace. Though tiny sparks crackled around her, nothing coalesced into a stable shield.

Frustration spilled out in a low groan. She sank onto the grass, ignoring the damp chill that soaked her knees. Ian's absence pulsed like an open wound, overshadowing any magical training. She gazed at the silent rows of trees, the same ones they had walked through, hand in hand, not so long ago. Her eyes threatened tears, but she refused to let them fall. She refused to be undone by longing.

When she finally rose to her feet, the moon had climbed higher, illuminating the orchard with a pale gleam. Wiping her palms against her coat, Emma cleared her throat and decided to push forward. She would not let heartbreak define her progress. Sadie had warned her about letting emotion rule her magic; she needed to shape it, feed it carefully into her spells, rather than letting it run wild. If Ian believed disappearing was the only way to keep her safe, she would train harder, so that his protective scruples lost their purpose.

She returned to the overseer's oak near the orchard's center, an ancient tree with runes carved into its trunk. She steadied her breathing and began one of Sadie's defensive sequences, pivoting her arms in a controlled circle while murmuring the incantation:

"Root and bough, across this space,
Empower my guard with steadfast grace.
Let no twisted fear confine,
Draw strength from orchard's quiet spine."

Again, she willed the orchard's magic to respond. Pricks of energy tingled over her palms and sizzled down her arms. She felt the beginnings of a protective shield shimmer in the air - a fleeting dome that hovered around her torso. For a moment, triumph flickered in her chest. Then her voice cracked on the last word, and the energy collapsed. The air was still, leaving her breath shallow with disappointment.

She let a tired laugh slip out at her own struggles. "I really need you here, Ian," she admitted to the empty darkness. Her voice sounded small. Yet he had made his choice, believing this to be best for both of them.

Eventually, exhaustion draped over her like a lead blanket, and she trudged back to the cottage, defeated but not ready to surrender. Inside, warm lamplight and the scent of herbal tea greeted her. Sadie must have brewed a fresh pot, though she had left none of her usual notes on the counter. Emma filled a mug and stood by the window, sipping slowly, letting the mild rosemary aroma soothe her raw nerves.

Her thoughts filled with the possibility that Ian's nightmares had grown so vicious he could no longer bear the chance of hurting her. She pictured him wandering the edges of Crestwood at night, or lurking near the forest's hidden groves, trying to escape illusions that haunted him. The idea carved an ache deep in her chest, and she resented that he had chosen solitude over leaning on her.

By the time she finished her tea, the night felt older, and the moon hung large above the orchard. The house lay quiet except for Sadie's muffled footsteps in the hallway. Emma heard her grandmother's murmur, probably reciting a final warding verse before bed. The knowledge that Sadie preserved these halting strongholds comforted Emma, yet it also reminded her that magical safety never lasted without practice and unity.

"I won't let him shoulder this alone," she whispered. The vow settled like a simmering coal in her core, heating her determination. Even if he walked away, she could prepare. She would learn to protect herself and him, whether he believed it possible or not.

She quietly walked to her room. Settling onto the floor, she spread her notebooks around her, determined to revisit the incantations Sadie had carefully outlined. The lines blurred now and then, tears pricking her eyes. Still, she rehearsed them under her breath, trying to contain the heartbreak thrumming in her veins.

"Focus," she told herself, speaking into the stillness. Each recitation felt incomplete; the words shaky with unspent sorrow. But as she repeated the spells, reworking syllables and rearranging runes, she felt the faintest flicker of resolve. If she couldn't find Ian physically, she could keep honing the craft he was so afraid might overpower them both. One day, he would see that love and skill could stand against any nightmare.

By the time she curled up in bed, the pages of her notebook lay halfway filled with fresh experiments in warding. Her eyes grew heavy, burning from more than just fatigue. She clutched her grandmother's silver amulet around her neck, the small weight anchoring her through the swirl of loneliness. Outside, the wind sighed across the orchard, as though unsure whether to mourn or to offer comfort.

Emma didn't know when she would see Ian again. He might remain hidden until he believed her safe from every monstrous illusion. She hated that he thought she needed shielding from himself. But she couldn't chase him down tonight. All she could do was train, gather strength, and wait. That single purpose numbed some of the anger, replacing it with a steely spark of hope.

She pressed her notebook to her chest, feeling the hum of potential spelled out in each line. The orchard waited beyond the drapes, a silent ally she would return to at first light. For now, she closed her eyes. Despite the ache of his departure, she braced her heart for the next sunrise. The night pressed in around her, heavy with bitter truths, yet she repeated one last chant in a ragged whisper, letting her final vow hang in the still air.

No matter how far Ian ran, she would be ready when he returned. Until then, she would master these spells for them both.

EIGHT

Moonlight settled over Crestwood with a subdued glow, illuminating the narrow path that wound along the coastline. Emma moved with silent determination, each step carrying her closer to the sea's rhythmic pulse. Spray hung in the air, tinged with the scent of brine. She focused on the subtle gleam that shimmered at the edge of her vision. These ward-runes, etched into her memory from Sadie's teachings, felt like invisible threads guiding her through darkness. Tonight, they led her to a secluded cove well beyond the usual beaches. She picked her way carefully across slick rocks, ignoring the swell of anxiety that crept into her chest.

She recalled the last time she saw Ian vanish. That memory still stung. A fragment of the memory seemed to cling to her as she left Sadie's cottage, heartbreak pressing against her ribs in an unrelenting ache. She pushed it aside, determined to locate him. Days without words had turned her agitation into fury, sharpened by longing. The ocean wind buffeted her hair, whipping it into her eyes, and she tucked stray strands behind her ears with trembling fingers.

Dark silhouettes of rock formations rose before her, sculpted by centuries of crashing waves. She climbed over uneven terrain, boots scraping against the damp stone. In the distance, the water crashed against the cove's barrier in a steady roar. The moon sat high in a cloud-streaked sky, its reflection flickering across restless surf. Her heart pounded as she rounded a final boulder and caught sight of a solitary figure crouching near the tide line.

Ian. His hair clung to his forehead, strands matted by the night's spray. The moon's glow revealed the taut line of his shoulders as he stared at the ebb and flow of waves. At her approach, he twisted around, eyes shadowed but unmistakably filled with that familiar mix of guilt and desperation. For a moment, neither of them spoke. The only sound was the sea rolling forward to greet their ankles, licking the rocks with hissing foam.

She closed the distance in three strides, swallowing the knot in her throat. Beneath her anger lay a fierce wave of relief. She had spent countless hours replaying his abrupt retreat, analyzing every word in his last note. Now, seeing him in front of her, she felt her composure falter. "You left," she said, voice urgent with the weight of everything she had been unable to express.

He stood, face stricken by her tone. "I had to," he whispered. "I'm too dangerous. Every time I close my eyes, I see you trapped in my nightmares."

"Stop deciding for me," Emma bit out, tears prickling

behind her eyes. "Taking yourself away doesn't magically erase the danger. You only guaranteed that I'd worry myself sick, imagining the worst." She lifted her chin, determined to show she wouldn't settle for half measures. "You can't keep me safe by running."

His breath rattled as he exhaled. The tension across his brow suggested he had little fight left. "I can't watch you hurt because of me," he said. "The illusions, the curse... it's all interwoven. I convinced myself that if I cut every tie, the curse might stop using you as leverage."

She inhaled sharply. The ocean's tang stung her lips. "And you really believed that?" she asked, voice shaking. "That leaving me in the dark about your suffering would help? You promised me we'd work through this together."

He winced, shoulders sagging. His silence spoke volumes about embattled nights and raw guilt. Only the wind and the relentless surge of waves gave the moment any sound. Emma felt a pulse of anger. She refused to lose herself in heartbreak. She brushed damp hair away from her face, stepping so close she could see the faint gold in his eyes. "If you keep believing you have to shoulder this curse alone," she muttered, "you'll break."

Ian swallowed, jaw tight. "I know," he whispered, shoulders trembling with some deep, suppressed emotion. "I tried to let go of you, to set you out of the path of my nightmares. Then every time I closed my eyes, the illusions latched onto your face anyway." His voice cracked. "I've missed you more than I can stand."

A stark vulnerability underpinned his words. His apology lay unspoken, but Emma heard it all the same.

The nearby waves lapped across their feet, and she stepped closer until their breath mingled in the salt-laden air. When she lifted a trembling hand to his cheek, he leaned into her touch as if drawn by a magnet. She felt the slight rasp of stubble against her palm.

"I'm angry," she said, eyes brimming with unshed tears. "But I'm relieved you're here. I thought you might vanish for good." When he closed his eyes under her fingertips, she let the swirl of lingering frustration slip free in a ragged sigh. "I can't bear it if you disappear again."

In a rush of emotion, that fragile composure dissolved. He pulled her against him with startling fierceness, as though reassuring himself she was real. The tide rose around their ankles in a cool swirl, but she scarcely noticed. Her fury melted into an overwhelming surge of longing, and her sob escaped before she could stop it.

His arms cinched around her waist. "I'm sorry," he rasped. "Every time I turned away, I told myself it was for your good. But it only tore me apart." He lifted his gaze, eyes haunted. "I'm so tired of lying to myself. I can't stay away anymore, not when being near you gives me the only moments of peace I've tasted in ages."

She caught the tremor in his voice and felt tears stinging her throat. "Then stop fighting me," she whispered. "I don't need you to protect me from your curse by shutting me out. I need you to trust that I'm strong enough to face this with you."

Ian swallowed hard. A sheen of moisture gathered in his eyes. "I'm afraid," he admitted in halting words. "I'm afraid that if you stand too close, the curse will use you up.

But I'm more afraid of facing it alone. I don't know how to reconcile those fears."

Emma closed her eyes, pressing her forehead against his, sharing breath in the hush. "The illusions can only torment us if we let them," she said. "We have magic. We have each other. Isn't that worth fighting for?"

Ian tightened his hold around her, breathing in the scent of her damp hair, the salt clinging to her skin. The wind howled around them, biting through their soaked clothes, and the relentless spray from the surf chilled him to the bone.

"You're freezing," he murmured, his lips brushing her temple. He pulled back just enough to look at her, tracing his fingers lightly down her arms, feeling the cold seeped into her skin. "We need to get out of this wind before we both turn to ice."

Emma nodded, shivering as the breeze tangled her hair around her face. She hadn't noticed how cold she was until now, her body trembling not just from emotion but from the relentless dampness of the sea air.

"Come on," Ian said, slipping his fingers through hers and tugging her gently inland. "There's a cottage not far from here. The fishermen use it sometimes when storms roll in. It should be empty this time of night."

The promise of warmth was all the encouragement she needed. They trudged over the rocky path, their steps hurried but careful, the wind pressing against their backs like an unseen force urging them forward. The coastline disappeared behind them as they climbed a narrow incline, cresting a small bluff where the land leveled out.

Nestled against the trees stood a modest stone cottage, its dark shape barely visible against the night sky.

The old wooden door groaned as Ian pushed against it, but it swung open easily.

"No lock?" Emma asked, her breath visible in the chill as she stepped inside.

Ian shook his head. "Nothing here to really steal. Everyone who uses it understands its meant to be a refuge. Everyone who stays takes care of it, so the next person has what they need." He glanced around the space before meeting her gaze. "Tonight, we need this."

The door clicked shut behind them, muffling the roar of the wind outside. The air inside was cool, tinged with the scent of seawater and aged wood, but at least it was dry. Moonlight filtered in through a small, salt-streaked window, illuminating a modest interior. A sturdy wooden table and a few chairs stood near the hearth; their surfaces worn from years of use. There were two folded cots against the wall and some cushions and blankets under-neath them and another cot already set up with a thick mattress. Shelves lined the walls, sparsely filled with mismatched tin mugs, a few earthenware bowls, and the remnants of supplies left by previous visitors—mostly dried herbs, a tin of loose tea, and a handful of well-used fishing tools.

A pile of split logs sat near the fireplace, remnants from someone who had stayed here before. Emma wrapped her arms around herself, rubbing warmth into her skin as Ian knelt near the hearth, stacking the kindling with practiced ease. The rough scrape of flint against steel echoed in the quiet room, followed by the sudden spark of flame.

Emma exhaled as the fire took, the small glow illuminating Ian's face, casting flickering shadows over the sharp angles of his cheekbones. The strain that had weighed on him earlier still lingered, but at this moment, he looked focused—determined. The muscles in his forearms flexed as he coaxed the flame higher, feeding each stick of wood carefully, as if willing the fire to burn away the chill that had settled deep into their bones.

Emma turned toward the shelves, searching through the scattered provisions. Her fingers curled around a small tin of tea, and relief warmed her at the familiar scent of dried chamomile and mint. She reached for the old iron kettle resting near the hearth and carried it to the water basin in the corner, filling it carefully before setting it on a grate over the growing fire.

"I found tea," she said, glancing at Ian as she worked. "What some?"

He exhaled softly, rubbing a hand over the back of his neck. "Something hot would be nice."

When the kettle had boiled, Emma worked quickly, scooping tea into two mismatched mugs before pouring the steaming water over the leaves. She added a spoonful of sugar she'd found in the cupboard to each, stirring until the granules dissolved, then set one beside Ian.

She settled beside him, stretching her hands toward the heat as the flames crackled, the warmth already seeping into the air. A quiet stillness settled between them, broken only by the occasional pop of the wood and the distant howling wind outside. Emma curled her fingers around the mug, savoring the way the warmth seeped into her chilled skin. The scent of chamomile and mint drifted upward, mingling with the faint smoky tang of the fire.

She lifted it to her lips, blowing softly over the surface before taking a careful sip, the heat unfurling in her chest like something steadying, grounding. Across from her, Ian did the same, his hands wrapped tightly around his mug, as if absorbing every bit of warmth it offered. His shoulders had relaxed slightly, the tension that had gripped him easing in the quiet crackle of the fire and the simple comfort of hot tea between them. He exhaled, a slow, measured breath, his gaze flicking toward her over the rim of his cup. For a long moment, they simply sat there, letting the fire chase away the last of the cold.

Ian let out a slow breath, resting his forearms on his knees as he stared into the fire. "I almost can't believe we're here," he admitted, his voice barely above a whisper. "That you found me. That you... still want to."

Emma turned her gaze to him, watching the firelight dance in his eyes. The vulnerability in his expression sent a fresh wave of warmth through her, something deeper than the fire's heat.

"I told you," she said softly, reaching out to brush her fingers lightly over his hand. "I'm not running."

Ian swallowed hard, his fingers flexing beneath hers before he turned his palm up, lacing their hands together. He held on, his grip just a little tighter than before.

And for the first time in days, Emma saw the flicker of something steady in his eyes.

The tea had warmed her, but it wasn't enough. Not compared to the fire in Ian's gaze.

Emma watched as he took another slow sip, his fingers tight around the mug, his jaw taut. The flickering light painted shadows across his face, highlighting the sharp edges, the tension still clinging to his body despite the quiet moment they had carved for themselves.

He looked at her then—really looked at her—and the heat in his eyes sent a sharp thrill down her spine.

It was the same tension that had coiled between them for weeks, for months, restrained by guilt, by fear, by every excuse they had convinced themselves was reason enough to hold back. But none of it mattered anymore. Not when she could still feel the imprint of his body against hers from the beach, the way he had clung to her like she was the only thing tethering him to the world.

Not when she could feel his hunger, barely contained, barely restrained, even now.

Emma set her mug down with deliberate slowness, her heartbeat thundering in her ears as she closed the space between them. Ian's breath hitched, his knuckles whitening around the ceramic in his grasp, but he didn't stop her.

He wouldn't stop her.

She reached for his cup, prying it gently from his grip, and set it aside before straddling his lap in a slow, deliberate motion. His hands landed on her hips instantly, fingers digging in like he wasn't sure if he meant to pull her closer or hold her at bay.

A shiver ran through him when she flattened her hands against his chest, feeling the solid warmth beneath his damp shirt. The rise and fall of his breath was uneven, shaking slightly as she dragged her fingers upward, slipping beneath the fabric, seeking the heat of his bare skin. She reached for him, tangling her fingers in his wet hair. He let out a shaky sigh and closed the final gap between them, capturing her mouth in a bruising kiss. The air tingled with an electric current, a surge of released tension that crackled through Emma's mind. She tasted salt and longing in that embrace, felt the tremor of his body flush against hers, and let her own tears slip free. Every heartbreak, every panic-ridden night in the orchard, every lonely day waiting for news—she poured that ache into the kiss.

His hands splayed against her lower back, clutching her as if terrified she might dissolve into foam. The roar of the ocean outside was a backdrop for the frantic beat of their hearts.

"Emma," he rasped, his voice tight, almost pained.

She tilted her head, her lips just a breath from his. "No more running."

Ian broke.

His hands surged up her back, dragging her against him as his mouth crashed into hers with a force that stole her breath. There was no hesitation, no caution—only raw, desperate need. He kissed her like he had been starving for her, like he had spent every night alone fighting this, and now, he couldn't fight anymore.

Emma gasped into his mouth as he gripped her hips tighter, rocking her against him, pressing her down until the heat between them burned through the layers of fabric still separating them. His tongue slid against hers, claiming, unyielding, as if he meant to consume her whole.

She matched his urgency, fisting her hands in his shirt and dragging it over his head in one swift motion, her nails scraping lightly down his chest. Ian let out a harsh breath, his body shuddering beneath her touch. Then he was moving—standing in one fluid motion, carrying her with him as her legs wrapped around his waist.

The world blurred as he strode toward the cot against the far wall, his mouth never leaving hers, never slowing. When they tumbled onto the mattress, Emma arched against him, needing more, needing everything.

Ian's hands were everywhere—pushing up her sweater, sliding beneath the fabric to palm the soft curve of her waist, then higher, his touch branding her, igniting her. His lips left hers only to trail a searing path down her neck, nipping, sucking, until she gasped his name, her fingers threading into his hair, anchoring him to her.

He groaned against her skin, the sound rough, desperate. "I can't—" He broke off, pulling back just enough to meet her gaze, his pupils blown wide with hunger, his breath ragged. "I can't be careful with you right now."

Emma shivered, her pulse hammering. "Then don't be."

That was all it took.

Ian ripped the rest of their clothes away in a flurry of movement, his hands rough with need, his body pressing her into the mattress, surrounding her with heat and fire and him. There was no slow buildup, no teasing restraint. Just the frantic, unrelenting crash of bodies finally giving in, finally taking what they had denied themselves for too long.

Emma clung to him as he claimed her, their breaths mingling, their bodies molding together in a way that felt inevitable. Every thrust, every movement was wild, fierce frantic rhythm that bordered on desperation, as if they were making up for every moment they had held back.

Her name left his lips like a prayer, his voice wrecked, ruined as she came apart beneath him.

And when he followed—his grip tightening, his body trembling, Emma knew, without a doubt, that neither of them would ever let go again.

When they broke apart, both of them breathed heavily. Emma's lips tingled, and Ian's eyes glistened with more than moonlight. As the fire crackled softly in the hearth, its golden glow casting flickering shadows across the small cottage, the storm outside raged on. Wind howled through the cracks in the wooden frame, rain drumming steadily against the roof, but inside, everything was warm—quiet.

Emma lay tangled with Ian beneath the worn blankets, their bodies still entwined, skin flushed from more than just the lingering heat of their lovemaking. Her heart had yet to settle, her breath still uneven, but the urgency between them had melted into something slower, deeper.

The kind of closeness that wasn't just about desire but about belonging.

Ian hadn't spoken for a long moment. He lay on his back, one arm wrapped securely around her, the other resting over his forehead as if he were trying to steady himself. His chest rose and fell in slow, measured breaths, but Emma could feel the tension creeping back in, the weight pressing down on him now that the moment of passion had passed.

She traced her fingers lightly over his ribs, her touch featherlight, reassuring. "Ian," she murmured, pressing her cheek against his bare shoulder. "You're thinking too much."

A short, rough laugh escaped him, but it lacked humor. His fingers flexed against her skin, gripping her tighter for just a second before loosening. "I didn't hurt you, did I?" he admitted, voice hoarse. "I sort of..." He let out a slow, unsteady breath. "Lost myself for a second."

Emma's heart squeezed. "Well, I appreciate that you took the time to practice safe sex. But it wasn't my first time having sex, but it was my first time making love. Now I know the difference. That was a first for me."

She propped herself up on her elbow, studying him in the dim light. The sharp edges of his face were softer now, his expression raw, open in a way he so rarely allowed. The flicker of vulnerability in his eyes made her ache—for everything he had been through, for the war he still waged within himself.

She reached out, brushing damp strands of hair from his forehead. "You do deserve this," she whispered, letting her lips graze his temple, lingering there as if she could press the words into him, make him believe them. "And so, do I. I'm not going to let you convince yourself otherwise."

Ian turned then, rolling onto his side so they were face to face, his hand sliding up to cup her cheek. His thumb traced slow, reverent circles along her skin, his touch hesitant in a way that was entirely different from before. This wasn't desperation—it was worship.

His throat bobbed as he swallowed. "I don't know how to keep this, Emma," he admitted, barely above a whisper. "I don't know how to hold onto something good without ruining it."

She caught his hand, pressing it flat against her chest, right over her heartbeat. "Then let me show you," she murmured. "Let me stay."

Ian's breath hitched, his fingers trembling slightly against her skin. And then he kissed her again—not frantic, not hungry, but slow and searching, like he was trying to memorize every part of her, trying to trust that she wasn't going anywhere.

"I hate how powerless I feel sometimes," he confessed, voice raw. "Lately, it's all illusions and nightmares. I keep seeing the orchard twisted with shadows, hearing your voice beg me to—" He couldn't finish, but she knew what haunted him.

She cupped his face again, thumbing away the tears he tried and failed to hide. "You're not powerless," she said with firm conviction. "You have me, and I promise I'm not leaving. Let's figure out how to lighten this burden. Let's do it together."

Finally, she placed a hand on his chest, feeling the wild thud of his heart. "I can't pretend the curse doesn't scare me," she admitted. "But I'm more afraid of losing you to your own self-doubt."

He brought his hands up, linking his fingers gently behind her back. "I want to believe you can walk this road with me." He sniffed, laughter threading through the last of his tears. "A part of me still thinks I'm so broken I can't be saved, but you're the only person who's made me hope I'm wrong."

Emma's vision blurred with fresh tears, but she smiled through them. "Then hold onto that hope," she murmured, pressing her palm flat against his chest. The vitality under her hand felt like tangible proof of the bond they shared. "I'm hoping too."

He leaned in once more, brushing his lips over hers in a softer kiss that made her heart lurch. "Emma…" He paused, as though uncertain how to form the words. Then he whispered, "I love you." The phrase trembled over his lips, charged with both tenderness and fear. "I'm sorry I tried to push you away."

Her heart soared. Relief and euphoria mingled like a warm tide in her chest. She let out a shaky breath, cradling him close. "I love you too," she answered quietly. "No more running. The illusions don't get to dictate our story."

He nodded; voice low. "I swear I'm done hiding. Even if the curse fights back, even if it throws nightmares at me every night, I won't leave you behind."

For a moment, the only sound was the crash of waves and the rattle of the tin roof over their heads. She rested her head on his shoulder, overcome by the cycle of raw emotion that had carried her from heartbreak to this night of briny confessions. The tension seeped from her body as she realized how close she'd come to losing him to his own despair.

"Emma," he murmured against her hair, "thank you for finding me." His voice held a quiet amazement, as though each second, he spent in her presence fell outside the nightmares that sought to claim his mind. "I felt so lost."

She closed her eyes, letting the words settle into her heart. "We'll figure out how to deal with the curse," she said. "But we'll do it together. Promise me one thing... stay, at least until sunrise."

He glanced out the window toward the horizon, where the glow from the moon lit the waves crashing against the rocks. "I'm staying," he said, voice resolute. "But I'll need to get you home before your grandmother starts worrying."

"Yes, we can't have that," Emma smiled lazily.

They circled each other's arms again, their embrace fierce enough to banish the lingering turmoil of the last few days. She felt the ocean's power churn outside but neither moved from that spot. He pressed his forehead to hers in a quiet moment of communion, and her heart fluttered with a heady rush of love, fear, and the promise of something stronger than both.

Time seemed meaningless in that cabin. She lost herself in the music of the surf, in the warmth of his hands, in the ragged edge of calm that they clung to with everything they had. The tears that slipped free were no longer just anger or frustration. They were tears that affirmed the depth of this moment, transcending disappointment and forging a new path forward.

He spoke again, quiet enough that only she could hear above the waves. "I can't promise all the nightmares will stop tonight, but I can promise I won't run from them." His voice shook with emotion. "I'll do whatever it takes to protect what we have."

She slid her arms around his body, letting the tension ebb from her shoulders. "I'll meet them with you," she said. "All of them. Nightmares don't stand a chance against the two of us together."

They stayed like that, watching the fire dance in the grate. Emma inhaled the salty air, each breath an attempt to steady the thrill of being so in love with this man.

Then, without warning, the air in the fisherman's cabin shifted. The temperature inside plummeted, and a prickling sensation crept down Emma's arms, as though unseen fingers skated across her skin. If she couldn't hear the fire crackling in the fireplace, she would've sworn it had gone out completely. Sharp fear stabbed her heart. She jerked upright in alarm, head snapping toward the dunes. The moonlight shining through the window, which had previously glowed with soothing brightness, now felt oddly harsh—like a cold lantern casting white-blue shadows along the sand.

"Ian," she whispered, voice trembling with uncertainty. "Something's coming. I can feel it."

Ian pushed himself up, taking Emma with him as he

rose swiftly to his feet. She followed, heart pounding, her limbs stiff from lying wrapped in blankets for so long. The fire still crackled in the grate, but it did nothing to dispel the sudden iciness pressing in around them, a creeping sensation that slithered over her skin like an unseen presence. They each grabbed their clothes and quickly dressed.

Ian reached for his coat, yanking it on in one swift motion before tossing hers toward her. "I feel it too," he said, his voice low but edged with urgency.

Emma caught the coat, her fingers fumbling slightly as she slid her arms into the sleeves. The weight of it did little to ease the cold sinking into her bones. She glanced toward the window. The fireplace no longer had the quiet glow that had bathed them in warmth earlier. Now, the air felt sharp, sterile, and the fire casted jagged shadows across the floor.

Ian was already at the door, his posture rigid, every muscle coiled tight. He hesitated for the briefest moment before glancing back at her, his eyes dark and unreadable in the dim light.

"Stay close," he murmured.

Emma nodded, swallowing down the fear rising in her throat. Then, together, they stepped outside.

Ian looked up toward the bluff; his muscles tensed. The wind changed direction, carrying a new scent of something stale and unsettling. Emma swallowed hard. A presence was there. She sensed it as if one might sense the moment before lightning strikes—electric, dangerous.

At the bottom of the rocky cliff, a shape materialized. Catherine emerged in a pale cloak that clung eerily to her slight frame. At first, she seemed as insubstantial as the wind, hardly more than a silhouette in shifting moonbeams. Then, inch by inch, her features sharpened, and Emma's heart lurched at the sight of eyes brimming with quiet malice.

Catherine's posture hinted at practiced composure, but there was an intensity in her stance that spoke of hunting. She took one measured step forward, her cloak brushing the gravel. A memory surfaced in Emma's mind: the braided twig she had found in her own garden, knotted with a strand of her hair and smeared with something foul. That moment had left Emma feeling violated, and now, seeing Catherine so unexpectedly ending such a wonderful encounter with Ian made her gut twist.

"Such a lovely evening," Catherine remarked in a voice both too soft and too pointed. She advanced with careful grace, salt-laden wind tugging the edges of her hood. "And such a dramatic storm of magic you two have summoned. I couldn't help noticing it from... afar." A cold smile tugged at the corner of her mouth.

Emma's throat tightened. Sadie had told her that Catherine was powerful. She also knew Catherine had tampered with illusions around Crestwood—subtle manipulations that rattled the orchard, spiked Ian's nightmares, and nearly shattered Emma's peace of mind over the last few days. The glimpses of hexes, the feeling of being watched: all signs pointed to Catherine's lethal brand of curiosity.

Ian stepped in front of Emma, as though shielding her from a sudden strike. Emma's pulse roared in her ears. She clutched the fabric of his jacket, drawing courage from the press of his shoulder blades beneath her palms.

Catherine's gaze drifted deliberately to Ian. "How touching," she murmured, eyes gleaming with predatory interest. "Such devotion." Her tone dripped with mock pleasure. "I must admit, I find your partnership... intriguing."

Emma gritted her teeth. Adrenaline pulsed beneath her skin, urging her to cast some kind of defensive spell on the spot. But she hesitated, uncertain if an outright attack would only feed Catherine's meddling. She forced herself to inhale deeply, trying to quell the nagging feeling that they were ill-prepared for this confrontation.

"Leave us alone," Ian said quietly, but there was an iron edge to his voice. The night air curled around him, stirring the sand at his feet. Emma recognized that flicker of tension in his stance—his warlock power, braced for a potential strike.

Catherine's thin smile deepened. She took another step across the dunes, arms folded neatly within the cloak's pale folds. "Leave you alone? But you two have created quite a spectacle. I must say, magic practically crackles when you stand so close." She cast Emma a side-long glance that reeked of condescension. "I couldn't resist tasting the echoes of it."

An urge to speak flared inside Emma, but her mind spun, torn between outraged fury and self-preservation. She could almost feel the orchard's protective wards miles away, as though calling out in faint alarm. If Catherine intended to strike, the open sand left nowhere to hide.

Ian's shoulders squared. "We don't owe you any explanation," he said, each word clipped. "Whatever you've done to torment us stops now."

"Torment you?" Catherine's voice floated closer to laughter than alarm. "My dear, if you believe that simple illusions and half-cast hexes are all I'm capable of, you're far too innocent to be dabbling in curses."

Emma's heart hammered. She thought of Sadie's many warnings, the hours spent fortifying the cottage's wards, and her own half-formed protective spells. Catherine might already know how to pick those defenses apart, if she had wanted to. The woman was cunning, and her illusions had proven disturbingly effective.

She cleared her throat and forced her voice not to tremble. "You're wasting your time," Emma said, stepping out from behind Ian to stand at his side. She refused to hide. "We've found ways to block your hexes before. We can do it again."

"It's adorable that you think so." Catherine tilted her head, her smile twisting into something more feral. "I do congratulate you on this new... bond. Romance under the moonlight is so enchanting, don't you agree?" Her eyes glistened with scorn. "But you should remember that lovers make each other vulnerable. Weakness in lovers is easy to exploit."

The words sank like a stone in Emma's chest. She knew exactly what Catherine was hinting at. The illusions that plagued Ian's sleep had always seized on his love for her as a tool to twist, turning every caring thought into terror. Catherine could do the same again, perhaps on a far more devastating scale.

A swirl of wind gusted through the inlet, fluttering Catherine's cloak. Emma tensed, expecting an attack, but all Catherine did was lift one hand in a mocking, half-wave goodbye. She parted her lips as though preparing another biting remark, but the wind snatched her words, scattering them into the night. Moments later, her figure seemed to shimmer.

"Stop playing games," Emma spat, desperation slipping into her tone.

Catherine's figure wavered, the edges of her outline flickering with silver threads of moonlight. "Games?" she echoed, voice distorted. "We're only just beginning, dear Emma."

Ian's hand clenched at his side, bright sparks forming near his knuckles. Emma could almost taste the surge of protective magic rolling off him, but Catherine gave him no target. One second she was there, her cloak flapping in the wind, and the next, she was gone. All that remained was a fleeting swirl of sand and a deeper chill in the salty breeze.

Emma stumbled forward with a frustrated gasp, but the only trace of Catherine was the lingering menace in the air. The back of her neck tingled, and she instinctively glanced over her shoulder, half-expecting the librarian's face to loom out of the darkness again.

Ian let out a trembling breath and turned to Emma. "Are you all right?" His voice tightened, betraying leftover adrenaline.

She nodded even though her heart still pounded. "Yes," she whispered, stepping closer to him. "You?"

He exhaled slowly, some of his tension unwinding. "I've been better," he admitted. "But as long as you're safe..."

They fell silent, scanning the bluff illuminated by moonlight. Emma rubbed her arms, trying to dispel the phantom chill Catherine had left behind. Her thoughts swirled with the witch's final warning. *Weakness in lovers is easy to exploit.* The phrase grated on her nerves, and she wished she could fling that cruelty right back in Catherine's face.

She caught Ian's gaze, reading his own tumult of worry. In that moment, they didn't need words to acknowledge the precarious tightrope they now walked. Their bond, so newly reaffirmed, might be the exact weapon Catherine intended to twist against them. Yet Emma refused to cower and let fear split them apart again.

She took Ian's hand, her chest knotting with defiance. "We won't let her tear us apart," she said softly, half to him and half to herself. "We've come too far." She recalled the ache of longing that used to consume her when she believed he had vanished for good. She wouldn't return to that lonely place, not for Catherine or any curse.

He squeezed her hand gently. "No more running," he murmured. "Whatever she tries next, I'm not going to abandon you."

Emma swallowed hard, her eyes stinging. The sincerity in his face stoked her resolve. She remembered

Sadie's teachings: illusions latch onto fear and friction; true love and trust can disrupt a manipulator's craft. Though she still felt small tremors of lingering dread, her determination flared stronger. Catherine might be skilled, but Emma and Ian possessed something more potent than fear.

They gazed at the vacant rocky bluff. Moonlight glinted off the tagged rocks, painting the landscape in shades of ghostly silver. Catherine's dismissal left Emma's ears ringing. The ocean's roar took on a quieter tone, as if the sea itself needed time to recover from the malevolence that had tainted the night air.

Ian inhaled, regaining some composure. Together, they turned, scanning the cove for any other sign of Catherine's illusions. Nothing stirred except the steady break of waves. Emma's mind strayed to the orchard—she imagined the runes carved into the trunks, the feel of the orchard's comforting energies, the protective wards Sadie often refreshed. She wished, fleetingly, that they were back in that orchard's warm protection. At least they knew that space, and it seemed far more prepared for magical intrusions.

She brushed sand off her damp legs, still holding Ian's hand. "She wants us trembling," she said, letting anger seep into her words. "She wants us separated, second-guessing ourselves. But we won't give her the satisfaction."

Ian's eyes flicked with renewed resolve. "You're right," he said, voice low. "We stand together. Always."

A fierce swirl of protectiveness welled up in Emma's

chest. She found herself remembering all the humiliations Catherine had inflicted: the hexed twig, the hair she'd used without permission. Those had been warnings, preludes to deeper games. Now Catherine's words about exploiting lovers hammered home just how far she was willing to go.

Emma squared her shoulders, letting the wind whip her hair across her cheek. She realized that perhaps, at some level, Catherine wanted them to cower. Sadie had told her that Catherine thrived on fear and rifts, on illusions that distorted self-trust. The best defense Emma and Ian could wield was their unwavering partnership, forcing Catherine to confront a unity not easily shaken.

They exchanged a single, solemn nod. The vow took root in Emma's soul: no matter how twisted Catherine's illusions became; she wouldn't bow to them. If Catherine thought love was a weakness, Emma would prove otherwise.

Keeping their fingers intertwined, they walked down the path and back toward Sadie's cottage. Though goose bumps still blanketed Emma's arms, the worst of her terror had subsided. Catherine might lurk in the shadows, but she no longer had the advantage of surprise.

She stopped and took one final look at the vacant stretch where the witch had disappeared. Silence hung thick in the air, but Emma's thoughts whirled with renewed purpose. True danger lurked beyond the gloom, that much was certain. A determined spark ignited in her core. Catherine had chosen the wrong night, and the wrong pair, to threaten with those cryptic warnings.

Ian's breath warmed the side of Emma's face. "Emma," he murmured, voice taut with resolve. "Let's get you back home."

"Yes," Emma agreed, swallowing the knot in her throat. "I hate that the witch interrupted one of the best nights of my life. I'm going to make her pay for that."

Ian let out a warm chuckle. "There will be more nights like this, don't you worry."

She moved toward him and gave him a soft kiss before turning back up the path. "Yes, there will."

They walked hand in hand, both still looking for the pale-cloaked figure who had threatened them. In that moment, the vow in both their hearts was unwavering: Catherine had meddled for the last time.

TEN

Emma caught her breath the moment she and Ian crossed the threshold into Sadie's cottage. The usually inviting scent of rosemary tea and dried mint felt oddly stale. A silvery hush blanketed the rooms, like the calm before a thunderclap. She set her foot on the wooden floor; it creaked from the weight of her nerves. Her muscles tensed further when she glimpsed Sadie in the small kitchen, arms folded tight against her chest.

A single lamp glowed on the countertop. Its muted orange light left shadows against the shelves laden with jars of herbs and half-labeled tonic vials. Sadie's jaw was set. She watched them enter as if she had been waiting for hours, eyes carrying a hurt that made Emma's chest tighten. On the table, Emma's journal lay open, pages splayed like a confession she had never intended anyone to read.

Emma's heart thudded, and heat prickled along her neck. The notion that Sadie had read her private thoughts about Ian—the swirling confusion, the dangerous longing, her fear that his nightmares would link with her own—made her want to shrink. If Sadie had discovered everything, there was no hiding how her emotions fueled her magic.

"Welcome home," Sadie said, her voice calm in a way that felt sharper than open anger. The salt-laced breeze whispered through a crack in the window, carrying a faint tang of the orchard's damp soil. "I went into your room because I sensed a disturbance, an unraveling of wards."

Emma swallowed. She remembered leaving her journal in haste just before going to find Ian earlier that evening. Neither one of them had expected to return to confront Sadie right away. "You... found it." Her gaze flicked to the journal, inescapably direct.

Sadie's brows rose. "I did." She breathed in, then laid her palm gently on the battered cover. "Why did you not tell me your feelings toward Ian were... that strong? Do you realize how this might endanger us all?"

Her words struck Emma like a gust of chill wind. "Your wards? My room is my private space," Emma burst out. Her pulse galloped as she remembered the scattered lines she had jotted down just that afternoon, lines filled with confessions about how Ian's presence made her heart pound and how she feared losing him to the illusions. "You had no right to read them."

Sadie's lips thinned. "This wasn't about prying. I sensed unsteady magic. I went in prepared to reinforce your wards. Why were you funneling so much power into your emotions without telling me?"

Emma hesitated. She tried to slow her breathing, but the injustice surged. "Feelings aren't something you turn off. As for power—" She glared at the open journal. "That was my private way of coping."

Ian hovered near the door; tension evident in the way he clenched his hands at his sides. The low hum of his aura prickled at Emma's awareness. He looked as though he wanted to speak but didn't know where to begin. Instead, he took a small step forward. "Maybe we can calm down. This might be a misunderstanding."

Sadie kept her gaze on Emma. "It is not only about the journal. It is what the entries say. You talk about forging stronger spells with Ian by your side. You describe a longing that can tangle with illusions."

"Your illusions are my nightmares," he said gently. Yet his voice trembled, betraying his own worry.

Emma felt her cheeks burn. She had written about the magnetic surge when Ian kissed her, how she suspected that same surge stirred deeper magic in them both. She thought about the orchard at midnight, about the fear that Catherine might twist these feelings to create new horrors. Those words had been sealed away in her journal, not meant for Sadie's eyes.

"You don't understand how complicated this is," Emma insisted. Her voice edged higher than she intended. "You taught me that love can be a strength. Why is it suddenly a risk?"

Sadie's stance stiffened. "Because I can sense your power roaring beyond your control. Love is an asset if it steadies you, but it can also blind you. This bond with Ian could be exploited by Catherine. Do you remember how illusions thrive when emotion runs hot and unguarded?"

Emma's frustration snapped. "Stop acting like I'm a child who can't manage my own life." Her eyes burned. "Yes, I know illusions can twist what we feel, but I'm not ignorant. I feel what I feel, and I refuse to pretend it is not real just to make you comfortable."

Sadie's magical presence radiated in the small space, pressing on Emma's senses. The lamplight flickered, casting a dancing glow over the herb jars. "I'm not telling you to pretend," Sadie said, voice trembling with worry beneath the sternness. "I'm telling you that your vulnerability to illusions intensifies when you pour every thought into Ian instead of learning deliberate control. You wrote pages of longing, of willingness to risk anything for him. Emma, this is precisely how curses slip deeper into unsuspecting hearts."

A spark of raw power sizzled near the ceiling, a small snap of uncontained energy that ricocheted. Emma watched, wide-eyed, as it popped like a tiny firework, drifting to the kitchen tiles in a fizzled ember. Her anger whirled, both at Sadie for reading her journal and at the stifling sense that her grandmother still viewed her as incapable of measured caution.

Ian cleared his throat. "I understand your worry," he said, stepping between Emma and Sadie. "But I promise, I never intended to drag Emma deeper into illusions."

Sadie's gaze swung toward Ian. "I see your sincerity. Yet your nightmares persist. They intrude on her peace, whether you intend it or not. Do you believe I want to lose you both because of a bond that fuels illusions more than it guards against them?"

Her voice cracked. Emma stole a glance at Ian. His brow creased with turmoil, and a faint bead of sweat glistened at his temple. Sadie's question about illusions cut close to the fear that had haunted him for weeks: that the curse would devour him and, by extension, devour Emma.

Emma tried to swallow the swell of indignation. "I'm not some naive girl." Her words came out raw. "Maybe it looks reckless to you, but I need to make my own choices. You told me power responds to truth. Ian is part of my truth whether you approve or not."

Sadie's eyes flashed. "And if that truth leads you to ruin?"

Emma let out a ragged breath. "Stop policing my heart. Every time I let you guide me, you hold back important details until it is almost too late. You don't trust me to handle what I feel, or to protect myself. You have never fully trusted me with knowledge of this magic—like I'm forever a child."

The tension in the cottage thickened, and the overhead light sputtered as if the electrical current mirrored their emotional storm. Ian lifted his hands, palms outward in a gesture that begged calm. "We can all talk through this without raising voices."

Emma's temper refused to subside. Sadie had withheld crucial truths about the orchard and that stoked the flames of her resentment. She turned toward Ian. "She read the entire journal, everything I wrote about you. She read my private thoughts, the anxieties I had no one else to share with." Her voice shook.

Sadie extended her arms. "I don't want secrets between us. If you felt alone, you should have come to me."

Emma's hand curled into a fist. Lightning lanced under her skin, a crackle of half-formed wards itching to break free. "That is exactly the problem. You only share knowledge on your terms." She forced herself to breathe slowly. "It was my room. You had no right to do that. No right at all."

Ian stepped closer to Emma, searching her gaze. "We don't have to—"

"And you," Sadie interjected, her voice sharper than Emma had ever heard it around Ian. "You keep luring her into illusions. I see the notes you leave, then you vanish, then you return. Every time you reappear, her magic reels in some new crisis."

Emma's heart pounded in dual sympathy and anger. She was furious that Sadie blamed Ian's presence while also recalling her grandmother's exhaustion from warding spells night after night. She thought of how the orchard had stirred beneath the moonlight, how it had responded to her tears for him, how it had thrummed with power when he kissed her among the trees.

"Ian is not some cursed monster you can scold away!" Emma practically shouted. The edges of her vision shimmered with tears. "Stop treating him like that. Yes, we have illusions to face. Yes, I love him." The words hung in the kitchen air, vibrant and unstoppable.

Sadie's face paled. The energy in the room crackled, sending another jolt through the overhead light. Dishes rattled in the sink. Emma had never voiced those three words so plainly until that moment, and the confession rebounded through her veins with a potent mix of terror and relief.

Ian stiffened, eyes flicking to Emma in shock that she had spoken so openly about her emotions in front of Sadie.

Sadie whispered, "Your devotion blinds you, Emma. You don't understand the darkness clinging to his family line." She locked her arms around herself, as though trying to contain her own trembling. "You see only the warmth in him, not the centuries of broken pacts that brought us to this point."

Emma wiped a stray tear from her cheek. She hated how small she sounded when she asked, "Do you really believe I'm that foolish?"

Sadie's chin rose. "I believe you're in danger of heartbreak and worse. Your entries made it clear how far you're willing to go for him. It scares me to the core."

Ian tried to lay a gentle hand on Sadie's arm, but she stepped back, turning away from him. The gesture left him standing awkwardly, sorrow and guilt shadowing his features. He exhaled a shaky breath and turned toward Emma. "Maybe this was a mistake. I shouldn't have come back so soon. Not if it causes this much strife."

Emma's heart twisted. "Ian, don't say that."

Sadie looked over her shoulder, eyes burdened with

regret. "I don't want either of you hurt, but this is spiraling. Catherine's illusions—"

Emma slammed her journal shut. The report of the cover against the table rang like a gavel. "Stop making Catherine the center of every choice I make. I'm here, making decisions for myself. You don't own my feelings, or my mind. I'm done being treated like your child apprentice who is too weak to carry any burden alone."

"That is not what I meant," Sadie said. "Your life does not just belong to you. You carry a legacy that protects this town. If you let illusions tear you and Ian apart, Crestwood will be more vulnerable than ever. This is not about you alone. It is about all of us."

Ian lifted his gaze, eyes filled with guilt. "She is not wrong, Emma. My nightmares aren't just mine. They shape illusions that can harm you, her—everyone."

Emma's cheeks flamed. She felt pulled in two directions, one by the love she had for Ian, the other by the loyalty she owed her grandmother. The frustration ignited inside her, a conflagration that made her want to fling the nearest object. Instead, her breath turned shallow, and her words came out unsteady. "No. I can't do this right now. I'm not some caretaker of illusions alone. I'm a person with a heart."

Her vision blurred with angry tears. She grabbed the journal off the table and clutched it to her chest. She hoped no more uncontained magic would spark overhead, but her frustration rippled in the form of shimmering motes near the rafters.

Sadie tried to speak, yet her voice cracked. "Emma—"

"I already know what you'll say," Emma snapped. She couldn't bear to see the disappointment in Sadie's eyes. This was the same grandmother who had shown her how to coax small seeds into sprouting with a gentle incantation, who had poured hours into teaching Emma protective wards. Now it felt like a chasm growing between them.

Ian cleared his throat, stepping forward with hands spread as if to quiet them both. "We have all been through a lot. Let me leave, Sadie. Emma is upset. Maybe some space will help."

Emma shot him a wounded glance. "You want to run off again?"

He swallowed, the hesitation stark in his features. "I don't want to make this more painful. I never wanted to wedge you and Sadie apart." He exhaled, gaze flickering between them. "But I see no solution right now. This argument is hurting everyone. I should go."

Silence fell, thick as difficult clay. Emma's fingers tightened on the edges of her journal. She couldn't look at Sadie's sorrowful face or Ian's tortured expression. It was too much, all of it.

Sadie closed her eyes, giving Ian a short nod. He turned toward the door. Emma almost wanted to call him back, to shout that they would fix it together, but each breath scraped her lungs, torn between fury at Sadie's intrusion and remorse for the heartbreak scrawled across Ian's face.

He rested a trembling hand briefly on Emma's shoulder. When she didn't stop him, he walked out into the dark. The front door opened and closed with a stark click.

Emma caught a glimpse of shallow moonlight outside before the door shut. Waves of guilt battered her, but she couldn't let them overshadow her anger at Sadie. She couldn't let them overshadow the sting of betrayal. She glanced again at Sadie, whose shoulders had fallen, as though awaiting some final condemnation.

"I can't look at you right now," Emma whispered, voice raw. The cottage felt too small, its walls pressing in with the weight of failed trust. She turned on her heel and rushed past the threshold before Sadie could respond.

Her feet carried her outside, the night air rushing over her heated face. Angry tears burned as she hurried off the porch. The orchard's ghostly silhouettes loomed behind the cottage, but she couldn't bring herself to venture there. Instead, her boots scraped across the gravel path, each step punctuated by her ragged breathing. Her heart thundered with conflict: the grandmother who had sheltered her, the warlock who had stolen her heart, and the illusions that turned love into something dangerous.

She stopped near the edge of the garden, a place where a meager patch of moonlight slipped through the thick canopy. She clenched her journal to her chest. How had everything unraveled so fast? Part of her wanted to run inside and beg Sadie to forgive her. Another part wanted to chase Ian, wrap herself in his arms, and let that shared magic soothe her.

But she couldn't endure a single moment more in that charged kitchen, nor face the grief in Sadie's eyes. She couldn't risk letting her tears fall in front of someone who had just dismissed her most private longings as reckless. In that moment, she felt torn open, uncertain which path to choose, or if either path had room for reconciliation.

She pressed her forehead against a wooden post near the fence. She pushed down a sob, and her shoulders shook. The orchard's wind brushed over her, hardly a comforting gesture. She wanted comfort and had no idea where to find it.

Caught between the guidance of the family magic she wouldn't forsake and her intense love for Ian, Emma let her tears flow. She closed her eyes, wishing the ache in her chest would subside. Yet the sting of betrayal, embarrassment, and heartbreak refused to lighten, and the night air gave no easy answers.

ELEVEN

Emma entered quietly, her pulse thrumming as she listened intently for any sound inside the cottage. A single lamp glowed in the living room, its light pooling over the floorboards, but she heard only the low whoosh of Sadie's breathing. An hour had passed since their argument, yet Emma's chest still felt raw from the words they had flung at each other. She clenched her journal against her side, remembering how Sadie's discovery of its contents—her private thoughts and unspoken hopes— had left them both reeling.

The cottage felt far smaller than usual. Stacks of old books loomed on shelves, and the faint smell of rosemary tea clung to every corner, as if it refused to let go of gentler moments. A few magical motes still flickered at the edge of the rafters, their glow a stark reminder of the grab-bag of stress and hurt that had sparked Emma's untamed energy earlier. Her hands trembled a little at the memory. She no longer felt anger, only an anxious ache in her stomach.

She stepped into the living room, careful not to make the floor creak. Sadie had retreated to her rocking chair, an old quilt draped over her knees. The older woman's eyes were closed, though her brow remained tight with lingering worry. Emma's heart squeezed with guilt. She still chafed at the loss of her privacy, yet she hated the sight of Sadie looking so worn.

Emma forced herself to turn away. Standing there forever would not fix anything. She slipped through the front door, journals and unresolved conflict pressed close to her chest, and stepped onto the porch. The night air collided with her cheeks, cool and briny. She let out a shaky breath, scanning the dark outline of the orchard.

She felt it before she saw him. A stirring of magic drifted from the trees, a subtle tug that set her pulse racing. She closed her eyes and focused, sensing Ian's presence somewhere within that tangle of branches. Her arguments with Sadie had overshadowed every rational thought earlier, but her bond with Ian tugged her forward now, coaxing her down the porch steps.

Patches of moonlight crossed her path as she navigated the orchard's overgrown trail. Gnarled trunks rose on either side, their twisted limbs reaching overhead as though to stitch the night sky shut. Leaves rustled in a restless breeze that teased the edges of her jacket. Despite the orchard's usual soothing calm, she felt a faint crackle in the air, a sign of magic that had never fully settled since they had left the cabin.

At last, she caught sight of Ian's silhouette. He leaned against a tree trunk near the orchard's far clearing, arms crossed tightly over his chest. Even in the dim light, she discerned the tension lining his jaw, the set of his shoulders. Relief flooded her so powerfully that her knees felt weak. She had feared he might have run off again, especially after the chaos from an hour before.

He stepped forward as she approached, the gentle crunch of fallen leaves underfoot the only sound besides the drumbeat in her ears. "Emma," he murmured. His tone hovered between caution and concern.

She managed a slight nod, realizing she was clutching her journal so hard her fingers hurt. She hesitated, unsure how to begin. In one breath, everything she had bottled up threatened to spill out: the fury at Sadie for invading her privacy, the guilt at hurting the one person who was now her family, the dread that every rope of tension in her life was about to snap.

Ian opened his arms a fraction, an invitation if she wanted it. She did. She crossed the distance and let her forehead brush against his collarbone. The orchard's earthy scent mingled with the soft hint of his aftershave, creating an odd comfort amid her churning thoughts.

His hand rested on her shoulder. "Are you okay?" His voice stayed low, as if he feared a single louder word might unravel her.

She answered with a humorless laugh. "Not really. I still can't believe...everything that happened with Sadie."

His chest moved in a silent sigh, the warmth of his body grounding her. "I'm sorry," he whispered. "I never wanted to put a wedge between you two."

Emma swallowed, her throat tight. "None of this is

your fault. She's panicked that my feelings for you might make me reckless, that they'll open me up to Catherine's illusions or something worse." She paused, chest aching with tension. "I can't pretend my magic isn't tied to you. Every time I try, it just gets stronger, and then I make mistakes because I'm afraid. I... don't know what to do."

Ian curled his fingers around Emma's. "I understand the fear," he said quietly. "At times I think my nightmares would vanish if I left Crestwood—if I stayed away from you. But that's a lie, isn't it? The illusions don't die just because I run."

She felt each syllable reverberate through his chest. The orchard flickered with a faint glow, as if the trees themselves leaned in to hear. Emma inhaled the crisp night air, tasting a hint of salted moisture on her lips. "I'm terrified," she admitted, her voice raw. "I'm worried I'll fail you. I'm worried about Sadie, about Catherine... about us."

Ian's thumb brushed the back of her hand in a slow, soothing gesture. The warmth that spread through her felt more genuine than any calming herb Sadie had ever brewed. "I need you to know that you help me more than you hurt me," he said. "I don't say that lightly." He paused, struggling for words. "Your presence is the only thing that eases the nightmares. It's like a guiding light. But if that weighs on you—"

She shook her head, pressing closer. This conversation felt like a precarious incantation; a string of confessions held together by bare courage. "I want to be there for you," she said, voice trembling with sincerity. "I'm just afraid that every step we take forward, Catherine will use it against us."

He exhaled, dropping his gaze to the journal pinned between them. "She might. But whether we stand together or stand apart, Catherine won't stop. Hiding might buy time, not safety." His eyes met Emma's, reflecting the silver glow of moonlight. "We can't face this alone. Haven't we tried that already, and didn't it end in more hurt?"

A wave of memories rushed through her mind: the painful nights she spent searching for him, the illusions that clawed at his sanity, the moment on the beach when they realized running never eased the curse. She tightened her grip on his hand. "You're right," she said quietly.

His breath hitched as he moved even closer. They stood amid ghostly swaths of moonlight, the orchard's silhouettes forming a natural cathedral around them. Leaves rustled overhead, offering no judgment, only gentle acceptance. Emma could sense the swirl of magic circling their feet, a silent promise of what they might achieve if they truly worked as one.

She decided to give voice to the doubts that had plagued her all evening. "Sadie thinks my heart is blinding me. She thinks that these feelings... that they make me too vulnerable." Her cheeks heated with the confession. She wasn't usually so explicit about the pull she felt towards Ian, but tonight demanded honesty.

He cupped her cheek. For the first time, she caught the glint of faint runic shapes on the bracelet around his wrist. "Love can blind us," he said softly. "But it can also be our strongest anchor. I'd rather trust our bond than pretend it's not there."

The next breath she let out was uneven, her pulse kicking up as if she had cast a spell without speaking a word. She reached for him, curling her fingers in the collar of his jacket. The orchard's shadows danced around them. She could taste his uncertainty, could feel the quiet desperation that matched her own.

She tugged him closer. The press of his mouth against hers sent a surge of warmth skittering across her skin. It felt more intense than any incantation. The orchard, the cottage, Sadie's anger, Catherine's threats, everything melted into the electric rush of that kiss. Her journal slipped from her grasp, tumbling to the grass at their feet.

Ian's arms slid around her waist, pulling her into the curve of his body. She could feel the thunder of his heart, could sense the raw desire in the way his fingers settled against her back. Her own pulse hammered against her ribs. A stray breeze swept through, stirring her hair and brushing it across his cheek.

Their kiss deepened, hungry and desperate, as if they could push away every fear by clinging tighter. The orchard seemed to pulse with gentle energy, the leaves whispering encouragement. Emma let herself sink into the sensation, let her trembling lips convey the apology she might never have the right words for, let her pulse do the talking.

When they finally broke apart, they both stood breathless. She let her forehead rest against his, noticing the faint sheen of moisture on his skin.

Ian brushed a stray tear from the corner of Emma's eye. "I hate that I've caused so much tension between you and Sadie," he murmured. "I wish I knew how to fix things."

She slid her hand along his arm, trailing her fingertips over the etched runes on his bracelet. "It's not on you to fix. Sadie and I… we'll have to talk it out eventually. Right now, all I can do is try not to break under this pressure." She inhaled deeply, letting the orchard's earthy warmth fill her lungs. "At least we have each other."

She bent down to pick up her fallen journal, rising to stand again with her back brushing the rough bark of the tree. "I came out here because I needed to see you, no matter what Sadie says." The confession sounded braver than she felt, but it was true.

He reached for her free hand, interlacing their fingers. "I'm glad you did. I've been waiting, not sure if I had any right to hope you'd show. You've done so much already."

Through the labyrinth of orchard shadows, she felt the restlessness of the night pressing in. The moon was sinking in the sky, coloring the leaves with silver edges. She knew that somewhere beyond the orchard, Catherine was likely watching, waiting for a moment to seize. She knew that Sadie was inside, perhaps even awake again, bracing herself for the next difficult conversation. High stakes, unrelenting tension. Yet right here in Ian's arms, Emma felt a whisper of strength she hadn't known she possessed.

They held onto each other as the wind murmured secrets through the branches and as the faint hint of a morning cast a new light on the orchard. She savored the press of his arms, his breath mingling with hers in the hush. The orchard's gentle hum reminded her that time still moved, that responsibilities and looming threats remained. But for this heartbeat in the moonlit clearing, Emma let her fears recede.

Her lips brushed Ian's neck, a tender graze that made them both start at the intensity still coiled between them. She drew back just enough to see his face: the shadows under his eyes, the softness in his gaze.

Beneath the orchard's canopy, they captured each other's hands once more, fingers entwined. Early morning dew started to dampen the grass, but neither of them seemed to care. She kissed him again, this time softer, as they faced a new day after a long night filled with love, fear, disappointment, and then back around to love again.

TWELVE

Emma and Ian watched the sun rise over the orchard that morning. He finally said goodbye with a gentle kiss on the front porch. He was smiling as he turned and waved from the gate just as Emma slipped back inside the cottage. Sadie was no longer in her chair but had probably moved to her room hours before. Emma crept to her room and laid down, fully clothed on her bed, pulling the quilt up around her. As she fell into a deep sleep, she could still smell Ian's scent, a mix of the forest and beach. For the rest of the morning, she slept soundly.

Around noon, Sadie knocked softly softly and entered with a tray of toast, tea and some bacon. Emma blinked twice and then sat up as Sadie put the tray in her lap.

"I know you had a late night and are probably sleepy, but I thought you might be hungry. Plus, I wanted to say I'm sorry that I was over-protective but that was no reason to invade your privacy, dear," Sadie said while tenderly running her fingers through Emma's hair pushing it off her face.

"I'm really sorry too for the things I said, Sadie, and probably over-reacted too. It must be a family trait," laughed Emma. "But nothing heals all wounds like bacon," Emma said while grabbing a crispy piece from the tray."

"So, all is forgiven?" asked Sadie.

"Yes, all is forgiven," Emma said as she washed the bacon down with a gulp of tea. "But you should know that I'm in love with Ian and I'm committed to helping him with this curse thing."

Sadie nodded. "I've been thinking about that and have been doing some research this morning. You take another nap and then we'll talk about it later," said Sadie placing the tray on the nightstand. She turned, smiling at Emma as she closed her door. Emma settled back under the covers and was soon back to sleep.

In the late afternoon, she finally got up and had a warm shower. Still in her robe with her hair wet, she found Sadie at the stove making a stew.

"That smells amazing," said Emma standing behind Sadie as she stirred the pot.

"It'll be ready in about 30 minutes so go dry your hair and then we'll sit down and eat and have a long chat and maybe play some cards, how does that sound?" said Sadie squeezing Emma's hand.

"Perfect," smiled Emma.

After supper of stew and vegetables from the garden, Sadie told Emma stories about her father when he was a boy. Some of the stories Emma had heard before but the story about his first try at magic when he was about eight was a new one.

"He came home from school and was really upset that Marianne, this little blonde girl he had always had a crush on had told him that she liked another boy better," Sadie recalled. "He came home crying and asked me to create a love potion he could give to the girl. "I told him that love potions weren't really my specialty. He got so mad at me and told me he would do it himself. He ran out to the garden and picked some herbs and bundled them up with some twine and then brought the bundle back and put it into his backpack."

"Then what did he do?" asked Emma smiling.

"He said he gave the bundle to Marianne. That little blonde girl who turned out to be your mother, Mary," Sadie laughed. "So, I think his love potion worked."

"I love that story so much but had no idea they had been together since childhood," Emma said tearing up. "I really miss them so much but I'm really glad they're still together...out there...somewhere."

"I am too," said Sadie as her eyes started watering. "Let's play some cards, what do you say?"

"Yes, let's do," said Emma looking fondly at her grandmother.

For the rest of the evening they played gin rummy until Emma finally yawned and kissed Sadie goodnight. "Thank you so much for the wonderful dinner, the stories and cards. Sleep, well," she said as she walked down the hall to her room.

An hour later, Emma was yanked out of a fragmented dream by the sharp, staccato sound of tapping against the window. Her pulse lurched. She blinked in the dark, trying to find the source of the noise. For a moment, she wondered if the orchard branches were scraping against the shingles again, shifted by the restless wind. Then it came again, more urgently this time. Tap, tap, pause, tap.

She slid off the bed and stepped over a half-opened notebook on the floor, crossing to the window with her heart pounding. Lately, the orchard whispered with unnatural noises, Sadie's wards strained by nightly efforts to repel intrusions. Any unexpected sound at this hour made Emma's nerves bristle. She braced her hand on the sill and pulled aside the curtain. The moonlight revealed Ian's face, slick with sweat, eyes ringed with desperation. He was half-bent beneath her window as though he had just finished climbing the narrow ledge.

Emma's heart skipped. She unlatched the window and pushed it open. "Ian," she hissed. "Are you all right?" She already knew from his ragged breathing and the haunted look in his eyes that whatever was happening wasn't a simple nighttime visit. He didn't answer at first, only crooked his trembling hand at her, his breath coming in frantic bursts.

"Let me in," he gasped, voice nearly hoarse. "They're behind me, Emma. Shadows... I can't shake them."

She opened the window and motioned furiously. "Climb through." She pressed her palms against the sill to steady him. Her arms buckled slightly as she tried to support his weight, and he managed a clumsy landing on the floor, nearly colliding with the foot of her bed. His hair clung to his forehead, damp with sweat, and sharp lines of panic traced his features. She caught him by the elbows before he crumpled, guiding him so he would not trip over her discarded shoes.

He swayed, gripping her wrists. "Lock it," he urged, glancing back nervously toward the window. "Whatever is out there... I saw it in the orchard. I saw... it looked like me, but it moved differently."

Emma's pulse hammered. She pushed the window shut, slid the latch with a resounding click, and flicked on the small desk lamp. Its warm glow illuminated Ian's pale face and the sheen of perspiration on his neck. "You passed the wards," she muttered, baffled that he had chosen to climb up to her window rather than approach the front door. "Are the illusions worse?"

He nodded, wiping sweat from his temple. "They started as nightmares, then I started seeing them even when I'm awake. I was walking near Sadie's fence, thinking maybe if I moved fast, the illusions would not catch up, but every time I glanced over my shoulder, there was a silhouette." His voice quivered. "I thought I heard it whispering with my voice."

Emma felt a jolt of alarm. She remembered Sadie's warnings that illusions often fed on an individual's personal fears, warping them into something more potent. She squeezed Ian's hand. "Sit down before you collapse. Let me grab some water."

She guided him to her bed, where he perched on the edge, chest heaving as though he had run a mile. Her room felt uncomfortably small all of a sudden, four walls now confining Ian's panic. She stepped out into the hallway, careful not to make the floor creak too loudly. Sadie's door was only half-closed. Lamplight from inside her room pooled onto the old floorboards, and Emma could hear soft shuffling. Perhaps Sadie was already stirring.

Emma hurried into the living room for a glass of water from the pitcher Sadie usually kept on the table. The low hum of tension weighed on her. Lately, nights are rarely calm. Having lived here for several months, Emma was used to the orchard and the gentle crackle of wards. Now, everything felt tight, as if the cottage's magic braced for an onslaught every single evening.

Returning with the water in hand, she peeked into Sadie's room and found her grandmother propped against the headboard in a rumpled nightgown. Her once-vibrant face looked drawn, her eyes hollow with fatigue. "Emma," Sadie said quietly, "what is happening?"

Emma lowered her voice. "Ian is here... nightmares again. He is seeing things even when he is wide awake."

Sadie exhaled. "Bring him in here, child. The wards are strongest in my room... or at least they should be."

Emma gave a quick nod, though the worry in Sadie's voice made her stomach twist. She loped back down the hall, water sloshing in its glass. She entered her bedroom to find Ian studying his own reflection in a small mirror on her desk. He had spilled a couple of notebooks onto the floor, probably from trying to shift around. He startled when she reentered, as if even her presence took him by surprise.

"Sorry," he blurted as soon as he noticed the mess. "I... saw something behind me in the mirror."

Emma tried to sound reassuring. "It's fine." She extended the glass, urging him to drink.

He took a deep gulp, water dribbling at the corner of his mouth. "I keep expecting that shadow to jump out," he said, voice cracking with humiliation at his own words. "I can't tell what is real and what is not anymore."

Emma's heart clenched. If Catherine was fueling these visions, that would make everything more dangerous. The illusions were no longer limited to nightmares that haunted Ian's sleep; they were creeping into his daytime perception. She gently tugged him up by the elbow. "Sadie wants to see you." She hesitated, glancing at his disheveled shirt, the collar damp with sweat. "She might be able to reinforce some wards, at least for tonight, so you can rest."

He let himself be guided out of Emma's room and along the hallway. His trembling hadn't subsided. The tension in his muscles thrummed beneath her hand, as though any moment he might try to bolt. Still, he clung to her, eyes flicking nervously over his shoulder.

In Sadie's room, a single lamp bathed the walls in gentle light. The small window was sealed with multiple runic inscriptions Emma recognized from earlier practice sessions. Worn candles littered the bedside table, half-melted stubs from Sadie's attempts to keep protective spells active. The older woman beckoned silently, leaning forward with visible strain.

"I'm sorry for barging in, Ms. Sadie," Ian whispered, voice laden with shame.

Sadie waved the apology aside. "Stop, child. You're always welcome here." Her eyes flicked to Emma, and there was that glint of grandmotherly concern overshadowed by exhaustion. "Tell me what you see."

Ian fidgeted with the empty glass in his hands. "I see... silhouettes. And they look like me, or a twisted version of me. Meanwhile, I hear my own voice echoing behind me whenever I walk in the dark." He tried to swallow, but his throat bobbed painfully. "I can't... I don't know if I'm losing my mind."

Sadie's brow furrowed, and she took a slow, measured breath. "This is not you losing your mind," she said. "Your nightmares have crossed the threshold from simple illusions into manifestations you can see at all hours. That is a sign the illusions are gripping you more firmly."

Emma couldn't hold back. "Catherine," she murmured bitterly. "It has to be her. These illusions are far more malicious than the usual nightmares."

Sadie nodded faintly. "Her dark energy does seem to be weaving into Ian's insecurities. She is exploiting the imprint his curse leaves on him." She reached for an herbal pouch on her nightstand, shaking it gently. It rustled with dried sprigs of lavender and a faint hint of chamomile. "I have a small incantation left in me tonight, but not enough to free you from these illusions permanently."

Ian glanced between them. "Ever since that last confrontation, my nightmares have just... escalated. I tried the protective runes on my bracelet but I had to rip it off, or it would have burned me."

Emma's breath caught. That amulet was meant to stabilize him, but evidently Catherine's power had dismantled it. She shot Sadie a questioning look—this was beyond what any of them had faced before. Sadie gave a minimal shrug, acknowledging the gravity of the situation.

The older woman pressed a hand over her eyes, massaging her brow. "The wards around this cottage might slow the illusions for a bit if you stay inside. When the sun rises, Emma and I will discuss a more permanent strategy."

But Emma could see the toll on Sadie. Every exhalation rattled in the older woman's chest, and the lines on her face looked deeper in the dim lamplight. Sadie had been reinforcing household wards every night for weeks, and it was tearing at her reserves of power and health. Since the confrontation, Emma had watched as Sadie forced herself to muster the energy to protect them. The woman's hands were shaking even now, but she straightened, rummaging for a half-burned stick of sage in a shallow dish.

"Here," Sadie said, offering it to Emma. "Light it, swirl it around him. Then recite the short incantation for clarity." She turned to Ian. "It might not banish the illusions, but it can reduce them enough for you to catch some sleep."

Emma cradled the sage in her palm, then looked around for the matches. None lay on the nightstand.

"Where are—I found them." She snatched the small box from beneath a stack of old letters. Striking a match, she lit the sage, which quickly released a faint, herbal fragrance that filled the cramped room with smoky wisps.

Sadie whispered the incantation, her voice carrying the smallest tremor:

"In branching dreams where shadows prowl,
Release the hold that darkness vows.
Let sight run clear, let hearts unbind,
Grant fleeting peace to troubled minds."

Emma repeated the words under her breath, drawing the smoke in a slow circle around Ian's head and shoulders. She watched Ian's expression for any sign of relief. He closed his eyes, inhaled carefully, and exhaled an unsteady breath. On the final line, Sadie's voice quavered, and Emma caught a flicker of dim golden light along the runes etched on the windowsill. Their synergy pulsed once, making the lamplight flicker.

Ian's shoulders sank a fraction, though wariness still glinted in his eyes. "It feels... a little clearer," he admitted, as if testing the air for illusions. Then he glanced at Sadie. "Thank you."

She nodded. "Rest if you can. Emma, help him settle in the living room. I would have him stay there or anywhere you can keep an eye on him." Her gaze darted to Emma, and Emma knew what it meant: Sadie was too tired to shoulder more responsibility tonight. Emma would have to handle Ian's next panic attack if it happened before dawn.

Ian dipped his head, face half hidden in the dim corner of Sadie's bedroom. "I'm sorry. I hate imposing—you both have done so much."

Before Sadie could respond, Emma stepped forward, placing a comforting hand on his arm. "You're not imposing. We want to help you. Let's get you something warm to wear. You must be freezing." She saw how his sweat-soaked shirt clung to his skin. He looked exhausted, as if any small jolt of fear would send him falling apart.

He smiled weakly, but it didn't reach his eyes. "Thank you," he said softly.

Sadie, went to her closet and found an oversized wool sweater and handed it to Ian who immediately pulled it over his head. Blinking with weariness, Sadie cleared her throat. "I will rest. Emma, come get me if any illusions break through the wards." She lifted a trembling hand in farewell and then sank into her pillows.

Emma guided Ian out into the hallway. She ran a hand over her face, feeling the weight of the situation. Catherine's illusions were no longer a background threat. They were actively shaping Ian's perceptions at every turn, even in the middle of the night. The knowledge rattled her more than she wanted to admit.

She led him to the living room, where the faint moonlight appeared through the front windows. A battered sofa sat against the wall. She grabbed a crocheted throw from a chair and wrapped it around his shoulders. He sank onto the sofa, blinking as though adjusting to the gloom. The shadows of the orchard wavered across the window, stirring a chill in Emma's veins. She noticed his immediate tension as he stared at those moving shapes.

"I keep thinking my reflection is crouching out there," he said under his breath. "It is like the illusions will appear if I blink too long."

Emma perched beside him on the sofa. "Can you see anything now... in this room?" She hated asking, but she needed to know exactly what they were dealing with at this moment.

He peered around and then shook his head. "Not like before," he said. "The shape followed me up to your window, though. It took a different face each time I glanced back."

She swallowed hard. Her chest ached with empathy. She wondered how many terrified nights he had already endured, refusing to burden her or Sadie. "Ian, you don't have to go through this alone," she murmured. "Whatever Catherine is doing, she is doing it because she knows you're vulnerable."

He let out a shaky laugh, though there was no real humor in it. "I can hardly argue that. I want to be strong, Emma, but my own mind... it is betraying me."

She pressed his hand between both of hers, feeling the damp coldness of his skin. "We'll find a more potent solution. Sadie's been reinforcing wards so constantly that she is running herself ragged, and now... I see how this goes beyond simple nightmares. The illusions are slipping into your everyday reality. That can't go on."

He took a breath, then squeezed his eyes shut. "I'm so

on edge all the time. The images taunt me, twist me, make me wonder if I'm looking at my own reflection or if it is something else entirely. I..." He swallowed his words, as if he were ashamed.

She shifted closer, letting him lean into her side. "I need you to stay with me. If that is what it takes for you to feel safe, you can stay here until morning. The wards in the cottage should prevent anything from breaching outright."

He opened his eyes and looked at her. In that moment, his raw vulnerability made her throat burn with sympathy. "You make it sound so simple," he said softly.

"We know it is not," she replied, her voice hushed. "But we have to start somewhere."

Outside, a breeze rustled the orchard leaves. Emma could picture the silhouettes of twisted branches, each a reminder of the illusions creeping in. She remembered glimpses of Catherine's magic from earlier run-ins: the reek of tar, the swirl of malevolent force. That same presence hung around his aura now, as if it had latched onto him like a parasite. Bile rose in Emma's throat at the thought. Catherine was feeding on Ian's insecurities, just as Sadie had warned.

Ian must have sensed Emma's rising anger at their invisible foe. He tightened his grip on her fingers and whispered, "Thank you for not giving up on me."

She exhaled slowly and looked into his eyes. "I will never give up on you." She studied the ragged lines of fatigue that etched his expression, determined to ward off the guilt that threatened to seep in. She forced a gentle smile and braced a hand on his shoulder. "You can try to sleep here. I will keep watch."

He hesitated, then laid his head back against the worn cushions. "Promise you won't vanish while I doze?"

"Not a chance," she murmured. She watched him close his eyes, breath hitching on each exhale as he tried to relax. The lines of tension across his brow eventually eased, though he didn't fully succumb to rest. Emma stayed at his side for many minutes. She listened to the faint whistle of wind outside, and the knowledge that illusions waited beyond the wards set her own heart racing. Her mind roamed through the spells Sadie had taught her, none of which felt strong enough to handle something that lingered at the very edges of Ian's consciousness, twisting his vision until he couldn't tell dreams from reality.

Her gaze traveled to the hallway where Sadie's door remained partly ajar. She could just make out a slice of lamplight across the floor. Sadie might be dozing or perhaps reciting incantations in a whisper, fighting to maintain the wards. Emma felt the ache of helplessness for her grandmother's draining strength. She thought of Catherine's face; the mocking smile the older woman had worn when they last confronted each other. That memory fueled Emma's anger, but there was another spark too: determination. If Catherine believed she could break Ian through illusions, then she was in for a fight.

Emma looked back at Ian. The faint lines of worry on his face signaled that he was still aware of the darkness swirling around him. Gingerly, Emma placed her fingertips at the side of his temple, brushing away a stray lock of his damp hair. "I will help you, Ian," she whispered. "We can't keep doing patchwork spells. We'll find something stronger."

He opened his eyes. They glistened with unshed tears —tears he was clearly fighting to keep at bay. "Every time I close my eyes, I see them," he whispered. "I see me but twisted. I see the orchard, only the trees are rotting, crawling with illusions."

A surge of protectiveness nearly choked Emma. She leaned closer until her forehead almost touched his. "I will not let the curse consume you." She spoke each word deliberately. He let out a shaking breath, as though that vehement promise lifted a small piece of his fear.

Sadie had mentioned a deeper synergy between Catherine's illusions and Ian's bloodline. Emma didn't know if it could be severed as easily as other curses. But she would not let that doubt creep into her voice tonight. She closed her eyes briefly, inhaling the smoky residue of sage. Her heart pounded with empathy and frustration. No mind—no heart—should endure what Ian was facing.

He set his hand over hers, their fingers interlacing gently. Even in his terror, his touch was warm, tethering her to the moment. She felt her own breath unsteady with the strength of her resolve. "We'll figure out a new approach," she said, each syllable uttered gently. "Sleep, or at least rest. I will not leave you."

Ian's voice was weary. "When I wake... if I see those shadows again... you'll still be here?"

Emma's throat tightened. "I swear," she said. "We'll not let this break you."

He nodded, as though mustering the last of his courage. As he settled back into the sofa cushions, his breathing evened out in fits and starts. Emma tucked the blanket around him and smoothed the hair back from his forehead. She could almost hear the wards hum faintly in the beams overhead.

Stillness settled for a few long minutes. She refused to let her vigilance falter, scanning the corners of the room for any sign of flickering illusions. At last, Ian dozed off, though not peacefully. Occasionally, his eyes twitched, or he issued a small moan as though chasing away lurking nightmares. Emma stayed close, ready to rouse him if he sank too deep into that terror.

A half hour trickled by in quiet tension. The top of Emma's head ached with exhaustion, yet she refused to sleep. Her mind whirled with half-formed ideas: searching for new spells in Sadie's trunks of diaries or combining wards with a personal incantation that might anchor Ian more firmly to reality. None of those solutions came easily, but at least she wasn't at a total loss. She resolved to comb through every page of Sadie's hidden references if that was what it took.

Ian stirred suddenly, muttering her name as if calling through the haze of a dream. Emma set a reassuring hand on his shoulder. The lines carved into his brow eased, and he sank back again. Her chest tightened at his vulnerability. There was no question that Catherine's illusions had grown bolder, strategic in attacking him at his weakest points.

She lowered her gaze to where his hand still clutched hers. Sadie might be at the end of her rope, physically and magically, but Emma had to believe they could find a path forward. She brushed her thumb gently across Ian's knuckles, mind spinning with a desperate urgency to free him from these nightmares.

He roused enough to open one eye. His voice sounded husky in the low lamplight. "Emma... promise me... you'll not let me fall too far." His words slurred at the edges, caught in the realm between waking and sleep. "Please."

Emma's heart pounded harder. She drew in a breath, banishing the sting of tears that threatened to form. "I promise," she whispered, smoothing her other hand across the side of his face. "I will stand guard all night if that is what it takes."

He closed his eyes again, quieter now, as though that one assurance gave him a moment of tenuous peace. She watched the slow rise and fall of his chest, reminded of how fragile everyone in this cottage felt. Sadie drained and half asleep in her bedroom, wards flickering at their edges, and Ian trembling under illusions that took his own like-ness to torment him. Yet somehow, Emma felt anchored to a fierce purpose she had never experienced before.

She resolved to gather every resource in the cottage. More amulets could be made, perhaps with new runes. She would scour Sadie's diaries for advanced spells. If Catherine's influence was weaving illusions that threatened to drive Ian to the brink, Emma intended to unravel them, no matter the cost.

She glanced toward the shuttered window. One small portion of the drape was crooked, allowing a sliver of moonlight to spill into the living room. Shadows of the orchard's branches rippled on the floor, but for now, they were only shapes of leaves and trunks, nothing more ominous. She gave Ian's hand another firm squeeze and whispered a vow only she could hear.

"We'll not lose you, Ian," she murmured. "I refuse to let Catherine sink her claws in you again."

Outside, the night breeze sighed against the walls. Emma sensed no immediate threat trying to breach the wards, so she exhaled a short, shaky breath. Then she leaned back on the sofa, letting his warmth reassure her that, for the moment, he was safe. His pulse thrummed under her fingertips, a reminder that he was alive and fighting.

The final thought that coalesced in her heart was simple and unwavering: she would face every illusion, every twisted shadow, if it meant keeping him upright. With the lamplight flickering over their entwined hands, Emma promised, in a voice so low it barely made a sound, that the curse would not defeat him. She quietly promised they would not let the curse consume him, if it meant she had to stand guard at his side day and night.

THIRTEEN

Emma felt a fragile relief settle over the cottage that morning. The air still carried a hint of old tension, but Sadie's renewed ward glimmered in the corners of each windowsill like threads of faint light. Ian's shoulders lost a fraction of their tautness as he sipped the tea Emma had pressed into his hands. She noted the way his gaze no longer jumped at every flicker of movement near the door. Gale had arrived earlier to join them for breakfast and to bring Ian some fresh clothes following Emma's telephone call from the night before. She now leaned against the kitchen counter and offered a bright grin at how Ian finally seemed able to breathe without panic lurking in his eyes.

The day felt calm enough for Emma to propose something scandalously ordinary: a trip to Crestwood's modest arcade. She explained it in excited bursts, as though it were a daring quest. Gale raised an eyebrow, joking that leading a cursed warlock into a neon-lit arcade was the perfect way to stir up small-town gossip. Emma only shrugged. She wanted Ian out of the cottage, if only for an hour, to remind him that his entire life need not revolve around battling illusions.

"Just trust me," Emma murmured. She brushed her fingers along the soft runes Sadie had etched into Ian's new warding amulet, which rested against his chest beneath his shirt. A faint warmth pulsed from it, like a comforting heartbeat. She hoped it would keep any illusions at bay.

Ian glanced at her with a hesitant smile. "I'm not sure the town is ready to see me acting normal," he said, voice quiet.

"We'll survive," Emma replied, trying to sound as confident as Gale usually did. "You deserve some sense of fun. Let them stare."

They set off in the late morning, walking side by side along Crestwood's narrow streets. Gale prattled animatedly about a new milkshake flavor at the local café, describing it as an abomination of whipped cream and sugary nonsense. Emma half-listened, more focused on the way Ian looked around as though each passing face might morph into an apparition. Glimmers of panic still twitched at the edge of his eyes, but she gave his hand a reassuring squeeze.

The arcade, named Neon Dreams, existed in an old storefront wedged between a dilapidated toy shop and a boarded-up music store. Outside, a flickering sign hummed in bright pink. Emma glanced around warily, noticing a handful of locals meandering past. They paused to look at Ian, then exchanged whispers before continuing on. She forced herself not to scowl at them.

Gale flung the door open. "Time to unleash your competitive spirit," she announced with a teasing grin. "Or in Emma's case, watch her rake in tickets at anything that requires weird aim."

Emma tried to laugh. She stepped into the stuffy, neon-lit space and inhaled air that smelled of stale popcorn and dust. Rows of retro game machines glowed under flickering fluorescent lights. Two teenage boys hunched over a pinball machine near the entrance, barely sparing Emma or Gale a glance. Ian, however, immediately drew their attention. One of them nudged the other, eyebrows lifting with a curious expression. Emma recognized the look. It was the look people gave a phenomenon they only half understood.

She took Ian's arm. "Let's find a corner and warm up with something easy," she said.

They made it a scant few steps before a middle-aged woman Emma faintly recognized from the produce stall caught sight of Ian. The woman's eyes lingered on him for a tense moment, flicking down to his hand, which Emma still clutched. Then she shook her head, turned on her heel, and hustled out of the arcade as though contamination might be catching. A trace of disappointment squeezed Emma's chest. She had hoped for a different reaction, but suspicion ran deep.

Ian swallowed hard. "I told you," he murmured. "I should have stayed at the cottage."

Gale appeared on his other side, deliberately linking

arms with him too. "Absolutely not," she said, voice bright. "People are just bored and nosey. Now, Emma, which game do you want to try first?"

Emma scanned the machines. She spotted a claw game blinking lazily in the far corner, next to an ancient racing simulator. She steered them that way. Each step brought more stares. A group of older teens, their arms crossed and eyes full of unsubtle curiosity, mumbled among themselves as Emma, Ian, and Gale passed. A couple of them adjusted their posture, inexplicably drawn a little closer. Emma recognized the faint flush in their cheeks, the subtle parting of lips. Sometimes, without intending to, Ian's warlock aura acted like a magnet for the curious. She had seen it happen at the market before, particularly with people more susceptible to spells or illusions.

A sudden wave of jealousy prickled across her neck. This wasn't Ian's fault, and yet her stomach knotted at the wide-eyed glances from two girls who looked around her own age. She felt a twinge of protectiveness and pressed closer to Ian's side. He flinched at the contact, not from discomfort, but from the flicker of dread that someone might see him and interpret the moment as something unnatural.

"Doing okay?" Emma asked, leaning up so only he could hear.

He nodded, though his eyes darted around at the watchers. "I'm trying not to let illusions slip in. The ward helps, but I keep expecting the walls to ripple or—" He shook his head, voice trailing off.

Gale cleared her throat. "I believe I promised to annihilate you both at the claw machine." She stomped forward, flipping a coin into the slot with dramatic flair. The gears whirred to life, and bright lights flashed around the glass box filled with plush animals.

As Gale maneuvered the claw, Emma let out a breath, trying to focus on the mundane thrill of picking up stuffed toys. She watched a battered plush fox slip from the claw's grasp just before it reached the chute. Gale scrunched her nose, muttering a theatrical complaint about rigged machines. A soft laugh rose in Emma's chest at Gale's antics. The ridiculousness of the moment felt oddly precious: a cursed warlock, an emerging witch, and their irreverent friend, all clustered in a dingy arcade corner. Emma wanted to tuck the memory away.

Then she noticed movement from the corner of her eye. A few more townsfolk had stepped inside, and each one seemed to stare at Ian. The group included a woman who shot Emma a sympathetic look, as though she pitied Emma for staying so close to someone rumored to be dangerous. Emma felt her cheeks heat.

"Maybe we should pretend we're just normal," she said under her breath, though she doubted normalcy was possible. "Play a racing game, laugh a bit, and show them we just average, crazy teenagers with raging hormones."

"Vroom, vroom," Gale said, making an exaggerated steering motion. She dragged them over to the dusty racing simulators. The seats' pleather material squeaked as Emma and Ian settled in. Gale hovered behind them, poking at the back of Emma's seat as if offering coaching tips. Emma glanced sidelong at Ian. He looked as if he wanted to disappear, but he slid a coin into the slot anyway, the screen flickering to life.

She picked the green car. He picked the red. The countdown beeped overhead. For a few heartbeats, Emma actually lost herself in the game—fingers gripping the plastic wheel, foot on the pedal. The virtual track scrolled before her in bright, cartoonish colors. Gale laughed each time Emma's car swerved off the pixelated road. Emma risked a glance at Ian. He was leaning forward, brow furrowed, as though focusing intently on each turn. She grinned at how adorable he looked, fighting to keep his car centered.

But beyond the glow of the monitor, Emma could sense the crowd's eyes. A pair of older teens had come in, one of them crossing his arms in quiet disapproval. A girl in a pink jacket not far away stared at Ian with something akin to infatuation. Emma's car spun out and crashed into a fence. She sighed, letting the race end.

"Alright," Gale said, cheerfully patting Emma on the shoulder. "That was a spectacular defeat. You should at least blame your losing on love." She used a teasing voice, but her perception was spot-on. Emma's mind was nowhere near the game. She caught Ian's soft chuckle as he fought a smile, though it quickly dissolved into a worried frown.

They clambered out of the simulators and retreated toward a quieter stretch of the arcade. The outdated décor loomed around them, battered posters advertising local tournaments from years ago. Each footstep echoed on the scuffed floor. Emma felt the tension mount as more onlookers inched closer. She clenched her fists at her sides, resisting the urge to snap at them. The last thing they needed was to alarm everyone or stir up rumors of aggression.

A red-haired woman in her twenties brushed a little too close to Ian, standing in front of him for a moment as if confused. Ian offered a polite nod, then carefully side-stepped around her. Emma recognized the spark of dread in his expression. He probably worried his aura had inadvertently pulled her forward. She took his hand, letting him know he wasn't alone.

Gale led them to the corner with the row of claw machines. This time, nobody else seemed to be lurking at the far edges, though Emma could feel stares from across the room.

Emma exhaled slowly and glanced up at Ian. His breath hitched. He seemed on the verge of trembling. Fear, embarrassment, and leftover exhaustion radiated from him. She couldn't stand to see him so rattled. She rose on her toes and pressed a quick, comforting kiss to his lips. It was light, over in a moment, but it made warmth blossom in her chest. She felt him relax a fraction against her, as though that gentle contact reminded him he was more than a spectacle for the rumor mill.

He gave a hushed sigh. "Thank you," he whispered, fingertips brushing the side of her face.

Gale hummed, looking away with a half-smile. "I'll just be here, scouting the best claw prizes, as you two get a room," she said playfully. She inserted another coin, the mechanical claw clanking above the plushies once more.

Emma returned her attention to Ian. "You're okay," she murmured, searching his gaze for any hint of illusions creeping in. "Sadie's ward is holding, right?"

He lifted the edge of his collar and showed her the amulet. A faint glow pulsed in time with his heartbeat. "It's better than before. I just... feel the weight of everyone's eyes. I hate that they look at me and see either a monster or something so intriguing they can't stay away. The illusions feed off my insecurities, so I keep expecting the arcade floor to dissolve or the walls to slither."

Emma traced a gentle line across his palm with her thumb. "We'll leave if it gets too intense. But you're doing great."

A loud cheer erupted from Gale behind them. They turned to see she had successfully snagged a stuffed fox in the claw's clutches. "Yes!" Gale exclaimed. "Bow to my unstoppable skill!" She hoisted the plush triumphantly, as though brandishing a trophy. The comedic triumph drew a handful of side glances from watchers, but at least it diffused the tension in that moment.

Emma reached out to tap the fox's nose. "That is so rigged," she teased, trying to match Gale's lighthearted tone.

"Rigged with pure skill," Gale quipped, winking.

But even as they joked, Emma felt the flickers of attention intensify around them. She saw two young women near the racing machines whisper to one another, eyes pinned on Ian. An older man glowered pointedly, as though trying to decide if he should intervene. The mixture of fascination and fear tangled in the air, prickling Emma's senses.

Ian leaned closer, voice low in Emma's ear. "I think we've tested fate enough for one afternoon," he murmured. "I'm not sure how else to explain why so many are lingering. Let's find a quiet space outside soon."

Emma nodded, though disappointment webbed through her chest. She wanted to grant him at least twenty minutes of normalcy, but perhaps that was asking too much. She turned to Gale, giving her a grateful smile for the comedic relief, then squeezed Ian's hand, determination sparking inside her. If the illusions stayed at bay, that alone was a victory.

Glancing up at him, she offered a smile. "Just a little longer," she said gently. "Maybe we can pick a final game and then head out? Something that doesn't put us in the spotlight."

He exhaled, shoulders easing despite the closeness of the watchers. "Deal," he said, voice steadier.

Gale flashed them a grin. "I'll scout for a game that's tucked away from the main crowd." She spun around and took a few strides deeper into the back row, leaving Emma and Ian to share a quiet moment by the claw machine.

Emma reached up, resting a hand on his cheek. The music from the other games seemed distant against the frantic thump of her heart. "We'll get there," she whispered. "One step at a time."

He pressed a small, grateful kiss to her fingertips. "Thank you for not hiding me away," he said. "I appreciate being reminded I can have a life that isn't just—"

He paused as movement flickered near the edge of his vision. But it was only a couple of onlookers, drawn by the intangible magnetism. Emma frowned, swallowing down another wave of protectiveness. She laced her fingers with his, bracing herself. If illusions didn't emerge today, it meant Sadie's ward was indeed doing its job.

The two of them lingered like that for a second more, breathing in each other's presence. The tension in Ian's body eased. Emma felt it in the slight relaxing of his grip, the faint relief in his gaze. Then she spotted Gale popping her head around a corner, gesturing with exaggerated enthusiasm at an old punching-bag style game that nobody seemed to be using. Emma tilted her chin in acknowledgment.

Leading Ian by the hand, she guided him toward Gale, ignoring the watchers. A swarm of uncertain stares traced their every step, and a ripple of unease ran down Emma's spine. Yet she held Ian's hand a bit tighter, determined to show him that the world beyond illusions could be faced —even if the townsfolk had yet to accept him entirely.

They paused behind the game, finding just enough space for the three of them to gather without an audience creeping too close. Emma leaned against the wall, hot neon lights reflecting off the chipped paint behind her and gazed at Ian's eyes. She closed her eyes, pressing her forehead to his shoulder. Her lips curled in a tender half-smile.

"Thank you," he said again, breath warm against her hair.

"For what?" she asked.

"For dragging me into a moment of normal life," he replied. "Even if it's not perfect."

"It's still ours," Emma whispered. She lifted her head and dipped in to give him another comforting kiss. His breath trembled as he kissed her back softly.

Gale coughed, half-teasing, half-choking on her own amusement. Emma reluctantly pulled away from Ian's embrace, cheeks flushing. He offered her the slightest crooked grin, a touch of genuine contentment that pushed away the gloom in his eyes.

FOURTEEN

Emma stood at the edge of the orchard, eyes fixed on the wavering figure of Ian only a few paces away. The late afternoon sun cast long shadows through the rows of apple trees, illuminating petals still clinging stubbornly to certain branches. Crestwood's seasons had grown unpredictable, and these blossoms felt like an echo of defiance against the chill in the air. She watched Ian grip a nearby trunk in an effort to keep himself upright. His face looked ashen, and a faint tremor ran through his shoulders. Every instinct in Emma told her to rush to him, but she worried one wrong move might unsettle his tenuous balance.

He staggered a moment, blinking hard, and swayed on his feet. Emma darted forward, heart pounding. Her boots crunched on the fallen leaves, some still green despite the creeping autumn around them. When she reached Ian, she wrapped an arm around his waist. He was taller than her by half a head, yet he seemed frighteningly fragile in that instant, weight sagging against her.

He drew in a shaky breath. "I'm... sorry," he rasped. His gaze flickered over Emma's worried expression as he struggled to right himself. "It just crept up on me. Everything spun."

Sadie appeared from the cottage path behind them, her pace brisk despite visible fatigue. She clutched a small wooden box against her hip and gestured for Emma to help Ian move away from the orchard's uneven ground. Emma guided him, her shoulder bracing his as they navigated the soft dirt. The orchard stood eerily still, as though the last of its magic held its breath in sympathy.

When they reached the grass transition near the cottage's side door, Sadie adjusted the box in her arms and glanced at Ian's pale face. Her own face looked pinched with exhaustion; deep lines etched into her cheeks from too many nights spent reinforcing wards. She gave a tight nod of acknowledgment to Emma before gently coaxing Ian onto the low stone step. He lowered himself with a faint groan, pressing his hand to his temple.

"This will help," Sadie said softly, crouching beside him and lifting the lid of the wooden box. Inside lay a newly crafted amulet, a disk of driftwood inlaid with several freshwater pearls. Emma recognized faint runic symbols across the wooden surface, each carefully burned into place. She had seen Sadie whisk away to the cove the previous morning, presumably to gather the driftwood, but she hadn't realized her grandmother's plan involved a fresh attempt at stabilizing Ian's curse.

Ian's eyes flicked from Sadie's face to the amulet, uncertainty warring with hope in their depths. "You think it will hold stronger than the last one?"

Sadie drew in a measured breath. "I believe so. The freshwater pearls come from a calmer source, unconnected to the ocean's wild tides. They are reputed to repel illusions. And this driftwood was gathered at the cove that has sheltered Crestwood for centuries."

Emma listened carefully, noting the undercurrent of weariness in Sadie's voice. She wanted to believe that this new amulet would work. She had watched the others—previous charms and wards—fail one by one, each eventually overwhelmed by Catherine's dark illusions. Yet the careful craftsmanship of the driftwood disk offered a moment of cautious optimism.

Sadie placed the amulet in Ian's open palm. The pearls glinted in the sunlight, and Emma caught a faint glow along the runic carvings. "It is meant to stabilize your connection to the natural world," Sadie explained. "If your mind begins to spiral under illusions, the runes should ground your senses."

Ian nodded. He lifted the amulet toward his chest, and Emma helped him fasten the slender cord around his neck. Warmth seemed to pulse from the driftwood surface, enough that Ian took a slow breath, as if testing his steadiness.

A moment passed while he closed his eyes. Then he exhaled and straightened his spine. "It is already doing something," he said, voice quiet with relief. His tremor subsided to a faint tremble. Emma's heart twisted at the contrast between his earlier desperation and this new flicker of relief.

Sadie bowed her head briefly, murmuring an incantation under her breath. Emma only caught a few words—ocean, root, balance—before her grandmother's voice fell silent. Then Sadie stood on stiff legs and motioned for Emma to prop Ian against her shoulder, guiding them both inside the cottage. The air grew cooler, and the orchard's branches swayed behind them, as though the old trees had just released a collective sigh.

Inside, Gale was in the living room, flipping nervously through one of Sadie's less important diaries. She glanced up, eyes flicking over Ian. Her usual spark of humor dimmed, replaced by concern. She set the diary aside and crossed the room so quickly her sneakers squeaked on the floorboards.

"How bad?" she asked in a low voice.

Emma shook her head, pressing her lips into a thin line. "He nearly collapsed. Sadie gave him a new amulet."

Gale nodded, stepping aside so Emma could help Ian settle on the worn couch. He leaned back against the cushions, eyes closed as if every bit of energy was now devoted to staying awake. For an instant, Emma allowed herself to imagine this was just a case of normal fatigue—any ordinary teenage boy might suffer from a bout of dizziness. But the tension in her stomach refused to ease. This was no ordinary boy, after all.

"We should let him rest for a moment," Sadie said, voice hushed. She shot Emma a meaningful look. Emma nodded in understanding: they needed to discuss the amulet further, but not with Ian subjected to more questions right now.

Gale crouched near the couch, sharing a reassuring smile with Ian. He opened his eyes just enough to meet her gaze. "You'll be fine," she murmured, placing a hand lightly on his ankle, the closest bit of him she could reach without disturbing him. "No more sudden collapses. You're better at scaring me than a ghost story."

He managed a weak chuckle, and Emma took it as a promising sign. She touched Gale's shoulder gratefully, then gestured for Sadie to follow her into the hallway. They walked away from the living room, leaving Ian with Gale's watchful presence.

In the narrow corridor, the cottage's walls seemed to press close. The air smelled faintly of chamomile, a residue from one of Sadie's protective teas. Sadie leaned against the wall, eyes half-lidded in fatigue. Emma instinctively reached out to steady her grandmother's elbow.

Sadie spoke barely above a whisper. "He will be stable for a time, but I fear Catherine grows bolder. I sense her illusions creeping through the orchard each night, pressing against my wards. She is determined to torment him at every turn."

Emma swallowed. "Is that why you hammered new runes into the orchard fence? I saw the fresh carvings this morning."

"Yes," Sadie admitted. "They will not hold forever, but they might buy us some time." She closed her eyes for a long blink, then opened them to fix Emma with a serious stare. "The illusions feed on his fear. That fear flares each time he feels eyes on him—daytime gawkers, anxious townsfolk... The strain is constant."

Emma shivered at the thought of prying stares around Crestwood. She had seen it herself in the market and at the arcade. The moment some people saw Ian, their curiosity and wariness seemed to magnify his own unease. She clenched her fists at her sides, wishing there was a way to shield him from every wagging tongue and suspicious glance.

"We'll manage," she said quietly, though a tremor edged into her voice. "This new amulet... it is the best approach for now?"

Sadie breathed out. "Yes, for now. We might find more solutions if we delve deeper into my diaries, but we can't forget that Catherine's illusions aren't random. She is targeting his mind specifically. One ward, no matter how meticulous, might not be enough."

Emma nodded slowly. She feared her grandmother's eyes carried the weight of a truth that neither wanted to say out loud: Catherine would not stop until Ian's mind fractured beyond repair. They needed a stronger, more permanent fix. Yet that fix felt out of reach.

For the rest of the afternoon, the household stirred with tension. Gale fussed over the living room, bringing Ian a fleece blanket and urging him to sip water. Emma retreated to the kitchen, determined to do something useful. She recalled Sadie once mentioning that fish chowder warmed the body against magical chills. She rummaged through the small pantry, gathering ingredients for dinner. Chopped onions and diced potatoes piled up on the cutting board. The fish fillets, fresh from the local stall, smelled briny in a comforting way.

While she worked, she heard occasional murmurs from Gale, who tried to coax Ian into conversation. The normalcy of kitchen tasks soothed Emma's nerves, though she felt guilty pangs for even momentarily wishing for a simpler life, one free of illusions and curses. Each sizzle of the pot was a reminder that her troubles were not truly dissolving, just simmering in the background.

The chowder finally reached a creamy consistency, and the aroma lured Sadie out of her room. She gave a wan smile and helped Emma ladle portions into bowls. Together, they carried dinner to the table, setting down chipped plates and the savory meal. Ian, with Gale's support, rose from the couch. He still looked tired but steadier, the new amulet visible beneath the edge of his collar. Emma felt a glimmer of hope seeing that he could walk without leaning heavily on anyone.

They ate in near silence, the only sounds coming from spoonfuls of chowder and the occasional crackle of the hearth. Ian managed small bites, his hands no longer trembling. Emma found herself studying him, reading each subtle shift in his expression. His gaze, directed at the table, revealed how intensely he was trying to maintain composure. The runes on the amulet didn't glow at first, and Emma dared to imagine it was a good sign.

Then, halfway through the meal, the faintest flicker of light sparkled across the pearls. At first, Emma thought it was just the reflection of the light overhead. But Sadie noticed it too. The glow pulsed once, then twice, as if responding to an unseen ripple in the air. Emma heard Ian exhale sharply. He rubbed a hand over his sternum.

"Something is... shifting," he mumbled. His cheeks paled, and a thin sheen of sweat surfaced at his temple.

Gale set down her spoon. "Hey," she said softly, sliding her chair closer. "Deep breaths. Remember, the amulet is supposed to help."

Sadie pressed her palm gently over the wooden disk. "Catherine's illusions must be pressing against your aura," she murmured. The corner of her mouth tightened. "She is testing your defenses." Her eyes flicked to Emma, confirming this wasn't a benign sign. The amulet was working, but it was also overexerting itself.

Emma set aside her half-finished bowl and placed a hand on Ian's arm. "You feel them right now?" Her voice shook.

He hesitated. "They feel like... tendrils around the edges of my thoughts. So many prying eyes."

Emma closed her eyes, attempting to quell the surge of anger toward Catherine. She thought about how Sadie once taught her a grounding technique: visualize the orchard's roots, stable and strong, rather than Catherine's illusions. She opened her eyes to see Sadie gently removing her hand from the amulet.

Sadie's voice dropped to a near whisper. "His curse is pushing back. She is pouring power into his vulnerability again. The illusions aim to crack him open at his weakest point."

A gust of wind chose that moment to rattle the windows. The entire cottage seemed to groan in response, as though acknowledging the rising tension. Emma reached for the half-empty pot of chowder, but her appetite had vanished. She saw Gale's face pale. Ian looked as though he was losing the last of his strength. His spoon clattered against the table, and he bowed his head.

Sadie caught Emma's gaze. "We must be vigilant," she said. "No warding amulet will fully protect him if Catherine continues to pry at his fears."

The rest of dinner passed in strained silence. Eventually, Emma and Gale cleared the dishes, giving Ian time to breathe. Sadie retreated to her room, presumably to rest or attempt another quiet incantation. Emma could tell from her grandmother's drawn features that each new charm drained precious energy she could scarcely spare.

When the plates were washed, and the kettle set for tea, Emma returned to the living room. Ian sat hunched in the same corner of the couch, his face turned toward the dim glow of the hearth. Gale stood next to him, flipping through one of Sadie's less intimidating diaries. At Emma's approach, Gale offered a small, tired salute and slipped out of the room, likely hoping privacy might help Ian unwind.

Emma sank onto the cushion beside him. The faint light showed shadows under his eyes. She gently laid a hand on his knee. "I'm here," she said. "Tell me if the illusions intensify."

He breathed slowly and gave a near-imperceptible nod. "I'm... trying to hold on." His voice was laced with a raw edge that shredded her composure.

The way he said it, the strain in his voice, made her

ache with something deeper than worry—something fierce and protective.

She tightened her grip on his knee, grounding him. "You don't have to do it alone," she whispered.

Ian let out a slow, unsteady breath, his gaze slipping from the fire to meet hers. His eyes were dark with exhaustion, but beneath the weariness, there was something else; a quiet, unspoken call for help.

Emma inhaled, steadying herself. She couldn't take away the illusions that haunted him, but she could strengthen the protections. Her magic alone wasn't enough—Sadie had made that clear—but maybe together...

She shifted, reaching into the small pouch at her waist, fingers brushing over the smooth stones and dried herbs she had gathered for protective charms. She pulled out a slender thread of woven copper and silver, one of Sadie's simplest warding materials.

"Let me reinforce the warding," she said. "With your help."

Ian frowned slightly, his fingers flexing against his thigh. "My magic—"

"Is yours," Emma interrupted gently. "Not Catherine's. Not the illusions. I trust it, Ian. I trust you."

A muscle in his jaw twitched, but he gave a slow nod, his hand coming to rest atop hers. The contact sent a faint pulse of warmth through her, the familiar sensation of his power responding to hers. It was subtle, always lurking beneath the surface, restrained out of fear.

Not tonight.

Emma pulled the woven thread between them, looping it loosely around their joined hands. She inhaled deeply, centering herself, and murmured the first lines of Sadie's warding spell. The magic in her veins stirred, rising to the surface, wrapping around the copper and silver like vines weaving through iron gates.

Ian hesitated, then closed his eyes. Emma felt it immediately—the moment he let go. His power surged forward, tentative at first, then steadily growing as it merged with hers. It didn't crash or overpower—it fit, seamlessly, as if it had always belonged there. A warmth spread between their hands, spilling into the air around them, sending a faint shimmer through the dimly lit room.

The weight pressing against Ian's shoulders seemed to lift. His breath steadied, the crease between his brows easing.

Emma whispered the final words of the spell, feeling their combined magic settle like a second skin over the house, reinforcing the protections that had begun to fray. The candlelight flickered, then stabilized, as if the air itself had drawn a deeper breath.

When she opened her eyes, Ian was watching her.

There was something different in his gaze—not just gratitude, but something deeply personal, something that sent a shiver down her spine. He turned his hand beneath hers, lacing their fingers together.

She sifted through her memory for something comforting to offer him. She recalled a simple bedtime story her mother once told her—a silly tale about dancing starfish on a moonlit shore. It wasn't grand, but it had soothed Emma during lonely nights. She decided to try. He listened with his head bowed, eyelids drooping. Her story was meandering and gentle, describing starfish that glowed under the moon, skipping across the wet sand as incoming waves emerged in shimmering arcs beneath them.

He let out a soft huff of amusement at the mental image. "I never pictured starfish dancing," he murmured. He attempted a smile, though it trembled at the corners. For an instant, Emma thought the quiet ridiculousness of the story might bring him that childlike comfort she once felt.

Then his brow furrowed, and he pressed his palm against his temple. A pained grunt escaped his lips. Veins stood out at his temple, and his breath came in short gasps. Emma's heart twisted as she realized the illusions must be tightening their grip, refusing to let him float in a peaceful moment. She placed her hand over his, hoping somehow her presence might steady him.

"It hurts," he admitted, voice wavering.

Emma's throat constricted. "Focus on me," she urged. "Think about the orchard's roots, or the cove, or anywhere that feels safe. Ignore... ignore everything else."

He tried again to steady his breath. After a few moments, the tension in his jaw loosened, but the lines of pain remained etched in his forehead. Emma glanced at the amulet. It flickered erratically, as if warning them that its initial success was already being tested to the brink.

She rose to fetch him more water, and he managed a quiet thanks, cradling the glass with shaky fingers. When he sipped it, color returned to his cheeks in faint measure. She coaxed him into leaning back against the pillows on the couch. Guilt gnawed at her, wishing she had a stronger incantation or some direct way to exorcise the illusions from his mind.

Outside, the wind had taken on a restless sound, rattling the loose shutters. Crestwood itself seemed perched on a nervous edge, braced for another strike from the illusions that had begun plaguing not just Ian, but everyone who crossed his path with wary eyes. Emma understood this torment would only intensify if Catherine was determined to shatter him. A single ward or amulet felt like patchwork against a storm that raged from deep within.

When Ian finally closed his eyes, exhaustion pulled him into a fitful doze. Emma stood watch, gaze flicking between his tense features and the flickering lamplight. She wished she had a real cure for those illusions, not a temporary shield. She recalled Sadie's pained confession that illusions this personal needed to be severed at their source, or they would keep burrowing into Ian's mind.

One day, Emma told herself, they would root out the curse behind these horrors. She told herself Catherine's manipulations couldn't last forever. Yet, as the night wore on, and each rattling gust made her chest tighten with worry, she wondered if they might be running out of time. The orchard outside felt like a silent guardian, but even it couldn't repel illusions forever.

She continued her quiet vigil. Ian's features never fully relaxed, small twitches disturbing his rest. Still, she stayed beside him, determined to ward off the nightmares that lurked at the edge of his awareness. Her eyes drifted to the amulet's unsteady glow, and she reminded herself, fiercely, that she would not abandon him. If Catherine thought she could isolate him through terror, she would learn otherwise.

Emma inhaled, conjuring the faint smell of fish chowder still hanging in the cottage. She tried to recall the starfish story again, imagining bright, playful creatures dancing free in the open sea. She pressed her lips to the back of Ian's hand in a gentle gesture, hoping her presence might tether him to calm. Glancing at the window, she found herself silently daring the illusions to approach. She was no master witch, but she had enough raw determination to face them. She refused to let this curse hollow out the person she cared about the most.

The breeze outside swelled to a sharper gust, rattling the glass once more. Emma looked down at Ian's complexion, still tense with lingering pain. The amulet's flicker settled into a faint, uneven pulse. She exhaled, a wave of harsh realization hitting her: if illusions this powerful could burrow past every ward, the path to relief lay farther than driftwood and pearls. Sadie's repeated warnings echoed in her mind. She wondered silently how much more strain her grandmother could take before her own health gave way.

The lamp flickered, and Emma gently adjusted the pillow beneath Ian's head, then leaned close. She whispered, "I will try another story. Maybe it will help distract you." She was unsure if he heard. His eyelids fluttered, and his breath emerged in quiet, ragged intervals.

Steeling herself, she began another simple tale from her mother's repertoire, this time about a battered boat that found its way home through a constellation's glow. She spoke softly, voice unsteady but determined to give him something to hold on to. In her mind, dread coiled tighter with each passing minute, each flare of runic light. No matter what comforting words she offered, she felt Catherine's presence gnawing at the margins of her thoughts, prowling like a feral thing outside the wards.

She kept speaking, weaving words about stars and drifting tides, stroking Ian's palm as he tried to hold onto slivers of rest. At some point, Gale peeked into the room, offering a silent question in her eyes. Emma gave a faint shrug, indicating there was little more to be done. Gale lowered her gaze and withdrew, leaving them to endure one more night of illusions together.

Emma continued until her voice ran hoarse. Eventually, she paused. Ian had slipped into a fitful sleep, brow knitted. She listened to the wind outside and the faint pulse of the amulet's glow. The night wore on with no sign of calm. Emma pressed her hand against Ian's, as though creating a bridge across whatever nightmares threatened him.

In that moment, she knew that sooner or later, they would have to confront the source of his curse, whatever the risk. She bent her head close to Ian's, closing her eyes in silent resolve. She would guard him through the night, and tomorrow, she would seek a deeper remedy. There was no other choice.

Outside the cottage, the orchard's blossoms swayed in the shifting moonlight, stubborn flickers of life in the face of encroaching darkness. The wind hissed through the branches. Emma tightened her grip on Ian's hand, determined not to let the illusions tear him away from her. If Catherine wanted him to break, she would find Emma standing in the way.

CHAPTER

FIFTEEN

Several days later, Emma woke with a dull ache behind her eyes, the residue of another sleepless night. Her thoughts sifted through the events of the previous days. She recalled Ian trembling against the orchard fence, Sadie fashioning yet another ward, and the unsettled tension that draped the cottage as night deepened. Embers of worry still crackled in Emma's mind. She sat up in bed, rubbing grainy exhaustion away from her eyelashes. Outside her window, the morning sunlight diffused through low-hanging clouds, giving the air a muted glow. She hadn't seen Ian since Catherine's attack, and she was worried.

She dressed quickly, pulling on a loose sweater and well-worn jeans. The chill in the cottage's corridors pressed against her arms as she opened her bedroom door. She inhaled the faint smells of dried rosemary and burnt candle wax. She had left a half-finished warding candle burning the night before, hoping its smoke might keep nightmares at bay. It hadn't helped much, yet the act of trying gave her something to cling to.

When she emerged into the hallway, she found Gale waiting by the foot of the attic stairs. A battered canvas backpack sagged off Gale's shoulder, filled with who-knew-what. Pale morning light slanted through the small window near the ceiling, washing Gale's pastel-streaked hair in a faint rainbow glow. She offered Emma a lopsided grin, though dark circles rimmed her eyes. "What do you need help with?" she asked softly. "Let me guess, Ian?"

Emma nodded. "I appreciate it. I'm not sure I have the energy to figure this out alone. I just wish I knew where Ian was. I just want to know he's okay."

Gale shrugged. "He's a big boy and he can take care of himself. But if he doesn't show up the next day or two, we'll go looking for him. For now, we've got to make use of the time we have and read through whatever diaries we can find."

They headed up the narrow attic steps. Cobwebs brushed Emma's shoulders as she ducked under a low beam. The attic smelled of musty paper, dust, and an underlying tang of old magic. She used to think the faint crackle in the air was her imagination, but with everything she had witnessed in the past weeks, she no longer doubted that these shadows carried leftover traces of Sadie's spells. Sunlight tried to stab through the small attic window, but heavy curtains filtered it into hazy bands. Stacks of boxes lay unevenly around the space, some tied with twine, others half-opened. Close to the far wall, a large trunk was sealed with runic etchings. Emma recognized it as one of the hidden caches Sadie had warned her about during some earlier discussions.

Gale set her backpack down near a pile of discarded journals. "I don't know exactly what we're looking for," she admitted, "but I have practiced some magic when I was much younger with my mother, but she sent me to Sadie for training early on. Sadie taught me some beginner stuff, nothing to advanced and I wasn't any good at it. But I do remember Sadie mentioning something about specialized healing or protective approaches. If that information is anywhere, it's probably in one of her diaries she keeps." She let out a breath and knelt, pulling free a trembling stack of old notebooks bound in worn leather.

Emma joined her. The first notebook she opened sent a puff of dust into her face, making her cough. Inside, Sadie's looping handwriting covered entire pages in dark ink, many lines smudged by age. Emma squinted, tracing a finger over cryptic phrases about orchard runes and the synergy between certain herbs. She found references to an "unstable aura remedy," which intrigued her. She flipped pages, scanning paragraphs. "Something about the mind's resilience being tied to scents," she murmured. "Protective aromatherapy, maybe?"

Gale stirred, brushing studs of dust off her knees. "I saw mention of that in another journal," she said, rummaging through the pile. "Check the spine of that teal one. It might connect the dots."

Emma set aside the first notebook and picked up a teal-bound journal with brittle corners. She opened it and found rows of carefully drawn sketches: plants labeled with Sadie's cramped script. More than half of it was incomprehensible, either in code or half burned, as if the pages had been exposed to a flame. "She definitely experimented a lot. Look at this." She held the journal toward Gale, showing illustrations of sprigs of thyme, rosemary, and something spiky labeled coral blight. "I've never heard of coral blight," Emma said quietly.

Gale peered at the drawing. "Neither have I. Maybe it's a local name for something else? Sadie did mention that some of her folksy terms didn't align with standard herb lore."

"Could be. But I see references to using it in steams or mixing it with salt to heighten protective wards." Emma's brow creased in concentration. "Has Sadie mentioned an actual method for bridging the effect to illusions?"

"Not that I recall," Gale said. She rubbed a smudge of dust off her cheek. "She always told me to trust my instincts if illusions crept in, but that's hardly a formal technique."

Emma sighed and kept flipping pages. Her gaze landed on a note about *stabilizing warlock energies during acute illusions* scrawled in the margin, but the page ended abruptly, the next few lines burned and unreadable. The partial instructions teased an approach for *buoying an unsteady mind* through an intense scent. But there was no mention of the full incantation or the final ingredient.

Setting the teal journal down, Emma pinched the bridge of her nose. "We can't replicate half-finished instructions," she muttered. "This is so frustrating. It's like every clue we find is missing some crucial piece."

Gale offered a sheepish smile. "Maybe there's more in that battered leather diary. It looks older." She picked up a thick book whose spine was peeling. Its cover had a large glyph Emma recognized as a simplified orchard symbol. Gale carefully lifted the cover, eyeing the fragile pages. "I can flip if you want to read."

Emma nodded. She scooted next to Gale so they could pore over the text together. With delicate movements, Gale turned the pages. They found entries detailing Sadie's younger years: references to practicing healing spells on birds, mentions of restless nights where illusions threatened Crestwood, records of a conversation with someone named Patricia about warding the orchard's perimeter. After a few minutes of quiet study, some words caught Emma's eye near the top of a page: *aromatherapy for cursed individuals*. She leaned closer, heart thumping. "Hold on," she whispered, pointing at the line. "That's relevant."

Gale's eyes lit with curiosity. She read aloud: "The synergy of salt, ephemeral root, and an incantation involving layered scents can fortify a warlock's frayed spirit. My initial attempts found partial success. Further refinement needed. Additional herb or anchor unknown." She glanced sideways at Emma. "We're on the right track."

Emma exhaled, partly relieved. "There must be more details," she said, scanning the next lines. They discovered a mention of a gathering ritual in the orchard's north clearing, but the writing broke off in mid-sentence, the bottom half of the page blackened by a scorch mark. The next page carried only half-legible runes. Emma groaned.

"Of course it's incomplete. Just when we get somewhere…"

They set the diary aside. Silence stretched as they each processed the frustration. Emma felt a slow burn of desperate anger coil in her stomach. Every passing day, illusions seemed to tighten their grip on Crestwood, especially around Ian. She clenched her hands in her lap, remembering how Ian's breathing hitched whenever he thought illusions might swallow him. They needed to help him. They had to piece together these scraps somehow.

Gale ran a hand through her pastel hair. "Maybe we can guess how to fill the gaps or find another diary that clarifies the missing steps," she suggested. "Sadie always said that synergy spells rely on a bond between the people performing them. If we combine that principle with some of these herbal techniques…"

Emma lifted her gaze, noticing how Gale's voice wavered. She realized, at that moment, just how tired Gale looked. Her friend's usual glib demeanor was replaced by shadows under her eyes. "Gale," Emma said quietly, "you look exhausted. I'm sorry I dragged you into this attic first thing in the morning."

A half-hearted grin flickered on Gale's face. "I'd be more worried if you didn't want me here," she teased. Then her expression sobered. "Emma, I need to tell you something. I've been practicing magic behind the scenes since, well, for a while. Sadie said she saw the potential in me, so she nudged me to try small spells here and there. I didn't want people to freak out about me dabbling in witchcraft, so I kept it mostly secret." Gale inhaled, her voice trembling with an undercurrent of nerves. "But I was never fully honest about just how much I've been practicing."

Emma stared at her friend, the words sinking in. Slowly, she closed her mouth and nodded. "I... I guess I suspected you knew more than you let on, but I thought you were just humoring me." The swirling dust motes in the attic suddenly felt tangible, like a constellation of secrets dancing around them. "Why keep it hidden from me, though?"

Gale's shoulders slumped. "It wasn't about you. Not really. I was afraid I'd get it wrong. I was afraid that once people realized I could cast spells, they would expect me to fix everything. But I'm still learning. I don't have a powerful lineage like you, or that orchard legacy. Just random bursts of magic that Sadie helped me shape." She paused, swallowing. "I guess I didn't want to disappoint you."

Emma's frustration dissolved into a gentle wave of compassion. She placed a hand on Gale's shoulder. "Gale, you can't disappoint me. I'm just stunned you've been practicing for so long. That's incredible." Her face softened into a small smile. "Let me see what you can do."

Gale hesitated, chewing her lower lip. Then she lifted her hand, palm up. Her brow furrowed with concentration. A faint shimmer of pale blue light trembled above her skin. Emma sucked in a breath as that glow turned into a tiny flame no bigger than a candle's tip. The flame wobbled in the drafty attic, but it flickered bright, undeniably real. Gale let out a strained laugh, and the flame sputtered, vanishing a moment later.

"Holy--that was..." Emma began, smiling wide. "Wow. That's actual flame."

"Yeah," Gale said, her cheeks coloring. "It's small, and I can't keep it going very long, but it's real magic. Sadie taught me to draw on the orchard for a tiny spark, even if I'm not connected by blood." She fiddled with the edge of her jacket sleeve. "Still got a ways to go, though."

Emma beamed. The sense of wonder and relief that flooded her chest made her realize just how desperately she needed an ally who truly understood magic's depths. Ian had his own curse. Sadie was exhausted. Emma's frustrations often brewed into self-blame. But here was Gale, offering a flicker of hope right in her palm. "Thank you for showing me," Emma murmured.

Gale smiled sheepishly. "Might as well put it to further use." She nudged one of the diaries aside and lifted her other hand. "Let's see if we can do something else." Her gaze landed on a battered chair near a stack of ragged boxes. She scrunched her face in determination, lips moving in a silent incantation.

At first, nothing happened. Emma felt a subtle shift in the air, like a gentle static charge. Then the chair lifted a mere inch off the floor. Gale's eyes widened in triumph. "Look--look at that!" she exclaimed softly.

But the excitement broke her concentration. The chair crashed down, striking the stack of musty tomes. Books toppled in a chaotic spill, pages fluttering in a great dusty whoosh. Emma jumped up, arms raised in alarm as journals and old logs scattered across the attic floor.

Gale winced. "Oops. Guess I overdid it."

A laugh welled in Emma's throat--a genuine laugh that shook off her exhaustion and the tension she carried. She covered her mouth with one hand, trying to stifle the giddy sound. "We'll call that a minor success," she teased.

Gale snorted. "I just tried to flex and look at the mess I made."

They embraced the humor of the moment, collecting the fallen books. Emma's chest felt lighter, as if she had found a pocket of fresh air in the gloom. They soon sank onto the floor, leaning against each other's shoulders, both giggling in short bursts, letting relief wash away the heaviness that had followed them up the stairs.

Eventually, Gale brushed dust off her hands. "I know it's not much," she said, voice softer now. "But I want to help. If Catherine's illusions keep plaguing Ian, or menacing you in random ways, I don't want to sit on the sidelines. Sadie has done so much for Crestwood, and for both of us. I want to be part of the solution."

Emma reached out to place her fingertips lightly on Gale's wrist. "You already are," she replied. "You have no idea how relieved I am that you can do real spells. We need every advantage we can get."

Gale's smile turned humble. "Sadie said my magic is unrefined compared to yours, but it means I can dabble without the orchard's direct blessing. I guess the orchard doesn't judge me for not being a Turner. It just sort of shares a piece of itself if I ask nicely."

"That's special," Emma said, remembering how the orchard's energy sometimes pulsed under her feet. She used to think that it only recognized the Turner bloodline, but clearly, it had room for others too. The orchard responded to intention and an open heart more than specific lineage. "I'm glad you talked to Sadie about it. She wouldn't have let you practice alone if she didn't think you had potential."

Gale nodded. "All I want is to help find the missing bits of spells we've dug up. We can figure out that aromatherapy technique, patch it together, and maybe it'll stop illusions from chewing Ian apart. Maybe it'll help you too. Everyone is so on edge that any little boost would make a difference."

Emma shifted her attention back to the diaries scattered around them. She recalled how the partial instructions mentioned layering scents with an incantation. If they found that obscure herb or the correct ritual line, perhaps they could conjure a protective effect strong enough to steady a mind caught in illusions. "Let's keep at it," she said, her gaze returning to the diaries. "I don't want to wait until something dire happens again."

Nodding, Gale grabbed the battered leather diary from earlier. Her eyes flashed with determination. "We can do this. We'll go page by page, try to see if Sadie wrote something in the margins. Maybe she scribbled a second mention somewhere else."

They continued their search, flipping through journals, cross-referencing incomplete notes, and brushing off the occasional spider skittering across the floor. Time slipped away in that dusty attic, the two of them murmuring snatches of incantations or herbal references. Emma found a few more mentions of aromatic synergy. Gale discovered a partial incantation that might bolster one's mental shields, though the final lines remained stubbornly missing.

At one point, the old trunk in the corner caught Emma's attention. The faint runes carved along its lid glinted in the gloom. Sadie had explicitly warned her to be cautious with that trunk, given the wards placed on it. Emma's fingers twitched with the temptation to open it, but she decided to hold off for now. They already waded hip-deep in confusion, and she wasn't eager to trigger powerful wards while Sadie was still drained from repeated spells.

Eventually, they exchanged a long look. Emma's shoulders sagged as she exhaled. "We're finding fragments, but not a full answer yet." She rubbed a bit of dried ink off her hand. "Still, I feel better knowing we're approaching this together."

Gale settled on the floor, hugging one knee. "Listen," she said softly, "I know I'm not the best at earnest speeches. But I promise you this: I'll help you and Sadie unravel Catherine's illusions. I'll keep practicing. If it takes me all night, I'll figure out how to keep these illusions from ripping Crestwood apart."

Emma felt the corners of her mouth turn up, a flutter of gratitude in her chest. "Thank you," she whispered. "I know it's not just about me. You're risking your own peace to face illusions. But you're here anyway. It... it means a lot."

They shared a moment of quiet understanding, broken only by the sound of a floorboard shifting under the attic's weight. Somewhere downstairs, the wind rattled a windowpane, reminding Emma that the outside world was still anxious and uncertain. For a brief second, the attic felt like a secret fortress where two friends offered each other comfort and a plan for the battles to come.

Gale gave a playful smirk, reached out, and swatted at the nearest fallen book. "I guess we'd better pick these up. Sadie won't be thrilled if she finds the attic in shambles."

Emma nodded, summoning renewed energy. They gathered the scattered diaries into manageable piles, setting aside the ones that looked relevant to the half-burnt ritual logs. As she smoothed the cover of an old notebook, the faint smell of chamomile and dust drifted up. She closed her eyes, thinking of Sadie's healing teas and that unwavering gentleness in her grandmother's eyes. She also remembered Ian's nervous smiles, the tension that coiled in his body whenever illusions loomed. She refused to let them all drown in fear.

Gale stood with a grunt, grabbing the final stack of logs. "We can come back tomorrow too," she suggested. "I can practice lifting bigger objects. Maybe I'll float the entire trunk just to show off."

Emma laughed, letting that spark of humor banish her lingering angst. "Just warn me first so I have time to brace for flying furniture."

They finished tidying the space. Dust motes still spun

in the angled daylight, but the diaries were sorted now, and Emma felt more purposeful. She turned to Gale with appreciation in her gaze. "Let's head downstairs. I'll make us some tea, and we can share whatever we found with Sadie after she wakes."

"Sounds good," Gale said. She stuffed a few vital pages into her backpack, then readjusted the straps on her shoulder. "I'm definitely craving something warm and less dusty."

They descended the attic steps, leaving behind the shadows for the slightly brighter corridor below. Halfway down, Emma paused on a creaking stair and murmured, "Gale... for what it's worth, I'm proud of you. Showing me that flame was the bravest thing I've seen in days."

Gale offered a fleeting look of gratitude. "It's scary, you know. But it also feels amazing, like... like I can be part of something that matters."

"You're part of it," Emma said, expression solemn. "I need you. Sadie needs you. Crestwood might need you too. So, keep that spark alive, okay?"

Gale pressed her lips into a determined line. "I will." Then her features relaxed into a small grin. "And, if I accidentally set the curtains on fire, I trust you to rescue me."

Emma let out a soft laugh. "Deal."

They reached the main floor. The morning chill remained, but Emma felt the warmth of hope thrumming in her chest. Gale's revelation lit a new path forward. They had no complete solution, but they had the promise of synergy, the promise that they could combine their strengths to stand against illusions. Emma silently prayed that these new insights would stitch themselves together into something powerful enough to help Ian and preserve Sadie's hard-won protections.

As they walked toward the kitchen in search of tea, Emma glanced over her shoulder, imagining the attic's half-burnt pages and half-written spells waiting for them. A pang of determination throbbed in her heart. She would piece together this ancient protective aromatherapy, or she would find another method entirely. Either way, she and Gale were no longer fumbling alone. A subtle resolution steadied her step: they would chase down every missing clue, every hidden line of incantation, until Catherine's illusions had no place left to hide. She and Gale would make sure of it.

SIXTEEN

Emma stood outside the cottage, her back pressed against uneven boards that still carried the lingering smell of chamomile incense. She hugged her arms as she stared at the orchard's dim silhouette. Dusk had settled too quickly. Only minutes ago, the sky had streaked with orange light. Now a smoky twilight cloaked everything, and the orchard felt tense, its shadows deeper than usual. Sadie's labored breathing seeped through the cracked windows behind Emma. Her grandmother needed rest. Every day of reinforcing wards and chasing after illusions had sapped her strength. Yet Ian was nowhere to be found.

"Seriously, where did he go this time?" Gale stepped onto the porch, adjusting the straps of her backpack. She wore her usual bright hoodie, but tonight she tied off the sleeves at her waist. The set of her mouth looked grim. "He told me he'd stay in the cottage living room, but he's not there."

Emma's chest tightened. "He must have gone into the woods again."

Despite her worry, she masked how unsteady she felt. She had spent the day reading Sadie's diaries and half-translated texts, searching for ways to bolster Ian's mind against illusions. None of that mattered if he wandered off alone. Emma pushed off from the cottage wall and grabbed a flashlight that hung from a hook by the door. "Sadie's in no condition to help. We have to track him ourselves."

Gale swallowed, glancing at the orchard's edge. "Fine, let's go." Her voice didn't snap with sardonic humor this time. Instead, she spoke in a thin hush, as though the orchard might be listening. Guilt flared in Emma's stomach. Sadie had nearly collapsed from weaving new runes around the orchard perimeter. She needed to sleep, not chase illusions. If Catherine's illusions had pulled Ian deeper into the Enchanted Woods, Emma and Gale would have to be enough.

They ignited their flashlights and hurried away from the cottage. Even the familiar rows of fruit trees felt eerie. The apple trees shuddered in the wind, leaves rustling like hushed warnings. Emma's fingers trembled around the flashlight. She steadied herself with a breath, reminding herself that letting fear root too deeply would only feed the illusions.

They reached the boundary of the orchard and followed an overgrown path into the Enchanted Woods beyond. The shifting silhouettes of pine trunks and tangled underbrush made their way forward slow. Emma recalled how these woods had once felt mysterious but alive. The air smelled of damp soil and a pungent, acrid tang. Faint wisps of magic wove in slow spirals through the pines, just visible at the edges of her flashlight beam.

"Do you smell that?" Gale's voice was tight. Her pastel hair, usually bright and carefree, was pinned back in a messy bun as though preparing for a fight. "Like burnt sage and... something rotten."

Emma nodded. She recognized the scent of twisted illusions clashing with the forest's natural energy. She paused a moment, searching for hints of Ian's aura. Over the last few days, she had started sensing his presence in a way she couldn't fully explain. When he stood close, she often felt a subtle tingle in the air, like a half-formed static charge. Now, it was as if that current flickered somewhere ahead. "He's that way," she said softly. "We have to hurry."

They pressed onward, flashlights bobbing among the pines. The wind carried a low whistle, or perhaps that was the illusions themselves, hissing in the dark. Emma fought the urge to call Ian's name. She feared that speaking aloud might alert whatever malignant force had lured him here. She and Gale crept between mossy trunks, stepping over curled roots that seemed to snag their ankles.

After what felt like too many tense minutes, they glimpsed a faint glow ahead. It flickered, ill-defined. Emma felt her heart stutter. They stepped into a clearing far gloomier than the rest of the forest. The ground sloped downward, ringed by blackened stumps that jutted up like broken teeth. Emma's flashlight revealed an uneven patch of earth, charred decades ago by some curse. The diaries had labeled this place a site of deep inversion, where the land itself was said to turn cold. Ian knelt at its center, slumped forward with his hands on the ground. His entire frame shivered as though trapped in a cold not of this world.

Emma sucked in a breath. "Ian," she whispered, but her voice stumbled.

At once, spectral shapes began to swirl around him. They looked like ribbons of pale smoke, though each wisp congealed into an eerie form. Emma's light caught a glimpse of Catherine's face among them—hair drifting in an invisible current—and then the face morphed, turning into something older, more monstrous. Cracks radiated over that visage, twisting it into a skeletal grin before it shifted again.

Gale shuddered. "Perfect. Nightmares made flesh." Her sarcasm faltered behind the real alarm.

Emma advanced, but the illusions swirled faster. A wave of intangible shapes arced up and lunged at her. She stumbled back and flung up her free hand. She tried summoning a protective bubble, recalling the incantations Sadie had taught her. She mumbled words under her breath, focusing on the orchard's memory of warmth and cyclical renewal. A pale shimmer flared to life around her, forming a translucent hemisphere.

At first, the illusions hissed against Emma's shield. She felt them clawing at the boundary like they sought to shred her protective magic. The strain rippled through her arms. She bit down on the inside of her cheek to keep from crying out. Ian lifted his head at that moment, eyes glassy. His lips parted in a hoarse apology, though Emma couldn't catch the full whisper.

She pushed forward, inch by inch, though the illusions thickened like a swarm of apparitions. They slammed against her shield with violent force, forcing her to recoil. The bubble wavered. Emma's muscles trembled. She felt her heart pound painfully against her ribcage. Gale pressed closer behind her; her flashlight discarded on the ground so she could raise her hands in a focusing gesture. Emma glanced over her shoulder, sweat beading at her temple.

"I'm going to try that new incantation," Gale said, voice quivering. She spread her fingers wide, arms braced. "Cover me."

Emma gritted her teeth, nodding. She poured every ounce of will into holding her shield in place, even as it flickered under the illusions' attacks. Gale took a shaky breath and began chanting:

"Threads of hope and light entwine,
Shield our friend from illusions malign.
Let truth hold fast through darkest fight,
And break the shades that haunt his sight."

Gale's trembling tone carried through the clearing, and Emma felt a surge of power swirl at her back. The illusions hissed anew, as though they recognized a fresh threat. They pelted Emma's flickering shield with renewed ferocity, but now Gale's conjured energy fed into the protective aura from behind. A second field of faint blue shimmered around Emma's bubble, preventing it from collapsing entirely.

Together, their combined shield pressed outward, forcing the spectral shapes to recoil. Emma could see them straining at the perimeter, each twisted apparition stretching into elongated limbs embedded with Catherine's hateful gaze. Emma swallowed her revulsion and pushed forward again. Each step rattled her legs, but she fixed her stare on Ian. He looked so pale. She feared he might pass out. The illusions flared in a last-ditch attempt to keep her away, but Gale's chant hit a crescendo, and the swirling specters parted just enough for Emma to slip through.

She dropped onto her knees beside Ian. The shield behind her crackled, flickering under Gale's effort, yet it held. She reached for Ian's shoulder. "It's me," she managed, voice tight with emotion. "Ian, can you hear me?"

He jerked as if startled from a delirious dream. His hands shook so hard that when Emma gripped them, she felt a deep chill as though a ghostly wind battered his senses. He spoke in disjointed gasps. "I—couldn't—I heard them call. I thought I could stop it."

"Stop talking," Emma ordered gently. "Try to breathe. We'll get you out of here."

The illusions renewed their attacks. Emma saw a swirl of them massing overhead, forming a partial ring that flashed with Catherine's features, only to shift into a tall, robed nightmare. She could practically sense Catherine's voice whispering in that swirling gloom, mocking Ian's vulnerability. She refused to let it seep further into his mind. Gritting her teeth, Emma clutched him against her chest and drew on the orchard's memory once more. This time, she pictured apple blossoms rustling in a gentle breeze, carrying vitality and warmth into every corner. She recalled her grandmother's gentle voice, reminding her that illusions thrived on fear.

"Stay with me," she whispered into Ian's ear. "We won't let them take you."

A final push of energy pulsed through Gale's incantation. The illusions overhead screeched without sound, as if a violent wind scattered them. Emma watched them peel back from the bubble's surface. The shapes thinned, the faces twisted in silent rage, and then the entire mass of nightmares receded. Their departure left a biting chill in the clearing, as though the earth itself exhaled sorrow.

Emma guided Ian onto her lap. He sagged, breath rasping, shame tracing his features. She pressed her lips to his brow, ignoring how sweat slid down her temple and made her jacket collar stick to her neck. "We have you," she whispered. "You're safe. Don't apologize. None of this is your fault."

He shivered, his forehead clammy. "I tried to shut out the voices," he said in a daze, "but they whispered that everything is broken. They said you'd leave me if I learned the full truth."

Emma's heart clenched. She gathered the last of her composure and smoothed back his dark hair. "They lied," she assured him. "I'm right here."

Behind them, Gale dropped her arms with a sharp gasp. She stumbled, nearly falling on the uneven ground. Emma saw how the draining spell had left Gale's face pallid. Her shoulders shook in small tremors. Emma gave her a grateful nod. Without Gale's focusing incantation, the illusions would have overpowered Emma's shield. Gale tried to smile, relief shimmering in her tired eyes.

The clearing fell eerily silent. The black stumps glistened with moisture under the faint light of Gale's dropped flashlight, as though coated in dew that never fully evaporated. Emma felt sick at the sight of them. Sadie's diaries had warned that some curses left the land permanently wounded, turning these trees into husks. She reached for Gale's hand and gave it a squeeze. "Thank you for that incantation," she murmured.

Gale exhaled shakily and cleared her throat. "At least we know I can do something right." Her tone held a wafer-thin attempt at humor. She bent to retrieve her flashlight, glancing warily around the clearing in case any illusions remained.

Ian tried to stand. His legs wobbled before Emma steadied him, wrapping an arm around his waist so he leaned on her shoulder. "They won't go away," he said in a tortured whisper. "They only get stronger."

Emma's heart twisted. "We'll figure it out." She hated that these words sounded flimsy under the lingering fear in her voice.

The three of them huddled together, scanning the clearing for any sign of a renewed assault. The biting chill remained, sinking into Emma's bones. She could scarcely imagine how badly it gnawed at Ian. She let him cling to her. The orchard, the diaries, all of Sadie's knowledge, they had to find something that would block illusions more permanently. What they had now felt like patchwork.

She and Gale exchanged a silent agreement: they needed to get Ian back to the orchard fast. They couldn't let him linger in this cursed hollow. Slipping an arm around each of Ian's sides, they guided him forward. Their footsteps crunched on scorched undergrowth. When they were beyond the black stumps, the gloom seemed less oppressive, though the night was still thick, and the Enchanted Woods swarmed with half-seen movement in the corners of Emma's eyes.

Gale puffed a quiet breath. "I never liked this part of the forest. It always gave me goosebumps."

Emma nodded, scanning the path for hidden roots or twisted illusions. She still felt the tension in the air, but at least the vicious swirl from moments earlier had receded. They stepped briskly, supporting Ian's weight. The hush pressed in, broken only by a rustle of branches overhead.

Despite her own exhaustion, Emma found enough strength to keep a protective awareness. She tried to sense any sign of the illusions creeping closer. She felt occasional flickers but nothing as menacing as before. Perhaps Catherine couldn't sustain her illusions after they had been repelled this time. Emma held on to that small hope.

They emerged from the Enchanted Woods onto the edge of the orchard. The crooked apple trees seemed almost welcoming in comparison to the stumps behind them. Ian clutched Emma's hand, knuckles white with leftover dread. He remained jittery, as though a single stray shadow might pull him back into horror. Emma stroked his forearm. "We're nearly safe," she said. "Just a bit farther."

Gale paused to catch her breath, casting a last look at the darkness behind them. "We can't keep doing it like this, Em. Next time, Ian might not come back if the illusions trap him deeper."

Emma's stomach twisted. "I know. We have to strengthen our wards. Find something that truly severs Catherine's hold."

They fell silent as they entered the orchard rows, stepping around scattered leaves. The wind kicked up, fluttering a few leftover blossoms. Though it was late in the season, those blossoms had clung stubbornly, reminding Emma of the orchard's defiance. She tried to let their soft fragrance calm her mind. Ian's breathing steadied a fraction with each yard they covered, but Emma felt persistent tremors in his grip.

As they approached Sadie's cottage, Emma noticed lights through the windows. Sadie must have woken from her restless sleep. She didn't want to add to her grandmother's exhaustion with more bad news, yet there was no choice. This incident proved that Catherine's illusions had grown bolder. The cottage door swung open before they knocked. Sadie's lined face, lit by the glow of a single lamp, appeared in the doorway. The concern in her gaze stabbed Emma's heart.

"It's all right," Emma whispered to her, though she

couldn't hide the tremor in her voice. "He's shaken, but we got him out in time."

Sadie lifted a hand, fingers trembling, to beckon them inside. Her expression carried the weight of her own fatigue, but her eyes glowed with quiet relief. Emma helped guide Ian over the threshold. Gale closed the door behind them, casting the orchard back into nighttime stillness.

One glance at Sadie's drawn features confirmed that she had little strength left to chase illusions, but perhaps they still had enough combined resolve to plan a better defense. Emma reflected on the blackened clearing's chilling presence, the wraithlike illusions that coiled around Ian, and the twisted shapes that had flickered with Catherine's sneer. A cold dread uncoiled in her chest. They might have won this round, but the illusions had carved deep into Ian's psyche.

She gripped Ian's hand and met Gale's gaze across the small living room. Gale looked shaken but resolute. Sore arms or not, she would brace herself for whatever came next. Emma exhaled slowly, the night's tension draining from her limbs but lodging in her heart. She resolved to unearth every clue in Sadie's diaries, no matter how cryptic. They had to piece together a stronger counterspell. They had to protect Ian from being lured away again.

Emma held Ian steady, her hand at his back, and gently lowered him onto the couch. Gale hovered near, eyes flicking from him to Emma with worry. Emma knelt, pressing her palm against Ian's cheek. The illusions had left a sallow pallor on his skin. He shut his eyes, leaning into her touch. For a brief moment, she let herself rest her forehead against his shoulder. She breathed in his scent, ignoring the tang of sweat and leftover fear. Their bond felt fragile but vital. She intended to guard it fiercely.

"Don't even think of wandering off alone again," she whispered. Her tone was part plea, part command. She felt him nod weakly.

In that moment, she vowed that they would not simply treat the symptoms. They would root out the illusions at their source, or they would all be devoured by the darkness Catherine had unleashed. The orchard waited outside, its branches stirring restlessly, echoing her firm decision. This threat would not fade on its own. If illusions could drag Ian into that cursed clearing once, they could do it again.

Emma felt Sadie's soft hand on her shoulder. The older woman didn't speak, but her presence alone gave Emma a flicker of reassurance. Gale stood a short distance away, raking a hand through pastel-streaked hair. The cottage felt cramped, full of tension, yet no one dared break the hush. In the quiet, Emma heard Ian's ragged breathing slow. The brief calm would not last. She lifted her head, exchanging a glance with Gale.

"We'll find a way to stop this," Emma said. Her voice emerged with more conviction than she expected to feel. "We have to."

Gale nodded, face pale but determined. She still breathed heavily from the spell she had cast. "We'll keep him safe. Let's figure out how."

They settled around the small living room. Outside,

the orchard's darkness stretched on, and Emma thought of the blackened stumps in the cursed clearing. The image of those writhing illusions churned in her mind. She closed her eyes, recalling the shape of Catherine's twisted expression, the half-rotted grin, and the deeper malevolence that prowled behind that façade.

Emma opened her eyes and focused on Ian, who rested against the couch cushions. Despite the night's ordeal, he was here, alive, and leaning on her. She pressed her lips together; breath unsteady but resolute. They had escaped the illusions for now. Tomorrow, they would arm themselves with whatever knowledge Sadie's diaries contained. This path of illusions would not devour him again. She refused to allow it.

Wordlessly, Gale sank to the floor beside Emma, both of them close enough to Ian that they could sense his heartbeat steadying. Sadie lingered in the doorway, eyes reflecting both worry and steadfast love. The hush in the cottage was fragile, but it was theirs. For tonight, that was enough. And though Emma's pulse still thundered, she clung to the faint hope that came from standing together, determined to forge defenses strong enough to thwart any dark enchantment that haunted the Enchanted Woods.

SEVENTEEN

Emma pressed her palm against the rough bark of a mossy apple tree as her heart thudded with leftover adrenaline. Everything felt oppressive in the wake of the recent chaos. Only yesterday, she and Gale found Ian slumped in a haunted clearing deep in the forest, illusions swirling around him in wild shapes. Gale's shaky incantation had helped drive back the nightmares clinging to his mind, but Emma could still taste the tang of dread in the back of her throat. Ian was safe now, at least physically, but every movement felt fragile, like stepping over cracked glass.

She made her way along the winding rows of apple trees toward a more open clearing. Her boots snapped through fallen twigs scattered over the soft ground. The orchard's subtle magic usually calmed her, but this morning it only sharpened her unease.

When Emma finally spotted Ian leaning against a crooked trunk, her breath caught. He stood with his arms folded and shoulders hunched, as though trying to become part of the bark pressing into his back. The soft early light revealed fresh bruises under his eyes, and he stared at the ground as if it were an enemy poised to attack. A chill lodged in Emma's stomach. She had never seen him look so wholly defeated. Only hours ago, they had coaxed him away from those illusions. Now, he seemed determined to walk straight back into their jaws.

She drew closer, careful not to rustle the dried leaves too loudly. He noticed her anyway. His gaze flicked up, a flash of guilt confirming that her presence was both expected and dreaded. Neither spoke for a long moment. The orchard's quiet felt unnatural, as if the trees themselves held their breath.

"You shouldn't be here," he said eventually. His low voice carried a ragged edge, reminding Emma of the illusions that had nearly consumed him. "I need... distance. For your sake. And Sadie's."

A current of frustration rippled through her. She tried to keep her tone even. "Ian, you can't just—"

"I can do exactly this," he broke in. He straightened with a wince, as though every muscle in his back had knotted. "Emma, listen to me. Those illusions are getting worse. The forest... I saw things." His expression twisted, and Emma's pulse sped up. "I saw illusions of me hurting you. And hurting Sadie. They weren't just vague shapes. It was my face. My hands. Every time I blinked, there was a flash of you, injured on the ground." His voice cracked, but he forced out the words, neglecting any pretense of calm. "Those illusions might become real if I stay nearby."

Emma's chest tightened in rebellion. She hated that he believed he carried all blame like a cursed brand. She also hated the surge of terror that sprang up in her own heart because she had glimpsed that destructive potential. She recalled the swirl of illusions in the clearing, how they had twisted his features into something monstrous. Yet the memory strengthened her resolve. She saw how illusions had battered him, and she had fought to pull him out.

She stepped closer, ignoring the sting of dried branches scraping her ankles. "Isolation is not the answer," she insisted. "Pushing me away won't make the illusions disappear. They feed off your fear. What do you think will happen if you're out there alone, with no protection?"

He almost laughed, but it came out as a hollow rasp. "Maybe I'll get lost permanently," he said. His gaze fell to the orchard floor, where an overabundance of fallen leaves gathered around his feet. "At least I wouldn't drag you down with me."

Her frustration flared, and she pressed her hand into the trunk behind her. "Stop it. Stop acting like you're the only one fighting this." Her voice rose despite her effort to stay calm. "I can't stand by and watch you tear yourself away."

"Emma, please—"

"And what about Sadie?" she shot back, her words trembling with pent-up emotion. "She's exhausted, but she hasn't given up on you. She's forging new wards, risking her health to keep illusions from swallowing Crestwood whole. She believes in you. I believe in you."

For a moment, his shoulders tightened, and she heard his breathing shift. He folded his arms tighter. Emma's anger mingled with heartbreak as she watched him wrestle his own terror. The orchard's wind turned restless, rustling leaves overhead in a rising sky. Light glinted along the runic carvings on one of the apple trees, a subtle reminder of the orchard's magic. She felt that quiet pulse in her bones, urging her to stand her ground.

Ian let out a short exhale. "You think it's easy for me?" he asked. His voice cracked on the last word. "I see these horrifying visions of you in pain, Sadie screaming, and I'm the cause. If it's not illusions feeding on me, then it's my own nightmares. I keep failing to hold them back."

She stepped closer, but he jerked away, making her frustration spike. "Ian, stop that," she snapped. "You don't get to decide my safety without asking me. We're in this together. You can't shut me out because you're scared of losing control."

He lifted his gaze, and a flash of anguish crossed his face. "That's exactly it—I'm losing control."

She saw the torment behind his words. The orchard's air felt thick, pressing around them like a turning storm. Her next words came in a rush. "Then let me help you hold on. We'll figure something out. We have the diaries. We have Gale practicing spells. Sadie is... well, she's doing everything she can. Do you think I haven't considered the risk? I know illusions might hurt me. I know I could fail. But I'm not going to walk away."

He shook his head. "You should. I'm one step from snapping. If these illusions get any stronger—"

His sentence broke when his eyes clenched shut. She moved forward instinctively, but he held out a hand, blocking her path. Fury and sorrow knotted inside her. She hated the illusions that turned him into a walking wreck and hated his idea of noble self-sacrifice even more.

"Get out of my way," she growled. Instead of waiting for him to lower his arm, she slipped around it. Shadows flickered in his eyes for an instant, as though the illusions tensed, ready to flare.

"Stay back," he warned again, but she refused.

"No," she said, her voice shaking from reined-in emotion. "We're done with that. I can't watch you retreat into some lonely corner of Crestwood, waiting to self-destruct." She gripped his wrist hard, ignoring the alarm in his eyes. "You're not going to vanish from me."

He tried to pull free, but she dug her heels into the soft ground, channeling every ounce of fury, grief, and desperate love into that hold. A spark of tension flashed between them, his yearning to protect her and her fierce insistence on not letting him go. She sensed the orchard's wind swirling around them in a sudden gust, rattling branches overhead.

"Emma, let go—"

She didn't. Instead, she yanked him forward, surprising them both. Her lips crashed against his in a rush of heat and desperation. Everything roared within her: the orchard's restless magic, the pounding of her own heart, the ache to keep him tethered here. She felt his body tense for an instant. Then his resistance crumbled, and he kissed her back with a bruising force that spoke of every emotion he'd tried to bury.

She tasted salt and fear in that hard press of his mouth. The wind whipped her hair across her cheeks, and a low moan of anguish escaped them both. With the illusions so close to the surface, she half-expected some monstrous haze to tear them apart. Instead, they clung to each other like drowning souls. Her breathing went ragged, and his arms slid around her waist, pulling her tighter until she could feel the thud of his heartbeat matching hers.

The orchard trees swayed overhead, as though caught up in the same tumult. Leaves trembled, and for an instant, Emma imagined entire arcs of illusions snapping overhead, unseen but lethal. She didn't care. All that mattered was the ragged sound of Ian's breath as he broke the kiss and pressed his forehead against hers, shaking.

"I'm so terrified," he muttered. His eyes fluttered shut, and she saw how his hands still shook at her waist. "I can't lose control, but I'm losing it anyway. Every time I think I'm done letting illusions feed on my mind, they come back. They show me hurting you, Emma. I'd rather cut myself off from everyone than risk that."

Her own tears pricked the corners of her eyes. She exhaled a trembling breath, lifting a hand to cup his cheek. "I'm scared, too," she admitted, voice barely audible. "I'm scared I don't have enough training to protect you. My spells are untested. Sadie's diaries might not have all the answers. But I refuse to abandon you to face that terror alone."

He buried his face in the hollow of her neck, a strangled sob escaping his throat. The orchard felt more alive than ever, the wind swirling around them in a cacophony of rustling leaves. Despite the raw flood of emotion, Emma found herself blinking furiously, determined not to let despair bury them both.

For a moment, they remained like that, clinging to each other like a makeshift raft in a raging sea. The orchard's magic throbbed in Emma's veins, reminding her they still had hope. The illusions hadn't claimed him fully, not yet, and she intended to battle them with everything she had. She gritted her teeth, mentally reaffirming her vow to push her magic further, even if it meant diving into dangerous incantations. Sadie had warned about advanced spells, but Sadie hadn't seen Ian trembling like this.

Eventually, the wind died down—a quiet, uneasy hush. Emma loosened her grip on Ian's arms. His eyes glistened with tears he was trying to hide, and her own face felt hot from crying. The orchard rang with the echo of too many unspoken fears. She threaded her fingers through his, offering silent reassurance that no illusions could break that bond entirely.

Her voice emerged like a near whisper. "Come inside. Please. Sadie's awake. She and Gale have been pulling spells from the diaries, trying to craft something stronger for you. Even if it's not perfect, we have to try."

He hesitated, eyes darting over the orchard as though searching for a reason to refuse. At last, his chin dipped in a brief nod. Relief surged through Emma, though it mingled with a raw ache she couldn't ignore. She led him out of the clearing, careful to step around the scattered clusters of fallen apples that dotted the path. Each step felt like a precious victory, as if coaxing him away from the darkness nipping at his heels.

Their walk back to the cottage passed in subdued quiet, broken only by the crunch of gravel underfoot. Emma's mind whirled with a thousand half-formed spells. She wondered if she ought to push for a synergy incantation, or a more permanent ward. Gale was practicing new techniques in the attic, though everything they did remained experimental. Frustration pulsed in Emma's belly. She wanted solutions now. She wanted to guarantee Ian's safety.

When they reached the cottage, Sadie's drawn face awaited them at the threshold. Pale morning light filtered through the doorway, illuminating the worn lines around her eyes. She leaned heavily against the doorframe. Her posture looked steadier than yesterday, but fatigue stained her expression. Emma felt a pang of guilt for letting her grandmother see them in such a state—him trembling, her tear-streaked and windblown. Sadie's grim gaze softened with relief at the sight of them together.

Without a word, Sadie stepped aside to let them enter. Gale was nowhere to be seen, likely rummaging through diaries upstairs in hopes of finding a new approach. The living-room lamp glowed with a single, flickering bulb that failed to chase away the gloom.

Sadie motioned them to the couch. "Sit," she said softly, her voice rasping with exhaustion. She turned toward the small wooden table in the corner, where half a dozen scattered runic sketches lay. She picked up a narrow chain with trembling fingers. A lacquered symbol dangled from the end, etched with a transition of runes Emma vaguely recognized. The polished metal glinted with something akin to warded energy.

"I adapted Gale's incantation from the diaries," Sadie explained, her voice faint. She crossed the room and pressed the new ward into Ian's palm. "We layered it with protective runes to steer illusions away from your mind or at least dull the edges of them. It's not a cure. But it should help for a while."

He stared at the ward in his hand, and the trembling of his fingers became more obvious. Emma's heart twisted when she saw tears brighten his eyes again, but he nodded, grateful. Slowly, gently, he slipped the chain over his head to let the ward lie against his chest. He clenched it there, chest heaving with a ragged breath.

"Thank you," he whispered. His voice wavered, but sincerity shone through. Sadie released a tired exhale and placed a cautious hand on his shoulder. Her expression carried both relief and a silent message that there was only so much more she could give.

Emma watched them, her own thoughts spinning in frantic circles. She felt the orchard's presence pulsing just beyond the cottage walls. She recalled the anguished desperation of that kiss less than twenty minutes ago. And despite her tears, she felt a smoldering determination to protect him, to ensure that illusions would never twist him into a weapon. Perhaps advanced ritual spells truly were the next step, no matter what the diaries warned. She swallowed, letting her breath steady. Then she gave Ian's hand a reassuring squeeze.

Emma tried to shake off the lingering sense of dread. She leaned against the couch cushions. Her arm brushed close to Ian's and she closed her eyes. Sadie's quiet presence radiated a weary kindness, and Emma let that comfort sink in. Here, at least for a moment, they were safe. The illusions were not vanquished, but they were at bay, and Ian wasn't alone in the orchard, wrestling them in solitude.

She listened to the slow rhythm of his breaths. The new ward glinted faintly under the lamplight, echoing the runes Sadie and Gale had tested in the diaries. Emma knew that as vital as those runes were, she would need to push harder, learn faster. Ian's safety, and maybe her own sanity, depended on it. For now, she held on to him and made a silent promise that she would not let him slip away into the illusions' hold. She would not let fear claim him. Sadie looked on, her own exhaustion overshadowing her usual gentle smile, and Emma saw the unspoken warning in her grandmother's eyes: this reprieve was fragile. They had to keep fighting—together.

Outside, the orchard's branches swayed in a muted breeze, as though acknowledging the fragile victory inside the cottage walls. And in that stillness, Emma rested her cheek against Ian's shoulder, letting their combined warmth hold back the dark for as long as the ward allowed.

EIGHTEEN

Emma gasped awake, heart pounding so fiercely that her ribs ached. Darkness clung to the edges of her vision as she fought to steady her breathing. The image of Catherine was still acute: the librarian's face, drawn in triumph, gliding through a moonlit graveyard. Emma could almost taste the chill of damp grass under her feet and smell the tang of overturned earth. Nameless tombstones had stretched in neat rows, but the only ones she clearly remembered bore the Turner name. She had recognized her own family's granite markers, pitted and rough. Catherine's voice had echoed all around them, promising sorrow so absolutely that Emma's blood felt cold even in her dream.

She tugged the thin blanket tighter around her shoulders. Weak morning light seeped in through her bedroom curtains, pale and watery, as if it hesitated to fully illuminate the fear that coiled in her gut. Her mind reeled, trying to parse how Catherine's illusions had reached her, especially in a nightmare. Until now, the illusions had centered on Ian's mind, twisting his perception. But Emma had just relived something so vivid that her mouth felt dry.

She blinked, forcing her eyes to adjust to the dim interior of Sadie's small cottage. The familiar shapes of her few possessions—her jacket draped across the chair in front of the desk, a dusty stack of diaries she'd skimmed last night—came into focus. Her pulse gradually slowed, but determination replaced the initial wave of panic. She couldn't let a dream keep her cowering, not when Ian suffered illusions far worse every night.

Emma tossed aside the blanket and planted her feet on the cool wooden floor. She whispered a calming mantra Sadie had taught her. It did little to settle her jangling nerves, but it reminded her how far she'd come. She was no longer the timid newcomer. Catherine had threatened her friends, subdued half the town with illusions, and driven Ian to the brink of despair. Enough was enough.

"Sadie," she muttered under her breath, pulling on the nearest sweater. If Sadie was already awake, she would likely be in the kitchen or rummaging through her study. Emma awoke right before dawn truly broke. A single lamp glowed near the living room, casting elongated shadows across the walls.

She found Sadie halfway down the corridor, leaning against the wall with one hand braced for support. Strands of silver hair pulled free from her loose bun. Her eyes flickered with concern when she caught sight of

Emma's drawn face. The older woman tried to stand straighter, but fatigue seemed to weigh on her bones.

"You felt it too," Sadie said quietly. Her words were hoarse, as if she'd just woken from her own restless doze.

Emma opened her mouth, uncertain how best to capture the unspeakable dread Catherine's illusions had woven into her dream. Instead, she pressed her lips together and nodded. She could practically see the question in Sadie's eyes: was this how Ian endured those twisted visions night after night?

Sadie touched Emma's shoulder gently. "Come to the kitchen," she said. "We need tea and a plan."

They settled around the scarred wooden table. The flickering overhead light revealed just how tired Sadie looked. Purple shadows gathered beneath her eyes, and her face appeared more lined than Emma remembered even a few days ago. Sadie busied herself with a kettle, hooking it onto the stove's small flame. Moments later, fragrant herbal steam drifted around them. Yet the old comfort of tea felt hollow this time.

Emma clasped her hands around a chipped mug, letting the rising warmth penetrate her numb fingers. "Last night," she began, voice trembling, "I saw Catherine among Turner tombstones. She spoke as if... as if everyone I love was doomed. I could almost feel the moist soil under my feet. I..." She paused, swallowing the stiffness in her throat. "It felt so vicious. I don't think she was just trying to scare me. She wanted me to see it, to know that she can strike in my own dreams. I can't stand aside anymore, Sadie."

Sadie gazed into her own mug, the hot liquid swirling. "I'm sure of it," she said softly. "You've crossed into her sights now. Catherine wants to break your spirit before you can act. She's accelerating her illusions. Perhaps she thinks it will sap your willingness to fight."

Emma absently traced her finger along the edge of the table. "She's wrong." Adrenaline pulsed in her veins, defying the tremor in her voice. "I'm done relying on wards alone. We keep reinforcing them, and she finds new ways in. If she can get into my dreams, we can't stay passive. I want to go after her illusions at their source. Something offensive, Sadie—something that targets her. We can't just block illusions forever."

The older woman's gaze flickered with alarm, though she tried to keep her tone calm. "I expected this conversation. But you know well that pivoting from defense to offense is dangerous. Curses and illusions often reflect the caster's own psyche. If you lash out without care, you risk letting Catherine's darkness into your own aura. She will retaliate."

Emma exhaled through gritted teeth. "She's already retaliating, punishing us for trying to defend Ian. And look at you..." She broke off, noticing how Sadie's hands shook slightly on her mug. "You're exhausted. Catherine is wearing us down, day by day. I can't wait around for her next strike."

Sadie closed her eyes. For several moments, the only sound was the quiet hum from the stovetop. "I fear that going on the attack might open you to worse illusions. But I understand the choice you feel forced to make. Let's see if there's anything in my older diaries, or the Grimoire fragments, which describes an incantation capable of shredding illusions at their root."

A prick of determination lit behind Emma's ribs. She nodded and set down her half-empty mug. "I'll search everything," she said. "I refuse to watch Catherine feed on our fear. If she wants a fight, I'll make sure she regrets it."

They retreated into Sadie's study, flipping on a single lamp shining over the cluttered desk. Parchment scraps, half-finished translations, and an array of battered diaries filled every available surface. Emma recognized Sadie's careful script on most pages, while a few bore older, spidery handwriting that belonged to long-departed ancestors. The entire room smelled faintly of musty pages and dried lavender. As they worked, the early dawn light pressed against the window, lending the spines of books a grayish glow.

Emma soon lost track of time, rifling through journal after journal. Her eyes ached from squinting at centuries-old script. Sadie occasionally paused to rest against a chair, face pinched with fatigue. The sense of dread that followed Catherine's illusions hovered over them both, thick as the orchard mist. A quiet dread told Emma that if they failed to find anything, Catherine would escalate even further, perhaps using the dream angle to break Ian entirely.

Finally, Emma paused at a faded entry in a volume older than most. "Sadie," she called softly, beckoning her grandmother over. "Look here." She pointed to a passage scrawled in the margin. The words were in an archaic dialect, but Emma recognized enough to piece together meaning. "It references illusions, anchored illusions, and an act of severance."

Sadie peered at the writing. "Yes," she murmured, tracing the line with her fingertip. "It's reminiscent of that final section in the Grimoire I never wanted you to see."

Emma flipped a few pages, scanning more references about illusions that threaded themselves into unsuspecting minds. Her stomach tightened as she read the partial instructions. "It calls for 'entering the illusions' boundary grid and unraveling them from within the caster's tether'? That's... that means we'd have to forcibly connect to Catherine's illusions and then shred them at their source. I see repeated warnings about emotional recoil, maybe even nightmares that rebound onto the caster."

Sadie pressed a palm to her forehead, eyes clouded. "This is exactly the type of spell we sealed away for a reason. It's not just a matter of chanting a line. You must open yourself to the illusions' root. If you fail to keep your own mind stable, Catherine's illusions could infest your consciousness."

"But if I succeed," Emma ventured, flipping more pages, "it would sever them. It would mean she can't just slip into my dreams, or into Ian's. She'd have to rebuild her illusions all over again without that existing tether. That might buy us enough time to strengthen wards or—"

"That might also do you permanent harm!" Sadie's

voice, raw with worry, grew louder than she intended. She steadied herself on the edge of the desk, breathing unevenly. "Emma, I've tried to keep you out of dark spells for good reason. Guilt is too gentle a word for how I'd feel if this destroys you."

Emma set a hand over her grandmother's. "I'm not leaping into this without caution. But we can't let Catherine pick us off one by one. She's already sinking her claws into Ian's mind." The memory of his haunted eyes, ringed by exhaustion, flashed in her head. Catherine's illusions had left him with trembling hands and restless nights. Emma forced a swallow that felt like shards of glass. "I can't let him suffer alone."

Sadie gave no immediate argument. The weariness in her posture hinted that she knew Emma was right. Slowly, she nodded. "Then we'll do what we must. Let's see how that incantation is formed. But I beg you to hold a sliver of caution."

They carefully spread the diaries over the desk. Emma meticulously pieced together cryptic references from multiple volumes, matching fragments of runic script to faint notes in Sadie's own handwriting. Each new line of text felt heavier, as if the words carried a tangible threat. She realized the incantation demanded a personal sacrifice, a direct vow of vulnerability that would let her aura latch onto Catherine's illusions. The risk was that Emma's mind could be left open to malevolence, possibly giving Catherine a back door to manipulate Emma's darkest fears.

Hours later, they arrived at a coherent sequence of

lines. Emma ran a trembling fingertip down the margins, reading them aloud in a soft voice:

"In gloom of mind where nightmares dwell,
I breach the void 'twixt light and spell.
I tear illusions from their host,
And claim their root at heavy cost.
By blood and breath, by soul's own seam,
I cut the tether, scythe the dream."

Sadie's lips thinned. "That's it," she whispered. "It matches the half-buried instructions. It's short, but it demands precise focus. The last line especially... scythe the dream. It's forcing your aura to become like a blade aimed at Catherine's illusions."

Emma stared at the lines, heart hammering. "The diaries talk about emotional backlash. This is... intense."

Before Sadie could respond, light footsteps sounded in the hallway. Gale burst in, hair pinned into a messy bun, pastel streaks escaping around her face. She juggled an armload of random items—several half-full jars of dried herbs, a battered mortar and pestle, and a box of matches. Slight strain carved lines at her forehead, but she forced a breezy grin.

"Who wants breakfast?" Gale teased, setting her supplies down on a side table. "Because I'm pretty sure I've got everything except normal food. Wait... we have none of that." She frowned at the scattered diaries. "Please tell me we're not going all gloom-and-doom again. I was hoping for a bit of positivity."

Sadie pulled her gaze from the incantation and managed a faint smile. "We found something, Gale," she said. "It's... complicated."

"Great," Gale quipped, voice dry. "Because things in Crestwood are never complicated." She opened a tin of dried rosemary, sniffing it like she was checking for freshness. "Tell me quickly, so I can gauge how many comedic jokes I need to keep you from spiraling."

Emma explained the gist: a forbidden spell that could shred illusions at the root, but at the cost of risking her mind's stability. Gale's eyes widened, and she set the tin aside carefully, as though it might explode. "That's... wow. Not going to lie, that's terrifying, Em."

A chill fluttered through Emma's belly. "I know," she said softly. "But it might be our best chance to stop Catherine before she breaks Ian."

Gale nodded slowly, crossing her arms. "Yeah, well, in that case, I'm with you. I'll watch your back. Also, if you plan on chanting that, we'll need all the healing stuff we can gather, and a protective circle so strong that Catherine can't hijack the process."

Sadie touched Gale's shoulder in appreciation. Then she looked at Emma, who was already leafing through the diaries for references on protective circles. "I want to ensure you understand the potential cost. This might anchor Catherine to you, even if only for a moment. You could become the target of illusions you never imagined."

Emma pressed her lips together, steeling herself. She recalled the dream tombstones, the moan of the wind over her family's graves. Catherine's purr of satisfaction still haunted her thoughts. Emma imagined those illusions in Ian's mind, repeated nightly until he could barely separate real from false. "I won't let her do this," Emma said. "I won't let Catherine's illusions devour him. If this is the only way, I'll face the risk."

Sadie bowed her head. The room fell quiet except for the hiss of the stove's flame and the rustle of pages. Then the older woman whispered, "We'll need to prepare carefully. Tonight, whenever you attempt this spell, you can't do it alone. Gale and I will fortify you as best we can."

Nodding, Emma bent once more to the diaries. The incantation's words swam in her vision, each phrase as sharp as broken glass. She forced herself to breathe evenly. The corridor behind them carried the faintest hint of orchard air—earthy and damp. Somewhere outside, the wind stirred branches that seemed to whisper caution. But Emma's determination blazed stronger than before.

Gale cleared her throat, fiddling with the mortar and pestle. "Seriously though, let's not do this on empty stomachs. I can rummage for eggs or bread, if we have any left. Or maybe we have some cheese. Anything that'll give us a bit of a normal morning."

Sadie gave a nod, distracted by her own notes. "Yes, that would help." She turned a page in the diary, searching for additional instructions about staging the incantation. "We'll need clarity, not hunger. Gale, see what we can manage. And gather some thyme, basil, and dried lavender—for calming the aura."

Emma blew out a measured breath. She felt as though a hundred thoughts fought for prominence in her mind.

Catherine's illusions, Ian's exhausted face, Sadie's hoarse warnings, Gale's halfhearted jokes. Above all, Emma envisioned the possibility of severing Catherine's hold. She pictured Catherine's illusions snapping like threads under a decisive blade.

"It's worth it," Emma murmured, running a finger over the lines of the newly unearthed spell. Even if stepping onto this path risked exposing herself to Catherine's hidden nightmares, she had no intention of letting fear stop her. Her love for Ian, her loyalty to Sadie, fueled a need to end the torment that would only worsen if left unchecked.

The lamp's dim glow caught on the scrawled lines, illuminating each word like a silent dare. Emma squared her shoulders. She might be stepping into a labyrinth of illusions, but she refused to surrender. She would fight Catherine's magic with her own, no matter the cost to her peace of mind.

Beyond the cottage windows, Emma pictured the orchard's roots, twisting deep, vibrant with Turner magic. Sadie's diaries insisted that their lineage was built on renewal and resilience. Emma clung to those beliefs, praying they would not crumble when she invoked this spell.

Gale returned carrying an odd assortment of bread, a wedge of cheese, and a bruised apple that looked ready to fall apart. She laid them on the side table and peered at Emma's pale face. "You sure about this?" she asked, voice uncharacteristically gentle.

Emma managed a small, determined nod. "Catherine's illusions are strangling us. I can't stand by and watch her torture Ian until he breaks. If we do nothing, her illusions will infect more dreams—even mine."

Gale gave her a crooked, reluctant smile. "Then I guess we're all in. I'm not letting you do this alone. I'll gather some protective wards, maybe re-check Sadie's chalk runes. If we're diving in, let's go prepared."

Emma glanced at Sadie, who still looked torn but nodded in agreement. The older woman's hand wavered over the diaries as if reluctant to let Emma bear this burden. But Sadie understood that Emma's resolve was unshakable. The longer they waited, the deeper Catherine would sink her claws into Ian's mind.

Emma tried to focus on practical tasks. She'd need time to memorize those lines perfectly and to prepare her own mental shields. She also wanted to check on Ian, to see if he'd had any rest. For now, she swallowed a bite of bread, ignoring how stale it tasted. She clutched her mug of tea, letting the bitter dregs remind her she was still anchored in reality.

Her gaze drifted to the diaries one last time. The forbidden incantation stared back like a reckless promise. Each verse reminded her that illusions could be dismantled if the caster dared face the source. There would be a price for such a bold strike—haunting dreams or partial possession. Something cold and uncertain twisted in Emma's chest, but she refused to look away.

Sadie finally cleared her throat. "We must plan carefully. You'll need a strong anchor to ensure your mind doesn't become a gateway for Catherine. That might mean drawing on the orchard's energy or forging direct synergy with someone you trust, so you don't slip too far into her illusions."

Emma's heart hammered. "I trust you. And Gale. And... Ian," she added softly, though she hesitated to involve him before he'd fully recovered from the illusions. She reached out and squeezed Sadie's hand, letting her grandmother feel how steady her fingers were. "I'm not afraid of Catherine."

Sadie sighed. "Let's not confuse determination with an absence of fear. Just promise me you'll remember your own limits, Emma."

"I promise," Emma whispered. Within her, light and dread coalesced. She inhaled, tasting the orchard's magic in the air. Then she folded the diaries closed, the lines of the incantation burned into her memory. "Show me how to do this right. I'll pay whatever price it demands."

Gale fiddled with a piece of cheese, lips pressed together. Sadie rubbed her temples, eyes tinged with both resignation and fierce love for her granddaughter. Emma felt the tension poised in that silent unspoken agreement that they would embark on this dangerous course. If Catherine had chosen to invade Emma's dreams, then Emma would tear Catherine's illusions apart from the inside.

At last, Sadie spoke, voice low. "We'll gather everything we need after breakfast. Then we'll figure out the next steps."

Emma nodded. The doubt in her chest felt as tangible as the diaries' battered covers, but her resolution held firm. "I'm ready," she said. And though her heart raged with the memory of Catherine's mocking voice, she embraced that anger as fuel. She squared her shoulders and prepared to face the day, well aware that once the incantation left her lips, there would be no turning back.

NINETEEN

Emma crouched over the table in the cottage's living room, scanning the scrawled notes from Sadie's diaries. Her pulse thudded in her ears, making it hard to concentrate on the cramped handwriting. The fireplace stood cold, and the air was thick with the tang of dried herbs and burned wax. Sadie was convinced a more offensive form of magic was required to confront Catherine, but no matter how many pages Emma pored over, she felt ill-prepared. She glanced at the array of open books, half-finished runic sketches, and the faint shimmer of protective wards Gale had drawn on the floor. She was about to rise and look for Sadie when she heard a ragged cry from the hall.

Sadie stumbled forward, bracing herself against the cottage wall. Instantly, Emma dropped the diaries, heart lurching into her throat. Gale rushed toward Sadie from her post near the back window, while Ian, who had been standing in the open doorway, seemed frozen in place.

"Sadie," Emma said, voice trembling. She slipped one arm under her grandmother's shoulder, and Gale steadied Sadie's other side. Sadie's normally calm face was etched with pain, her eyes clouded as she tried to speak.

"I only tried—" Sadie whispered, but her voice cracked. She pressed the heel of her hand to her temple, her breath coming in shallow bursts. "Only half...the incantation..." She swallowed painfully, then leaned more heavily against Emma. "I wanted to test it...before letting you attempt anything so dangerous."

Emma's stomach clenched. She could feel Sadie's pulse fluttering under her palm like a dying bird. "You should have called us," she said, frustration coloring her tone. "That spell—whatever you tried—was obviously too draining for you."

Gale's eyes were wide with alarm. "I thought we agreed to go step by step," she said. Her usual teasing was gone, replaced by raw concern. "I never said you should do this alone."

Sadie gave a faint, apologetic smile. The lines around her eyes, which once conveyed gentle wisdom, now carved deeper shadows. She opened her mouth, but no words emerged. Her hands trembled uncontrollably, and she coughed, shaking her head as though fighting dizziness.

"All right," Emma said, voice tight with worry. She guided Sadie into the living room, helping her sit on the worn couch. Gale hurried to bring a cup of water from the small kitchen area. When Emma glanced at Ian, he seemed paralyzed, guilt radiating from him so intensely she could almost see it shimmering in the air.

Ian slipped into the room behind them, eyes haunted. "Is she going to be okay?" he asked quietly, though his wary posture suggested he already knew the situation was serious.

Emma forced a steadiness into her response, pressing her lips into a thin line. "We'll make sure of it," she said. She lowered her voice and looked directly at Ian. "This is not your fault." She wanted to break through the swirling shame that kept tightening in his expression.

He flinched. "I don't see how it is not my fault," he said, voice hushed. "Sadie keeps pushing her limits because of this curse in my bloodline. Townsend illusions. Catherine. All of it leads back to me and my family history."

Sadie tried to raise her hand in reassurance, but the trembling was so severe she practically dropped it back into her lap. Emma exchanged a worried look with Gale before brushing a few strands of hair from Sadie's forehead. Her skin felt clammy.

"Let's breathe," Gale murmured, kneeling on the floor near Sadie's feet. She balanced the cup of water carefully, offering it to Sadie in small sips. "We can do something helpful right now, like a grounding technique. Remember the one with the salt?"

At Gale's mention of the salt circle, Emma slowly exhaled. She remembered the protective wards spaced around Sadie's cottage. Each line of chalk or swirl of dried rosemary was supposed to fortify them. But at this moment, it felt inadequate.

Sadie swallowed the water and gave a shaky nod. Her

voice, when she found it, stretched thin as thread. "I only read half the verses," she said, wincing as she spoke. "I wanted to gauge the incantation's...draw on my energy... before risking Emma or Gale. Thought it might be safer to test alone."

Emma's frustration blossomed. "You can't keep shouldering all the risks," she said. "Look at you." She gestured at Sadie's pale complexion and the faint quiver in her shoulders. "You're exhausted, and it will keep worsening if you push like this."

Ian crossed his arms, gaze downcast. "I should go," he said quietly. "If I remove myself from Crestwood, there will be no reason for Sadie to keep sacrificing her strength for me. You can all focus on defending the town, and I can handle the illusions alone."

Sadie tried to interject, but her voice rasped into silence. Emma glanced at her grandmother, heart pounding. She softened her tone, addressing Ian again. "Look, I understand your fear, truly. None of us wants to risk more harm. But leaving is not a solution. The illusions will follow, or Catherine will find another way to torment you, torment us."

He clenched his jaw, the guilt warping his features. "Every time I see Sadie like this—straining herself, drained, trembling—I feel like I'm forcing you all into a losing battle."

Gale rose from her crouch, setting the water aside. She gently placed her hand on Sadie's knee. "Let's at least get Sadie comfortable and check if there is anything we can do to ease this strain," she said. Her comedic relief flickered back in uncertain bursts. "Because I, for one, can't handle any more catastrophic drama before dinner."

A tense, half-hearted laugh escaped Emma. She allowed Gale's words to break the tension, just enough to let them breathe. Together, Emma and Gale helped Sadie up from the couch and guided her into the kitchen nook, seating her near the table where the light was better. The overhead lamp cast a warm glow on Sadie's trembling figure and her ashen expression.

Emma grabbed a lavender-scented cloth from a nearby cupboard, wetting it with lukewarm water. She pressed it gently to Sadie's forehead. The older woman exhaled, though her voice remained weak. "I had hoped… only a fraction of the incantation would not do so much harm," she croaked. "It is stronger than I expected. Catherine's illusions…they grow more potent by the day."

Ian hovered by the doorway, one hand braced against the wall.

Gale drummed her fingers on the table, eyes darting between Sadie and the scattered diaries. "We have got to do something about Catherine directly," she said, her voice crisp. "These nightmares, hexed objects, illusions— none of these are letting up. Every time we do a protective ward, something new happens around town. Did I mention the talk in town of that freakish cold spot in the bakery. Or the silent crows swarming the orchard."

Emma remembered that morning's unnerving sight all too well. Waking up early, she had peered outside to find more than a dozen crows perched around the orchard's edges, not a single caw among them, similar to the story

Gale had described someone in town. Just black eyes and eerie stillness. It was as if they were scouting the orchard or delivering a warning on Catherine's behalf.

"Flocks of silent crows," she murmured, rubbing a chill from her arms at the memory. "And the local market had those sudden cold drafts, where people's breath came out in puffs of fog even though it was sunny. It is like Catherine is testing how far her illusions can bend reality."

Sadie coughed softly, regaining enough strength to speak in a whisper. "That is precisely it," she said. "She is unraveling the threads of Crestwood's normalcy, feeding on fear and the power she leeches from Ian's unsettled aura." She tried to lift her trembling hand to gesture at him. "She thrives on your nightmares, dear. She will keep pushing."

Ian closed his eyes, pained. "I never asked for any of this," he said, voice low. "Believe me, if I could carve this curse from my bloodline and bury it, I would."

"We know," Emma said gently. Then she directed a question to Sadie, hoping to glean some reassurance about the incantation that had nearly collapsed her. "What was the preliminary test telling you? Is the spell workable at all?"

Sadie set her hand flat on the table, trying to steady the tremors as she talked. "It can work," she said. "But it demands immense focus and resilience. When I only chanted half the verses, it turned into a raw siphoning of magical strength—like a vortex with nowhere to go. It battered my defenses." She swallowed, eyes fluttering closed for a moment. "I'm not sure I can wield it again in my condition."

Emma felt a wave of dread cresting in her chest. "So, who will perform it?" she asked. She looked toward Gale, whose eyebrows shot up, though she didn't back away from the challenge. Then Emma's gaze shifted to Ian. The thought of him attempting such a draining incantation terrified her. If Catherine's illusions seized that moment of vulnerability, the backlash might be catastrophic.

Ian seemed to read her mind. "You can't seriously consider me," he said, voice shaking. "My illusions are so close to the surface most nights that I hardly recognize my own reflection."

Emma squared her shoulders. "We'll figure it out," she said, refusing to let doubt win. "If we need to combine our magic—me, Gale, you, whatever it takes—we'll do it. But we aren't going to let Sadie harm herself again, and you're not vanishing into the woods to get swallowed by illusions."

Sadie touched Emma's hand in gratitude, but her expression carried warning. "Emma, be cautious," she said. Her voice was regaining a fraction of steadiness, though it remained frail. "Powerful spells require skill, or the illusions could turn them against you. Catherine knows how to slip into a single stray thought if your guard is down."

Gale rubbed her eyes, looking much older than her usual playful demeanor revealed. "I thought practicing spells in the orchard was nerve-racking," she muttered.

"Now we are ramping up to advanced incantations while half the town is spooked by crows."

Ian exhaled a shaky breath. "This is all the more reason for me to go," he said quietly. His earlier guilt and frustration painted every syllable. "If Catherine is feeding on me, maybe I can draw her illusions out of Crestwood by acting as bait somewhere else."

Emma's temper spiked again. She slammed her hand on the table hard enough to rattle the teacup. "Stop it," she growled. "Stop trying to martyr yourself. That will not help anyone. Sadie's life is entwined in all this, and so is yours. The orchard is our strongest defense. All the runes, wards, and diaries cluster here. Helping you run away is basically tossing everything Sadie built to the wind."

He opened his mouth, but his retort caught in his throat. His eyes flickered with a mixture of anger and sorrow, and in that moment, Emma felt her resolve sharpen. She was done letting fear drive them into separate corners. If they didn't stand together, Catherine would win.

Gale cleared her throat, cutting through the tense silence. "At the very least, we need a plan for tonight," she said. "Let us make sure Sadie can rest. She needs to recover from that misfired test. Then we should reinforce wards around the orchard. It is the only place Catherine has not fully corrupted, and we can't risk illusions sneaking in here."

Sadie spoke in a faint murmur, "I can help with small wards. I just need an hour, perhaps two, to gather myself."

"Absolutely not," Emma said, pressing the cool cloth

over Sadie's forehead again. She exchanged a quick look with Gale. "We'll handle the wards. You rest. I mean it."

Ian took a hesitant step forward. "I can help with the wards," he offered. "At least let me do something productive. I may be a burden, but I know Catherine's illusions. I can sense them when they are near. If that helps keep them at bay…"

Emma nodded slowly. She couldn't deny that such help would be valuable. "Fine," she said. "But promise you'll not slip off."

He held her gaze, and a flicker of emotion, maybe relief or gratitude—crossed his features. "I promise," he said softly.

The four of them fell into a weighted hush. Outside, the hazy light that filtered through the windows told Emma it was late afternoon. Soon, dusk would seep across Crestwood, and illusions tended to thicken in the dark. She rubbed her arms, fighting off a chill.

She recognized that the group was dangerously frayed; Sadie had nearly collapsed from a half-finished incantation, Ian remained one breath away from fleeing, Gale was overwhelmed by the swirling chaos she tried to laugh away, and Emma herself felt the simmer of helpless rage whenever she recalled Catherine's smug illusions. Yet they had each other, and the orchard, and the diaries that might hold answers.

Gale set her hands on her hips, letting out a wry laugh that held no real amusement. "Honestly," she said, "if anyone had told me last year I would be stuck in a cottage, dealing with cackling illusions, cows on the rampage, and unstoppable curses, I would have demanded a refund on life. This is too much."

Emma almost laughed. She reached out and squeezed Gale's shoulder. "We didn't ask for any of it," she said. "But we'll see it through, absolutely."

Ian stilled by the doorway, his stance pained but resolute. Sadie closed her eyes, breath shallow, trusting Emma, Gale, and Ian to handle the rest while she regained her strength. Emma realized they had reached a tipping point. The illusions circling Crestwood were only getting bolder, and Catherine's boldness would not ease up on its own.

Emma stepped away from the table, running a hand along the shelf containing every battered diary Sadie had rummaged through in these last few weeks. Her determination flared, fueled by her grandmother's wan face. She would not watch Sadie throw away her life in a doomed attempt to contain Catherine alone.

"Let us do this," Emma said. "Gale, we are going to reinforce every ward in and around the cottage. We are doubling the lines of chalk, the rosemary bundles, every pinched circle of sea salt. Ian, you can help us sense illusions. If anything creeps close, we'll adjust the wards. Then, once Sadie has rested, we figure out how to handle that incantation's final form."

Gale nodded slowly, dropping the hint of a smirk. "Yes, Captain," she said, mock-saluting. "I'm on it."

Ian's voice came out low but clear. "Understood."

Emma felt the pulse of her own heartbeat drumming in her ears. She spared one last glance at Sadie, praying that rest and the orchard's underlying magic would revive her. Then, gathering the diaries under one arm and inhaling the lavender-scented air, she strode toward the hallway to collect the warding materials.

Outside, the sky was shifting to a dusky palette, and Emma was certain crows might be gathering in the orchard. She thought of Catherine, likely relishing the group's growing desperation. But Emma refused to cower. If illusions kept stalking them, she would craft a spell powerful enough to end them at the source.

Whether she liked it or not, the day was waning, the protective wards needed immediate bolstering, and Sadie's decline was obvious. Catherine's hold was creeping across Crestwood, stirring silent birds and unnatural chills. Emma would not wait for more chaos to descend. They had lost enough ground, and she would not lose anyone else to illusions or curses.

She squared her shoulders and met Gale by the front door, chalk and bundles of herbs in hand. Ian lingered close, offering her a faint nod of support. Sadie's faint breathing from the next room reminded Emma that time was slipping through their fingers. She would do whatever it took to protect them, even if it meant confronting Catherine head-on, long before she felt ready.

With that conviction burning in her chest, Emma closed her eyes for half a second. The orchard's distant energy thrummed beneath her feet, and though her heart pounded in dread, a steely determination flowed through her veins. Enough was enough. She had a grandmother to protect, a friend to shelter, and a warlock she refused to abandon. Confrontation might be risky, but they were done waiting for Catherine to strike first.

She opened her eyes, hand tightening around the chalk. "Let us start," she said, voice calm but resolute. Gale nodded, and Ian moved closer. Together, they stepped over the threshold, prepared to fortify every inch of the orchard's boundary before nightfall.

Emma tried to ignore the prickle of fear at the back of her neck as the evening shadows lengthened outside. Soon, they would face illusions lurking in the dark, but she refused to let that fear consume her. As the final trace of daylight flickered across the windows, Emma resolved to stand firm. She would face Catherine's illusions, restore Sadie's strength, and protect Ian from the nightmares that haunted him. No matter the cost, she would not let Crestwood slip under Catherine's control.

The sky dimmed further, and a tension settled over the orchard's swaying branches. Despite the hum of dread echoing in her ears, Emma inhaled, letting the crisp air fill her lungs. Her heart echoed with a single vow: she would do whatever it took to keep them safe, even if it meant forging a direct confrontation with Catherine far sooner than anyone anticipated.

TWENTY

A bitter wind rattled the shutters of Sadie's cottage as Emma pressed herself against the fogged glass, peering into the darkness. Something sharp and restless churned in the orchard beyond, where skeletal shadows flickered near the tree line. Each swirl of movement sent her stomach twisting with dread. Beside her, Gale steadied the chalk in her trembling hand and began scrawling a fresh ward along the window's edge. Pale lines of runic script glowed under the faint lamplight.

Emma forced a calm breath. She could sense an even greater surge of tension in the air. In an unsteady voice, Ian repeated what he had already asked: "Emma, we should go. We should leave Crestwood tonight and keep running until Catherine can no longer find us." His hands shook at his sides, betraying the panic he tried to hide. She didn't blame him for suggesting that she escape. Catherine's illusions had hounded his every footstep, dragging him closer to the brink.

Yet Emma felt the orchard's pulse through the worn floorboards beneath her feet. She knew, deep down, that running would serve only to tighten Catherine's grip on them. If they fled into the night, the illusions would trail behind, converging on them whenever their guard slipped. She clutched the collar of her sweater, remembering the harrowing moments when Catherine's illusions had latched themselves to Ian's soul. The darkest images still haunted his gaze.

"We stay," Emma said, voice low yet unwavering. She glanced at Ian, heart lurching at the fear in his eyes. "Fleeing only helps Catherine chase us on her own terms. If we leave, we give her the power to strike when we are exhausted and alone."

Ian's posture sagged in defeat, but he exhaled slowly as if readying for a fight. He took a step forward, close enough for Emma to feel the warmth radiating from him —warmth that continued to anchor her even when she thought her courage might fail.

Sadie's voice rose weakly from the other side of the dimly lit living room. She had positioned herself near the hearth, arms extended over the flames. She murmured protective verses that crackled with the faint firelight. A sheen of sweat glistened across her forehead, and her normally steady hands trembled in sync with the flicker of her magic. Emma knew Sadie had been pushing herself too far for too many nights, reinforcing wards and rummaging through diaries for any advantage.

"You must listen," Sadie said, breath ragged as she completed another verse. "Catherine is not content to stay in the shadows. She knows Emma has found those forbidden spells, and she will stop at nothing to prevent us from using them."

Emma swallowed. She pictured the half-deciphered incantations scattered across the kitchen table. Only a day before, she had read them with trembling hands, half in awe, half in terror. The taboo knowledge of how to sever illusions at the root had cost Sadie dearly when she attempted a preliminary test. Yet Emma felt a faint current of power brimming inside her, drawn from heartbreak and anger in equal measure.

Gale finished her chalk sigil along the windowsill. She shot Emma a tight grin. "I always said I wanted to be in a horror film," Gale said, voice cracking with a laugh. "Turns out I changed my mind. I'm good with comedic relief, but real illusions ripping through our orchard? That's not on my bucket list."

Emma forced a small smile in return. She was grateful for Gale's humor, even if it came laced with fear. Without Gale's steady presence, Emma suspected she would have sunk beneath the weight of guilt and dread. She gestured for Gale to move on to the next window, and Gale nodded, stepping carefully around the scattered books on the floor.

At the fireplace, Sadie spoke another verse, her voice weakening. Emma turned to find her grandmother leaning heavily against the mantel. Each word from Sadie's lips crawled with magical sparks, flickering across the logs in the hearth. The incantation was a simple protective one, designed to cloak the cottage in a shell of low-level wards against illusions. Under normal conditions, Sadie could have cast it in her sleep. Now she looked as though the slightest gust of wind might knock her over.

Emma moved to Sadie's side and gently reached for her hand. "Please rest," she murmured, pressing the older woman's trembling fingers. "We can handle the rest of the wards. You have already done so much."

Sadie shook her head, determination shining behind her exhaustion. "I will see this through," she said, though her voice wavered. "Warding the cottage might buy us time if Catherine decides to unleash her illusions all at once."

Emma doubted Sadie would allow herself any rest tonight. She heard the shriek of the wind outside and tried not to flinch at the shapes crossing in front of the orchard's dark trunks. This was a storm of magic and fear, swirling around them, refusing to let go until someone held the line.

Ian approached, his footsteps careful. A stray gust rattled the rafters, and the cramped living room lights flickered. He caught Emma's gaze and curved his fingers around her wrist as if grounding himself. His features were etched with guilt and desperation, a look that squeezed Emma's heart. "Your grandmother shouldn't have to keep pushing beyond her limit," he said quietly. "She nearly collapsed days ago just attempting half an incantation."

Emma clasped his hand and looked at him with unwavering resolve. "I will not lose you, or Gale, or Sadie," she said. "Catherine has taken enough from us, from Crestwood." She turned her face toward her grandmother. "We'll end this."

Ian's grip tightened. She felt the tremor in his arm, saw how his jaw clenched as he struggled with the impulse to run again. She guessed he worried that Catherine would target him with illusions so vicious that he might lose control. The memory of his restless nights, the way illusions roamed through his mind, fueled her determination. She couldn't watch him suffer that torment forever.

Seconds later, Gale let out a sharp whistle from the front door. "Emma," she called. "Somebody is out there." Her voice faltered. "No, not somebody. It is Catherine. Look."

Emma braced herself and joined Gale near the door's small window. Through the glass, beyond the orchard's first line of apple trees, she saw movement. The silhouette of a lanky figure stood at the tree line; pale robe buffeted by a wind that seemed not entirely natural. Catherine's arm lifted, and faint arcs of energy crackled around her hand. The orchard branches rustled in agitation, as if recoiling from the magic pooling at the woman's fingertips.

Emma's pulse hammered. Catherine's illusions had always been insidious, creeping into dreams until her victims felt unmoored from reality. Seeing Catherine poised to strike openly brought a fresh shock of adrenaline. Fear warred with fury. Though Emma's stomach knotted, she lifted her chin.

"She knows," Emma whispered, voice tight. "She

knows we found the solution in Sadie's diaries. She does not want us to cast that spell."

Ian stepped closer, pressing a protective hand on Emma's shoulder. Gale clenched a stick of chalk in her fist as though it were a weapon. For a moment, none of them spoke. Then Sadie spoke from behind Emma, voice hoarse:

"If Catherine unleashes more illusions, she may be able to slip inside our wards." Sadie closed her eyes for a fraction of a second. "Once illusions penetrate the mind, you'll need more than chalk lines. You'll need that incantation you discovered."

Emma's pulse pounded. She thought of the scribbled lines on the scrap of parchment by the kitchen table, the very spell that had nearly shattered Sadie. The incantation was short but exacting, calling for emotional sacrifice and an unforgiving confrontation with Catherine's illusions. Even the diaries warned repeatedly of the dangers. Yet Emma knew, with unwavering certainty, that they had no other path.

Ian exhaled as if sensing her thoughts. "You plan to use it tonight," he said, more statement than question. His eyes flickered with dread and a flicker of hope. "Is that wise?"

Emma's hands clenched at her sides. "I see no choice," she said. "If Catherine stands out there waiting for us to make a move, the illusions will only get stronger as the night drags on. She is likely feeding on fear, weaving illusions into the orchard. This might be our chance to catch her by surprise."

Gale rubbed her arms to ward off a chill, then forced

an unsteady smile. "I will keep up the comedic commentary if it helps, but that might not cut it against illusions." With a softer voice, she added, "You're not doing this alone, Emma."

Sadie straightened, though exhaustion carved lines into her features. "We combine wards and spells," she agreed. "I will maintain a perimeter if I can, and Gale can reinforce from the windows and doors. Emma, you must be ready to cast that incantation at the first hint of an illusion breach."

Ian didn't argue. He didn't hesitate. He stood there, thinking, but not with the doubt that had plagued him before. Something had shifted in his stance, in the sharp focus of his gaze. He wasn't uncertain anymore—he was fiercely resolute, like a blade finally unsheathed, honed to its purpose. The air around him crackled faintly, his magic stirring just beneath his skin, no longer buried under fear but sharpened by it. He met Emma's gaze, eyes dark with something deeper than determination.

"I will help," he said, his voice low, steady, unshakable. "My warlock energy isn't just a shield. It's a weapon. I won't let Catherine twist this power, this whole situation, into something we can't fight."

Emma nodded, exhaling as determination steadied her hands. She thought of that earlier day in the orchard when they had tested minor spells and discovered how seamlessly their magic merged, how Ian's raw power amplified her own like an unspoken harmony. If they could channel that synergy now, if he truly let his magic unleash—maybe they could withstand Catherine's illusions long enough for Emma to cast the forbidden spell.

A crackle from outside shattered the quiet.

An eerie glow streaked across the cottage lawn. Emma flinched, startled, as Catherine slashed her arm sideways, the orchard branches convulsing as if gripped by unseen hands.

Gale whispered sharp profanity and darted toward the wooden coffee table, fingers flying over the scattered notes. She grabbed the parchment containing the ocean-salt runes, the quartz placements, and the incantation Emma had painstakingly translated from Sadie's diaries. "We have everything," Gale said breathlessly, knuckles white from gripping the parchment. "At least, I think we do."

Emma's heart pounded in her chest, an erratic rhythm that matched the pulsing force of magic rippling through the air. Outside, the orchard trembled on the verge of collapse, as if caught between two warring forces—Catherine's illusions and the desperate protections barely holding it together.

Failure meant devastation. Total obliteration. Catherine's illusions would shatter their minds, warping reality until Crestwood belonged to her.

Emma moved to the kitchen, where a neat row of quartz shards gleamed on the counter. Each crystal was a conduit, a focus point for energy during the incantation. Beside them, a shallow dish of ocean salt shimmered under the candlelight, collected that afternoon from the tide pools—a last-ditch effort to ground them, to strengthen their ties to something real.

She reached out, fingertips brushing over the crystals, their cool surfaces anchoring her spiraling nerves.

"You're certain about this?" Ian asked quietly from behind her, a tremor in his tone. "If something goes wrong, if that spell backfires, you could be trapped in illusions far worse than mine."

She turned to face him. One unsteady hand found his, clasping it with gentle determination. "I'm not certain," she admitted, voice softened by honesty. "But I'm done letting Catherine torment you and wreck our town. If this is what we must do, then tonight is when we do it."

Ian drew her closer, and for a fleeting moment, they stood embracing, their heads bowed together. Emma breathed in the faint scent of his skin, a reminder that there was still something precious worth defending. Gale's anxious sprint back into the living room ended the moment, and they stepped apart, faces set with resolve.

Outside, the roiling shadows intensified, creeping toward the edge of the cottage's front yard. Emma could just make out the outline of Catherine's cloak billowing in that supernatural gust. Sparks of dark magic arced around Catherine's trailing sleeve, reflecting her heightened impatience. Each spark made Emma's skin prickle.

Sadie braced herself by the hearth, reciting a short verse that flared the flames higher. Emma knew it was a final push to strengthen the wards, the last bit of magical security from inside the cottage. If Catherine's illusions strained enough to crack that barrier, then Emma would have to cast the offensive spell.

Gale paused by the front window again, gave a shaky laugh, and whispered, "This is too real. My stomach is flipping. I would rather be relaxing with hot chocolate." Her gaze flicked from Emma to Ian. "But if it means saving Crestwood, I'm here."

Emma forced steadiness into her voice despite the adrenaline scalding her veins. "We are all in this together. We have studied the diaries. We have drawn the runes. We have the incantation." She looked at Sadie, who nodded weakly. Then she found Ian's eyes one more time, quietly apologizing for any pain he might suffer if illusions struck him. His nod in return showed that he accepted the risk.

Emma walked to the center of the living room, the spot where they had practiced smaller spells for half the night. Gale hovered nearby with the chalk, ready to reinforce the boundaries at Emma's command. Sadie steadied herself against the mantel, and Ian steeled himself beside Emma, hands warm and certain. Leadership, Emma realized, meant not letting fear overshadow the determination that burned in her chest.

A glimmer of lightning lit the orchard. For an instant, Emma glimpsed the shapes of twisting branches and flickering illusions wreathed in jagged shadows. Catherine's silhouette stood in stark relief, her hand raised. That sight solidified Emma's resolve. She remembered the simplest moments: Gale's teasing, Ian's gentle kiss in the orchard, Sadie's unwavering love. She would not allow Catherine to tear any of it away.

She made for the table at the center of the room, where their half-finished circle waited. In the flickering lamplight, the chalk runes glimmered with potential energy. The quartz shards would form a ring of refracted power once activated. The ocean salt, sprinkled at each cardinal point, would further secure the boundary. All that remained was the final impetus to unleash the spell. Emma felt a spark of fierce determination surge through her veins.

Ian's breath caught behind her. Outside, the orchard moaned under Catherine's assault. Emma reached for the parchment of incantations, her fingers shaking as she lifted the sheet. Once they began, there would be no going back. The illusions would sense their defiance, and Catherine would fire back with everything in her arsenal.

She turned to Gale, whose eyes were wide with trepidation but bright with loyalty. In that shared glance, Emma found the last push of courage she needed. She drew herself up, raised her chin, and spoke in a quiet but firm voice.

"We combine the wards with that blasted spell—whatever it takes, we stand together." She looked down at the scribbled notes they had prepared that afternoon, confirming the ocean-salt runes, the quartz shards, and the exact verses they would use for tonight's stand.

This was the turning point. Either they stood their ground, weaving every ounce of magic and courage they possessed into a shield that could push Catherine back, or they risked sacrificing everyone and everything they held dear. As lightning illuminated the orchard, Emma and her allies prepared for a battle that would decide Crestwood's fate once and for all.

CHAPTER

TWENTY-ONE

Emma hadn't slept. She stood in the cottage's cramped kitchen with the first hint of dawn casting long shadows across the floorboards. Every breath felt tight, as though the weight of Crestwood's restless magic sat on her chest. She pressed a hand to her collarbone, recalling the lingering tremor from the night's chaotic illusions. Wards and runes sealed the doors but worry still gnawed at her. Ian hunched beside her at the small table, with circles under his eyes. Gale leaned against the counter, tapping her foot nervously.

Outside, the sky glowed murky gray. Emma thought she heard echoes in the distance: a deep rumble, unlike ordinary thunder. Her fingertips were cold. Something simmered beneath Crestwood's soil, and the orchard's wards felt painfully thin in her mind. She glanced at Ian. He remained pale, shoulders tense, as if expecting another onslaught from Catherine's illusions. Yet this urgency felt larger than illusions. This felt real.

Gale's voice snapped Emma from her thoughts. "I don't like that sound," she said, nodding at the window. "Is that normal storm weather or Catherine's new trick?"

Emma swallowed. "It is not normal. She has tested illusions. Now she might be testing the ground itself."

A slight quake rattled a mug on the table, sending it skittering to the edge. Ian caught it before it fell. His eyes met Emma's, filled with a mixture of exhaustion and dawning fear. "We should go to the ravine. I can almost feel it pulling at my magic, like something is urging me there."

Emma shuddered. The ravine had always looked precarious, but now the energy swirling around made her heart pound. She grabbed her jacket, though it did little to fight the chill growing inside her. "Let's not wait here," she said. "If Catherine is truly messing with the earth, we need to see for ourselves."

They left the cottage in a rush. Damp air greeted them, and overhead, the clouds seemed to boil with trapped light. The orchard's trees rustled as they passed. Emma could almost sense them straining to warn her, their branches trembling with tension that mirrored her own. A swirl of crows rose from distant apple boughs as they cut across the property.

Gale stayed close by, flicking her gaze from Emma's drawn expression to Ian's stiff movements. "Your wards are still in place, right?" she asked Emma, voice hushed. "Because I really don't want a mountain of illusions crashing in on us while we're gone."

"They should hold for now," Emma replied, trying to

sound confident. The protective chalk lines she and Gale had drawn earlier still ringed Sadie's cottage and the orchard's central paths, but illusions had never been Emma's only worry. The ground beneath her feet felt unstable, as if unsettled by the undercurrent of Catherine's emerging power.

They turned onto the winding path toward the ravine, stepping past fallen branches and loose stones. Streaks of pale sunlight fought through the brooding clouds, casting everything in hazy half-light.

Ian stopped abruptly. His breath shuddered, and he pressed a hand to his temple. "She is definitely here," he said, voice tight. "I can sense her magic everywhere. It is like the earth itself is humming with it."

Emma scanned the path ahead. "Stay close," she whispered. "We have no idea where the ground might crack open."

Gale managed a shaky grin. "Lovely. Just the morning hike I wanted, with a side of potential disaster." Her humor at least eased some tension in Emma's chest.

They crept onward. Each step felt precarious, as if the path itself might crumble. Another quake rippled under Emma's feet, more insistent than before. Stones clattered off to the side, tumbling down into the half-hidden depths of the ravine. The vegetation's drooped leaves were coated with a strange film of dust that gave the entire area a haunted feel.

A low groan rumbled from the ravine's edge, making Emma's stomach tighten. She heard the rasp of shifting earth, then saw the ground split into a hairline crack that zipped across the path.

Gale gasped, stumbling backward. "That is not just an illusion," she breathed. "That is real."

Emma's pulse hammered so loudly she almost didn't hear Ian shout. He was further ahead, standing where the ravine's lip crumbled in small avalanches of soil. Sharp rocks tumbled into the chasm below. Through a haze of panic, she realized the fissure raced straight toward him, splitting the ground beneath his feet.

"Ian, move!" Emma yelled. Her voice trembled, but she forced her legs to surge forward. Gale was right behind her.

The crack widened. A sinkhole opened directly under Ian's boots, as if drawn by Catherine's will. Ian tried to jump back, but his momentum faltered on the loose soil. One foot slipped, sending him nearly waist-deep into a sudden drop of collapsing earth. Sheer terror tore across his features.

Emma sprinted, heedless of the shifting terrain. The quake intensified, and she felt the shape of Catherine's dark magic rolling through the ground. The entire ravine echoed with a thunderous roar, scattering dust and grit into the air.

She flung herself down at the edge and skidded onto her knees, reaching for Ian's forearm. "Ian, hold on!" Her heart slammed. She gripped his wrist hard, her nails biting into his skin.

He tried to brace himself, but the sinkhole started widening, pulling chunks of soil along with it. Emma strained her muscles, certain that if he slipped farther, the collapsing ground would bury him alive.

Gale dropped beside her, grabbing Ian's other arm. "We have you," she shouted, voice cutting through the roar. Together, they started to pull, but the earth kept shifting. Emma's boots threatened to lose traction in the streaming gravel.

"I can't hold on," Ian hissed, agony twisting his features. "The ground is giving way beneath my feet!"

Emma's mind raced. She remembered a technique Sadie had taught her, a type of mental call meant to summon help across distances. She pressed her lips together, chaos swirling around her as more of the path fell into the ravine. She closed her eyes and pictured her grandmother's face.

Sadie, please, we need you now, Emma called silently. She clutched the memory of her grandmother's clear eyes, the warmth of her voice, the soft crackle of her magic. Cold sweat trickled down Emma's neck. The rock under her knees threatened to give out, and Gale swore under her breath as another quake trembled through the ravine.

Then Emma heard footsteps behind them, light but sure. She twisted her head to see Sadie rushing forward. Her grandmother's hair was unbound, silver strands whipping in the wind, and her hands already glowed with the telltale sheen of powerful magic.

Sadie's voice rang out, resonant in the swirling dust. "Keep holding him," she called, eyes fierce. She thrust both arms forward, chanting words that vibrated through the air like unseen cords binding the scene. The ground shook again, but this time Emma sensed a new influence —a wave of protective energy surging from Sadie's outstretched hands.

Shoots of pine roots and tangles of greenery tore through the dirt around Ian's legs, weaving together into a makeshift lattice. Emma realized Sadie was commanding the roots to lock the ravine's collapse in place, halting the sinkhole's hungry pull. Thin shoots twisted into a rope-like barrier, bracing the edges of the crumbling ground.

Ian's trapped foot found a momentary hold between exposed roots, and he managed to push up. Emma and Gale, still clutching him, hauled with all their might. The ravine trembled again, sending one more shudder through the soil, but Sadie's magic held. Emma's muscles screamed in protest until, at last, Ian could swing a leg up and crawl free.

They tumbled in a heap, coughing on dust. The roar of collapsing dirt grew distant as the newly fortified edge held. Emma pulled Ian into her arms, adrenaline scorching her nerves. His chest rose and fell in frantic gasps, face streaked with dirt. Gale sprawled on the ground nearby, panting in relief.

Sadie exhaled a weary breath, standing not far from them. Her hands still glimmered with residual magic that pulsed faintly, binding the roots in place. She pressed her lips into a half-smile at Emma, although worry flickered in her gaze. "I sensed your call," Sadie said quietly. "Are you hurt?"

Emma shook her head, hardly trusting her own voice. She checked Ian for injuries, finding only scrapes and bruises. The quake's force drained away as if Catherine had retreated under the ravine's depths.

Gale leaned on one elbow, wiping a streak of dust off her cheek. "I'm never going near this ravine again," she said. Her attempt at humor came out shaky, but Emma flashed a grateful look. Anything to break the suffocating tension.

Ian's voice sounded unsteady. "Thank you," he choked, turning his gaze up at Sadie. "I almost believed the sinkhole would swallow me whole."

Sadie approached in measured steps, kneeling briefly to check Ian. "Catherine is growing bolder," she said softly. "Illusions once stayed in the mind, but she is funneling such power into the physical realm that the land obeys her. She is pushing beyond illusions, harnessing raw energy in ways that endanger us all."

Emma's stomach lurched. She remembered the silent crows, the cold spots in the marketplace, and the swirl of illusions that had haunted them. If Catherine could twist the earth itself, she would be more dangerous than they had imagined.

Gale got to her feet, brushing off her legs. She offered Ian a hand. "I guess your nightmares were just the warm-up, huh?" she muttered, gaze flicking around the ravine.

Ian rose, leaning for a moment on Emma's shoulder. He steadied himself and pushed the hair from his fore-head. "We can't keep waiting for Catherine to show up with new tricks," he said. "She nearly took me out in one blow."

Sadie took a slow breath, gathering her composure.

Her eyes momentarily closed, as if drawing in the orchard's energy from afar. "We may need stronger wards than the ones around the cottage," she said, glancing at Emma. "My daily castings are no longer enough. We'll have to try something else."

Emma hesitated, recalling how exhausted Sadie was the last time she attempted advanced protective spells. She didn't want to see her grandmother drained further, but the alternative was to leave the entire town vulnerable. She brushed the dust from her sleeves. "I can help," she said, voice firmer than she felt. "Whatever we must do, I'm with you."

Ian's hand slid over Emma's, his grip shaky but resolute. "We can't let Catherine make this entire town her battleground. If she can tear open the ground itself, nowhere is safe."

Sadie looked at them with pride mixed with sorrow. "Then we stand together," she said in a quiet voice. "We'll not allow her to crush us."

The ravine beneath them seemed to brood in uneasy silence, as though Catherine's magic still simmered below. Emma glanced back at the path, noticing the newly formed lattice of roots that formed a ragged but functional bridge over the worst of the sinkhole. Stones lay scattered, and the precipice remained perilously close.

Gale pressed a hand to her temple, her expression shifting from fear to a sort of determined exasperation. "I hate to bring this up, but if she can break open the ground around here, she can do it anywhere. The orchard. The marketplace. Even the library."

Sadie adjusted her stance, looking older than she had a day ago. "We'll need to bring the orchard into this," she said. "The orchard's bond with our magic might be the only reason your call reached me so fast." She cast a meaningful glance at Emma.

Emma drew a shaky breath, letting the presence of her grandmother and friends steady her hammering heart. "We'll reinforce every ward we can," she said, meeting Sadie's gaze. "We'll let Catherine know we're not backing down."

Gale gave a hard nod. "No more letting her pick us off or corner us at the ravine. We hold our ground, or in this case, we hold the entire town."

Ian's dark eyes flicked from the fractured soil to Emma's face, and she saw gratitude shining there. She clasped his hand in both of hers, pressing his knuckles to her cheek for a moment in silence that he stood beside her, not buried under a wave of cracked earth. The swirl of morning breeze carried the lingering taste of dust and fear, but also the faint promise of unity.

Sadie cleared her throat, looking around at the wreckage. Thin tendrils of her magic still bound the broken soil. "Let us leave this ravine," she said gently, voice carrying the note of finality. "We have done what we must here. We'll regroup at the cottage and plan our next move, whatever it takes."

Emma and Gale helped Ian step clear of any further breaks, ensuring the ground remained stable beneath their feet. Emma felt her resolve tighten. Catherine's assault had shown them all a terrifying truth: illusions were only part of her arsenal. If they wanted to protect one another and the people of Crestwood, they needed a plan stronger than hope, stronger than wards cast in a panic. They needed to face Catherine head-on.

Emma glanced at the distant horizon. The stormy clouds overhead still roiled ceaselessly, a warning that more trials were sure to come. She felt Sadie's hand on her shoulder, a small but comforting gesture. Gale stayed alert, scanning the terrain as though expecting the ground to erupt again at any moment. Ian stood close to Emma, his breath still uneven from shock.

They walked away from the ravine slowly, quiet but determined. Catherine might have unleashed a new weapon, but resolve glimmered in each of their eyes. Though shaken by what they had survived, they refused to retreat. Whatever illusions or earth-shattering force Catherine wielded next, they would stand firm together.

TWENTY-TWO

Emma tasted blood on the back of her tongue as she fought to steady her breath. Dust and swirling leaves choked the clearing, and her heart pounded an erratic rhythm against her ribs. All around them, the orchard swayed under an unseen strain, every branch trembling as if bracing for the inevitable clash of magic. Beyond the haze, Catherine's silhouette flickered with malevolence, robes billowing from the force of her illusions. Emma glimpsed her dark eyes sparking with a hatred that demanded more destruction than illusions alone could satisfy.

Sadie stood several paces in front of Emma, staff clutched so tightly her knuckles shone white in the half-light. Deep lines of exhaustion scored Sadie's face, but an unyielding resolve burned in her gaze. The orchard shuddered when she drew a ragged breath, an eerie echo of the life force she had woven into the very soil over decades. Emma's palms tingled; she sensed the orchard's energy rushing to Sadie, responding to her unspoken call.

A bone-deep groan reverberated across the glen, and the top layer of soil began to crack. Catherine's illusions swirled thickly, conjured shapes that lurched and snarled as if alive. The illusions clawed at the edges of Sadie's protective wards, sending sparks scattering near the orchard's mossy floor. Emma winced when one spark broke through and flared inches from her foot.

Sadie gritted her teeth. "Gale," she shouted, voice drenched in fatigue, "hold the western side. Do not let those illusions flank us." Her words quivered from effort, but she steadied herself and tightened her grip on the staff.

Gale positioned herself near a trio of gnarled oaks, rummaging in her coat pocket for chalk. She etched frantic circles on the ground, chanting a quick ward that flickered around her in uncertain light. Despite the tremor in her voice, her focus remained sharp. Each new line of chalk glimmered when she spoke, pushing back illusions that tried to slip around Sadie's flank.

Emma pressed a trembling hand over her racing heart, wishing she could do more. She had unleashed too many spells, her arms still hummed from a defensive incanta-tion she had cast moments earlier. Ian stood close to her side, casting uncertain glances at Catherine as if measuring the distance for a desperate counterattack. Emma felt his fear through the slight tremor in his hand. She caught his gaze, offering a silent promise that they would stand together.

Catherine pivoted her focus on Sadie, dark hair flung around her face as she unleashed a roiling wave of illusions. Phantom forms with ghastly mouths stretched across the clearing, clawing at any living thing. Emma's stomach twisted, and she stumbled back when one illusion snapped at her leg. Ian reacted instantly, letting a burst of kinetic force surge from his palm. The illusion dispersed, screeching in a shower of sparks that scattered across the roots.

Sadie braced herself. The orchard's branches rattled in a sudden gust, as if mustering the last vestiges of magic hidden among the ancient trunks. Emma felt the ground quiver beneath her boots. The orchard was alive, responding to Sadie's call for help. Sadie lifted her trembling staff, and her voice rang out clear and bright:

"In gloom of mind where nightmares dwell,
I breach the void 'twixt light and spell.
I tear illusions from their host,
And claim their root at heavy cost.
By blood and breath, by soul's own seam,
I cut the tether, scythe the dream."

The moment Sadie spoke, Emma felt a hot pulse of energy thunder through the clearing. It hammered into the earth, surging through the orchard's lattice of roots, right where Catherine stood. A sharp crack split the air, followed by a shriek of wood under immense strain. Thick vines erupted from the ground, twisting around Catherine's ankles. Where the vines touched, illusions fizzled or shattered apart, leaving behind disoriented swirls of shadow.

Catherine's eyes flared with alarm. She tried to unleash another wave of illusions, but the orchard's living force snapped them off at the source, each attempt sputtering in midair. Pale vines coiled higher, hooking around Catherine's knees, then her waist. A tremor raced over the clearing. The cracked soil opened into a deep fissure at Catherine's feet. Emma's heart pounded when she realized the orchard itself responded to Sadie's incantation, shaking the ground in an attempt to bury the threat.

"Sadie, that is enough," Ian called, voice ragged. Emma sensed his panic as the vines gained momentum, corded with lethal strength. "You cannot push yourself any further."

But Sadie didn't yield. Gasping for breath, she poured her love—for Emma, for the orchard, for everything that still drew breath in Crestwood—into the incantation. Her final syllables rippled across the clearing in a burst of emerald glow. The orchard soared to answer, wreaths of thick green tendrils looping around Catherine's torso and slamming her downward. Catherine's outraged cry rebounded off nearby tree trunks, echoing until it dissolved into a choking gasp.

Emma's vision blurred from the shock of so much raw magic. She clutched Ian's arm, struggling to maintain balance. He slid an arm around her waist, pinning her upright. She barely glimpsed Catherine's contorted expression of fury and disbelief. The orchard's roots churned like restless serpents, half dragging their prisoner toward the open fissure.

Suddenly, the entire clearing flashed with white light, so intense Emma had to shield her eyes. A thunderous crack followed, vibrating through her bones. Dirt and broken branches spun into the air, then collapsed in a ragged heap. When Emma dared to blink away the spots in her vision, she saw Catherine vanished from sight—only a few thrashing seedlings hinted at a shape pinned beneath the churned soil.

At first, disbelief clutched Emma. She exhaled a stunned breath, daring to hope that this final strike had subdued Catherine for good. The illusions vanished from the edges of the orchard, dissolving into thin wisps. Branches trembled, but not from fear—more like exertion, as if the orchard itself needed to catch its breath.

Her relief fractured the instant she heard Sadie's ragged cough. Emma swung around to see her grandmother buckle at the knees, staff dropping from limp fingers. Gale shot forward, sliding one arm around Sadie to keep her upright. Emma's heart stuttered, and she broke free of Ian's steady hold, running to Sadie's side. The orchard fell eerily silent except for the rasp of Sadie's breathing.

Sadie's skin glistened with sweat; her face ashen. She struggled for air, each inhale shallow and painful. Emma knelt, pressing her shaking fingers to Sadie's cheek. Terror seized her when she felt how clammy Sadie's skin was. The orchard's hush seemed to gather around them, as if it, too, sensed its guardian fading.

"No, no, you are all right," Emma half-whispered, blinking back tears. She brushed stray strands of silver hair from Sadie's forehead. "Please be all right."

Ian sank down on Sadie's other side, eyes dark with anguish. He placed trembling fingertips on Sadie's wrist, searching for a pulse. Emma could see the dread etched in every angle of his face. Gale was close, blinking fiercely to keep her own tears at bay.

Sadie's breath rattled in her chest. Her unfocused gaze flickered to Emma. The orchard's protective shield offered no comfort now, only a hollow aftershock—a terrible silence that felt like heartbreak.

Emma's eyes brimmed with tears. "We have to help you," she pleaded, voice unsteady. She remembered half-finished healing incantations Sadie had taught her. She tried to summon a spark of magic, but her own reserves felt dangerously low. Her palm glowed for an instant, then fizzled out, powerless against the magnitude of Sadie's drain.

Gale's lips trembled. "We can get her back to the cottage," she said, though the desperation in her eyes betrayed her doubt. She tightened her arm around Sadie's shoulders, trying to guide her grandmother upright. But Sadie's legs buckled again, the fight drained from her limbs.

A thin, rasping cough escaped Sadie's mouth, and she gave a small shake of her head. She tried to speak, but not a single syllable emerged. Despite her silence, Emma sensed the message her grandmother was struggling to convey. Sadie had poured every last drop of her strength into that final incantation, and the orchard had responded fully.

The clearing around them bore the scars of that power. Large patches of overturned dirt, uprooted brush, and scoured bark marred what had once been a stately grove. A swirl of residual green magic hummed around the vines that anchored Catherine below the churned earth, like a lingering shield to keep her imprisoned. Emma stole a glance at that fractured patch of ground. She prayed it would hold Catherine until they could find a way to reinforce the seal.

Sadie's breath came in shallow gasps. A final note of heartbreak knifed through Emma's chest when she saw her grandmother's eyelids flutter, too heavy to remain open.

"Sadie," Emma whispered, her voice cracking. "Gale, help me lift her. Ian—" She swallowed a sob. "We need to—"

Gale moved to cradle Sadie's shoulders, but Sadie's body twitched in a brief jolt of pain. The orchard, in turn, exhaled a sorrowful breeze. Leaves swirled down in a gentle confetti of wilted green, each flutter a quiet lament. Emma felt tears rolling hot down her cheeks.

"She is barely breathing," Ian said, despair gripping every word. He took Sadie's limp hand in his own, voice raw. "I am sorry, Sadie. I should have—"

Sadie let out a weak groan, scarcely audible. Her lips parted as though to speak, but only a broken breath escaped. Emma pressed her forehead to Sadie's, feeling a painful tightness clamp around her throat. She couldn't lose her grandmother, not after all the sacrifices and wisdom Sadie had shared.

Gale's voice trembled. "We can perform a quick healing circle," she proposed, fumbling for the chalk in her pocket again. "We can—"

"I do not know if that will be enough," Emma whispered, tears blurring her vision. She slid an arm beneath Sadie's shoulders, trying to keep her as upright as possible. Sadie's body felt so frail in Emma's grasp. Her chest rose and fell with painfully shallow motions.

Ian brushed a wavering hand through Sadie's silver hair. He looked on the verge of tears himself, although he struggled to keep composure. Emma understood his torment—Sadie had rescued him more than once, and now he felt helpless to repay that debt.

The orchard's stillness weighed on them, more suffocating than any swirling illusion. The wind had quieted to a mere whisper, as if the orchard had withdrawn its fury. Emma glimpsed Catherine's partial entombment. The vines remained, though flickers of dark aura still slipped between them, evidence that Catherine might not be fully defeated. Yet that threat paled in comparison to the immediate crisis pressing against Emma's heart.

Sadie's eyelids fluttered again. For a fleeting instant, her gaze found Emma's face. Love and weary acceptance shone in her expression. Then her eyes closed, her head rolling weakly against Emma's arm.

"Sadie!" Emma's voice cracked in a plaintive plea. She held her breath, terrified that Sadie had already slipped away. But a faint pulse still throbbed under her fingertips.

Emma clung to that small sign as if it were an anchor in a violent storm.

Gale placed a shaking hand on Emma's shoulder, and for several seconds, none of them spoke. The orchard's broken clearing surrounded them with evidence of Sadie's mighty sacrifice: uprooted earth, battered roots still quivering with leftover magic, and the land left gasping for reprieve. Emma's tears fell onto Sadie's tunic, soaking into the worn fabric. She felt Ian's presence behind her, close enough that she sensed the heat of his body and the tremor in his breathing.

Finally, Gale said, "We—maybe we can get her to a safer spot. It might be easier to cast a healing incantation closer to the cottage." Yet even as she spoke, Emma heard the uncertainty in her friend's voice. Sadie's energy felt so faint.

Emma forced herself to draw in a slow, steady breath. She tasted salt on her lips, unsure if it came from tears or from the air still charged with leftover magic. "Yes," she managed. She gently smoothed a damp strand of hair off Sadie's brow. "We have to try. We cannot leave her out here." She lifted her face toward the orchard's silent canopy, blinking hard.

Sadie made no sound, but Emma could tell that even the smallest movement jostled her limp form. Gale shifted, tucking a chalk stub into her pocket before kneeling down again. Carefully, she maneuvered around Sadie's other side, offering support. Ian stayed at Sadie's feet, ready to help lift her. No one mentioned Catherine.

The orchard's vines still held that threat at bay, but they all sensed the fragile victory could unravel at any moment.

Shaken, they lifted Sadie as carefully as they could, mindful of each shallow breath that rattled in her chest. With unspoken agreement, the three turned toward the distant path leading to the cottage, stepping gingerly around debris and uprooted soil. Catherine's dark aura still flickered beneath the prison of vines, but no illusions rose to stop them.

As if acknowledging her dwindling life force, the orchard's ancient trees quieted to a mournful stillness—no rustling leaves, no cawing crows. Only the rasp of Sadie's shallow breaths and Emma's shaken sobs penetrated the silence.

And in that stifling stillness, the wind died down, leaving only a quiet devastation in its wake.

TWENTY-THREE

Together, the three of them guided Sadie away from the clearing, stepping gingerly around fallen branches and tangles of vine that still bristled with magical residue. Emma dared one last look over her shoulder. Catherine's dark hair was barely visible above the churned earth. Though she remained trapped, Emma couldn't shake the feeling of those eerie eyes still upon them.

The forest rose around them with harsh shadows deepening under the failing light. Every gnarled tree looked sinister now. Emma remembered a time when this woodland path felt mystical but also comforting. Gale stumbled over an uneven spot, nearly toppling Sadie in the process. "I'm sorry," Gale murmured, voice high with panic. Emma brushed Gale's arm in silent reassurance and tried to distribute more of Sadie's weight onto her own shoulders. Sadie's head lolled, and the older woman's eyes fluttered open just long enough to look at Emma.

A soft, dry sound escaped Sadie's lips. Emma bent her head closer, straining to hear. Sadie's voice was barely above a breath. "Keep... your guard," she whispered, the words dissolving into a ragged cough.

"We will," Emma promised, though she doubted Sadie could fully grasp her answer in this state. Everywhere Emma looked, the ground threatened to pull away, leaving dangerous holes. She had never felt so powerless.

They continued through the darkening woods, forced to pick their way over exposed roots and clusters of broken branches. Once, Emma spotted a fallen trunk that blocked the usual path, forcing them to circle around a cluster of thorny undergrowth. Each detour cost time, and each minute weighed on them like a physical burden. Sadie's moan of pain drove daggers into Emma's heart.

Gale's breathing turned uneven when they reached a narrow stretch of ground littered with jagged stones. She spoke as if to fill the silence with anything that might lighten the crushing dread. "You'd think... this lovely forest could cut us some slack," she said, stumbling through the words.

No one replied, though Emma's lips twitched in the faintest attempt at encouragement. A part of her knew Gale joked because she, too, felt terror snapping at her heels.

Eventually, the trees thinned, giving way to the far edge of Sadie's property. Emma's chest constricted at the sight of the orchard's final row, branches sagging as though they mourned their keeper. The cottage lights glimmered faintly ahead—even from here, Emma could see the window glass trembling from the aftershocks of magic.

Emma bit down on her fear and murmured a healing incantation that she had practiced only days before:

"In hush of eve, in breath so light

Let wounds find solace through this night."

The words faltered halfway out of her throat, and though a flicker of warmth glowed at her fingertips, it fizzled uselessly. She swallowed a cry. Sadie remained lifeless against her side, and her shallow breathing didn't ease.

Ian pressed closer; his voice hushed so only Emma could hear. "You tried," he said. "She's just... she's lost too much energy."

Emma refused to tell the truth: her grandmother might be slipping further with every beat of Emma's frantic heart. She squeezed Sadie's hand harder and forced her feet to keep moving. Ahead, the cottage's outline stood in a swirl of dusk. The front door had been left unlatched, shockingly enough. Emma nudged it open with her hip, and they entered in a mad rush, stumbling inside with Sadie's limp body braced between them.

A coating of dust clung to the air, stirred by the trembling earlier in the day. The furniture had shifted slightly; a cabinet door stood ajar, and a couple of old books had tumbled from a shelf. Pale lamplight in the living room revealed how thoroughly the quake had shaken the cottage. Gale let out a quiet gasp. "Look at this mess," she whispered, but there was no heat in her remark, only fear.

Emma guided Sadie to the hearth. Her arms burned

from the strain, but she refused to let go until Gale and Ian steadied Sadie from both sides. A thick blanket, half-folded, lay crumpled nearby. Emma tugged it open and placed it on the rug.

"Careful," Ian cautioned, easing Sadie down so as not to jar whatever injuries lay beneath her battered form. Gale stood on Sadie's other side, sliding a cushion beneath her head.

Gale knelt, rummaging through the scattered items to find something that might help. She cursed softly when she came up empty. "I can try a... a minor incantation," she said, nerves making her words unsteady. "It's not for healing exactly, but it could calm her ground-level pain."

Without waiting for Emma's approval, Gale flipped her palm upward, her fingers trembling. A wafer-thin swirl of azure magic manifested, but the energy sputtered erratically before vanishing. Gale winced and whispered, "I'm sorry. I'm all nerves."

Emma reached out and clasped Gale's hand, giving it a gentle squeeze. "You did your best," she murmured. She understood the feeling of magic slipping away under stress. Her own attempt in the woods had failed similarly. The orchard's raw power had been exhausted, and so, it seemed, had Sadie.

Ian stood abruptly, sweeping his gaze around the room. "We need warmth." A slight tremble colored his voice. "A fire might help her body not go into shock."

Emma nodded. Though the night was cold, she suspected Sadie's chills came from more than a draft. Emma swallowed a surge of guilt and followed Ian as he worked to gather kindling. Broken twigs, torn from the orchard's outskirts, had been stashed in a basket by the hearth. Emma passed them to him, her breath still ragged.

He held out his hand, palm splayed over the scattered wood. Emma saw the faintest glow in his dark eyes, a reflection of the magic he channeled. Heat blossomed in the air, and then a spark flickered across the kindling, igniting a small flame that licked hungrily at the sticks. Ian exhaled sharply, as if the effort cost him more than usual.

A warm glow spread around the hearth, casting dancing shadows on the cottage walls. Emma gently pulled the thick blanket beneath Sadie's shoulders and positioned it so she was cocooned in the fabric. The older woman moaned softly again, eyelids fluttering. The fireside light revealed dark smudges under Sadie's eyes, and lines of pain wove across her brow.

Gale took a shaky breath. "Let me try conjuring some orbs of light, maybe lift the gloom a little." She lifted her hands and whispered a practiced phrase that Emma recognized as a simple focusing charm. This time, three faint golden orbs appeared, hovering near the rafters. Their dim radiance made the cottage slightly less oppressive. Emma heard no laughter from Gale, no triumphant exclamation about her magical success. Now, her eyes were bright with tears.

Ian crouched next to them; his expression tight. He placed two fingertips against Sadie's wrist, as if checking her pulse. After a few seconds, he looked at Emma, uncertainty etched in his gaze. The flickering light from the orb above caught the gold flecks in his eyes. "Still there," he whispered, voice heavy with relief. "It's faint, but it's there."

Emma nodded, tears burning the back of her throat. "I'll find anything that might help," she said firmly. She tried to stand, resolved to search the cottage for healing tinctures Sadie might have stored, but her knees wobbled from fatigue. Ian reached for her elbow, steadying her.

"Rest for a moment," he murmured. "We need to keep watch too. If the orchard starts trembling again... or if Catherine—"

A low moan from Sadie cut off Ian's words. Gale rested a trembling hand on Sadie's brow. "She's so cold," Gale said, desperation slipping into her tone. "Emma, do you remember that protective tea Sadie once made when you were feeling sick? The one with rosemary and, uh, those pinkish dried petals?"

Emma grasped at the recollection, though her mind reeled with exhaustion. "I think so," she managed. "Let's see if it's still in the kitchen cabinet. Or if the earthquake knocked it loose."

Gale nodded, shooting to her feet and hurrying toward the small kitchen nook. Emma heard rummaging, the chime of dislodged jars and the creak of half-broken boards. She clasped Sadie's hand, trying not to let worry paralyze her. Sadie's eyelids fluttered again. For a moment, Emma saw the faint glimmer of recognition in her grandmother's gaze.

"Stay with us, please," Emma murmured. "We'll fix this—somehow. We'll fix this."

She felt Ian's presence at her side, steady yet filled with sorrow. He lifted Sadie's other hand, brushing away a streak of dirt from Sadie's palm. The older woman's lips parted, and a faint, raspy breath left her chest. She didn't speak.

Gale returned, a small jar of dried petals in one hand and a bundle of slender green herbs in the other. "This is all I could find that wasn't smashed," she said, voice tight. "I'll try to brew something right here if the stove's not working. Maybe the fire can heat the water."

Emma nodded, grateful to have Gale's resourcefulness. She kept her eyes on Sadie's face, memorizing each shallow inhale. She wished she had honed her healing magic more thoroughly when they had the chance. She and Sadie always meant to revisit advanced spells once the orchard's tensions calmed. That chance had been snatched away by violence.

While Gale began preparing a makeshift infusion with a battered kettle, Emma coaxed Sadie's hand into a warmer position under the blanket. The cottage air felt stale, thick with the stress of their fight. Ian flicked his gaze to the door, then back to Emma. "No sign of illusions out there," he said softly, reading her unspoken fears. "The orchard is unsettled, but I think... Catherine is still stuck."

After a few moments, Gale placed the kettle by the flame, letting the water heat enough to steep the herbs. The faint aroma of rosemary and the sweet tang of dried petals wafted through the cottage. "It's not a proper spell," Gale muttered. "But maybe it'll help her body relax."

Ian slowly fed more scraps of wood to the hearth. The new flames cast dancing reflections across Sadie's still form. Gale let out a wavering breath and stood, one hand pressed to her sternum in a nervous gesture as though she could anchor her heart against the tragedy playing out before them. Emma could think of nothing else but how they had to keep Sadie alive, had to give her a chance to recover. Nothing mattered more than saving the woman who had risked everything to protect Crestwood.

Emma smoothed Sadie's hair away from her forehead, whispering the same fragile promise until the words formed an unbreakable vow in her heart.

"We're here," she said, voice trembling. "We're all here."

In the corner, Ian focused on the wood as he built up the base of the fire. With careful motion, he coaxed the flames into a steadier blaze, ensuring Sadie would have enough warmth. At length, Ian added a final piece of wood, turning to rejoin Emma at Sadie's side. The fire burned bright, its glow casting sharp shadows on the cottage walls. With the light dancing across them, the trio remained close, gazing upon Sadie's wan face.

No one moved from that spot. They stayed, huddled around Sadie's motionless form in the silent, dust-curtained room. Emma could find no words, and neither could Gale or Ian. At that moment, all they had was the warmth of the fire, the quiet swirl of herbal steam, and the fragile hope that Sadie might yet survive.

TWENTY-FOUR

Emma perched on the edge of her chair; shoulders tense as she flicked through another of Sadie's old tomes. Deep, ragged breaths filled the cottage's living room, most of them coming from her grandmother, who lay prone near the hearth. Sadie's complexion had turned an alarming shade of gray, her cheeks hollow, and her fragile frame struggling to draw each breath. Outside, rain beat steadily against the windows, a relentless percussion that only added to the oppressive dread clinging to the room.

Gale stood a few feet away from Sadie's makeshift bed, whispering a mild enchantment. She moved both hands in a small circle, coaxing several scraps of cloth into a lazy float around her shoulders. It appeared half comedic, half desperate—a child's attempt at conjuration. Emma's chest clenched at the sight. She knew Gale was only trying to keep their spirits alive, yet Sadie's labored breathing reminded her that nothing about their situation had any lightness.

"Come on," Gale muttered with forced cheer. She nudged one of the cloths, and it tumbled in midair, nearly colliding with the low-hanging lamp. The makeshift enchantment flickered like a spark about to die. Gale lowered her hands, and the cloth pieces dropped harmlessly onto the floor. "I tried," she said quietly, wringing her fingers as she glanced at Sadie. "Maybe I should, I don't know, brew more tea."

Emma pressed her lips together and turned another page in the tome. The old leather binding creaked in protest, as if the book had been silent for too long. Most of the text described arcane theories about reversing illusions. Despite scanning each sentence, Emma found no direct reference to an injury as dire as Sadie's. Everything read like half-coded instructions, requiring knowledge of advanced runes or unfamiliar incantation lines. She stifled a frustrated groan.

"Thank you, Gale," Emma murmured, trying to sound grateful. "We need any bright moment we can get." She paused, eyeing the living room's clutter and the scattering of magical texts. If there was a secret to healing someone on the brink of collapse, it had to be in these pages. Yet the instructions were either incomplete or garbled with warnings about how the orchard's magic might complicate results.

Ian chose that moment to step quietly into the room, a wide tray balanced in his hands. Steam rose from a large bowl of stew, and the aroma reminded Emma that she had not eaten more than a few bites since early morning. The bread and cheese perched on the edge of the tray sent her stomach into an uncomfortable growl. She glanced at Ian's face and spotted the same regret she had glimpsed earlier—a heaviness lining his eyes, as though he carried blame for the storm raging around them.

"Please eat," he said gently, voice pitched low to avoid startling Sadie if she drifted in and out of consciousness. "You both need to keep your strength up, and I can do more in the kitchen if necessary."

Emma watched him set the tray on a small side table near Sadie. The tang of herbs and cooked vegetables swirled into the air, making Gale inhale in anticipation. Neither of them hesitated, hunger and worry combining into a frantic edge. Emma accepted a chunk of bread while Gale tore off a piece of cheese.

As Gale handed Emma a wooden spoon, Emma lifted it to the stew pot, filling it with warm broth. She felt an odd sense of gratitude she didn't have the words to articulate. Ian's presence had a reassuring effect on her, even though she knew he felt undeserving of any thanks. Whatever storms swirled inside him, he was here, offering more than just food. He was offering her a measure of hope.

Emma took a sip of the stew, warmth sliding down her throat. For a moment, her vision blurred with emotion or maybe pure exhaustion. She braced her palm against the edge of Sadie's tomes to steady herself. The pages lay as if mocking her inability to decode them.

"Let me feed Sadie," Ian offered. He prepared a smaller bowl and spoon, then knelt beside Sadie with careful reverence. Gently, he lifted her head enough so that he could coax a few spoonfuls of broth to her lips. A flicker of comprehension crossed Sadie's gaze. She emitted a feeble whimper, her mouth barely parting to accept the liquid.

Tears prickled in Emma's eyes. "Thank you," she whispered to Ian, forcing a smile when he glanced in her direction. In truth, Emma's heart stung, caught between sorrow for Sadie and tenderness for Ian. She had seen what fear had done to him, how illusions had threatened to twist his mind. Now, he poured his concern into every careful motion of that spoon. Outside, lightning lit the orchard with a cold flash, revealing the twisting silhouettes of branches. Thunder rumbled an instant later, shaking the cottage windows and sending ripples through the broth in Ian's spoon.

With a shaky breath, Emma tried again to search the tomes. She turned a few more pages, scanning passages that mentioned advanced rituals requiring synergy with orchard blooms, or spells that demanded energies Emma didn't yet comprehend. The paragraphs blurred. When she reached the end of the page, she realized she couldn't recall a single meaningful phrase. Frustration burned her eyes. Many times, she had attempted to rouse Sadie into offering a clue, but all she received were half-lidded murmurs or the faint shift of Sadie's fingers.

Gale must have noticed Emma's despair. She set aside her cheese and stepped toward the hearth. "I can try warming the place more," Gale suggested, her voice attempting a bright note. "It might make her breathing less, well... anyway, a bit of heat might be good. Let me see."

She snapped her fingers and spoke a gentle word of magic. The flames in the hearth flickered higher, crackling with new life. It shed more warmth across Sadie's cheeks, but her breathing stayed too shallow. Emma silently thanked Gale for at least attempting a stable incantation, since so many of Gale's comedic conjurations collapsed under stress.

Ian eased away from Sadie, setting the half-empty bowl on the tray. He stood and hovered near Emma's shoulder, gaze sweeping over the open tomes with quiet concern. "Any luck?" he asked, voice low enough for Emma alone to hear.

Emma shook her head, swallowing the knot in her throat. "These references keep pointing to techniques I have no real training to perform," she admitted. "Half of them mention synchronicities with orchard blossoms or advanced runes that Sadie never taught me in detail. I am missing something crucial." Her frustration bled into each word.

Ian's expression tightened. "You aren't the only one who regrets not learning more while Sadie had the strength to teach," he said. "Maybe there is a simpler remedy stashed among her journals."

Gale, overhearing, cleared her throat softly. "I have rummaged through everything this side of the cottage and only found mild healers. She must have hidden the advanced knowledge somewhere secure." She hesitated, biting her lip. "Like that warded trunk you mentioned before, Emma."

Emma stilled. She recalled the warning Sadie had given her at least twice: never open the trunk unless you have no other options. The memory snapped into sharp focus, mingling with the raw desperation that coiled in her belly. Sadie was barely clinging to life. They absolutely had no other options left. She steeled herself and set her spoon aside. The stew, no matter how comforting, couldn't solve Sadie's crisis.

With trembling hands, Emma reached out and brushed a damp compress over Sadie's brow. The older woman's eyelids twitched. A faint moan escaped her. Emma leaned closer, lowering her voice. "Grandma, please... let me know if you can hear me," she whispered. "We're not giving up, but we need something stronger. Do you... do you have a key? Or a word that might unlock something?"

Sadie's murmur dissolved into shallow coughing, then she slipped back into fitful silence. Tears ran down Emma's cheeks, and she pressed the cool cloth again, feeling her grandmother's forehead. "She is so cold," she said, voice thick. She rose from her spot and turned to face Ian and Gale fully. "We have to find the trunk. The trunk, or at least the wards that guard it."

Gale nodded, determined. "We'll do whatever you need."

Emma hugged her arms to her chest, trying to keep her composure. She recalled overhearing Sadie once mention the trunk's location behind certain wards or possibly beneath a floorboard. Yet there was no certainty. The house was not large, but it had more than enough nooks and secret compartments to hide something so important.

Ian set the food tray on the table, next to Emma's scattered books. "I'll help you search," he said. His usual calm tone carried a current of urgency. "This time, we check every corner."

Gale's eyes glistened with lingering tears she refused to shed. "We're a team. Sadie taught me a few tricks for wards, so once we find that trunk, I will do what I can to break or disarm them carefully." She paused, lips trembling. "We cannot lose her, Emma.

"All right," Gale said softly, stepping back from Sadie's bedside. "Let's find this trunk." She reached to pick up the few scraps of cloth she had dropped earlier. The mild enchantment had fizzled, but at least the cloths would be ready if Sadie needed them for comfort or support.

Emma nodded. "Ian, do you think you can help me check the upstairs? Gale, you could start near the basement. Then we can meet and compare notes if neither place works."

"At least the trunk might not be small enough to hide in a drawer," Gale attempted to joke. Her soft laugh died quickly. Their fear weighed too heavily on them all.

"Emma," Ian said quietly, glancing at the cottage door. "If something is warded, it might be dangerous to meddle with it alone. So, no matter what, we search together."

Emma exhaled, a slight nod of agreement. Gale folded her arms, eyes steeled with purpose. Together, they turned their faces from Sadie's bedside to the rest of the cottage. The wards, the chest, the Grimoire's missing pages, everything they needed might be waiting just out of sight. With full hearts and trembling anticipation, they prepared to open door after door, rummage under every floorboard, and unravel the mysteries Sadie had warned Emma about since she had arrived.

In the cottage living room, Sadie remained on the makeshift bed with the damp cloth resting gently on her brow. Her breathing came shallow and raspy, yet the faint rise and fall of her chest continued. Quietly, the group drew closer to the door, each of them united in a single goal: they would find the hidden trunk, open it, and reclaim any knowledge that might save Sadie's life.

CHAPTER

TWENTY-FIVE

A distant rumble of thunder coursed through the beams of the cottage as Emma guided the flashlight's glow along the basement's concrete floor. She tried to keep her breathing steady, though her heart pulsed with trepidation that mingled with a flicker of hope. The air tasted stale down here—faintly of mothballs and old cardboard.

"This is the last row of boxes," Gale announced from beside a tall shelf stacked with musty crates. Her voice cracked just enough that Emma glanced over in concern. Gale was forcing a brave front, arms crossed, pink-streaked hair catching the light.

"I'll check over there," Ian said, stepping carefully around a wooden crate that threatened to collapse under its own age.

Emma set the flashlight on a rickety table and knelt to rummage through an open box. A breath of dust stung her nose, bringing her back to the moment. Inside lay a neatly folded quilt, its fabric pattern long faded to dull browns. Another quilt rested beneath it, plus two crocheted blankets with moth-bitten edges.

She gently lifted one corner of a crocheted piece. "I don't think Sadie hid anything down here," she said, voice soft. Part of her hated sifting through these personal effects, but fear overrode any guilt. Sadie's trunk had been mentioned only in passing, though it was rumored to hold spells too dangerous for casual study. At this point, they had no choice but to look.

Gale expelled a weary sigh. "Same story here," she said, flipping shut a lid on the next box. "There's nothing but musty doilies and stained aprons."

Ian straightened with a quiet inhale. He had the next crate open, but the disappointment on his face told Emma that it, too, contained only ordinary items. "At least we're thorough," he murmured, though his eyes flicked anxiously toward Emma. She recognized a flicker of self-blame there, a silent worry that every moment wasted threatened them all. In the hush, thunder murmured again, making the overhead lamp tremble.

Emma pushed aside her own frustration. "Maybe the trunk isn't here," she said. "Let's head to the attic. Sadie kept old furniture there, right? Some of those wardrobes might hide compartments." Her voice shook, but she forced determination into it. They had endured illusions, storms, and heartbreak. If the trunk existed, they would find it together.

Gale tucked a loose strand of hair behind her ear. "I'm

game," she said, picking up a flashlight. "The spiders better watch out."

The three ascended the narrow stairs, footsteps echoing like muted drumbeats. A cold draft greeted them in the hall. The attic door loomed ahead, a pad of old paint flaking from its surface. Emma braced herself for more dust. She gripped the tarnished handle and pushed the door open.

A dank, musty scent enveloped them. Gale lifted the flashlight higher, exposing the cramped space. Layers of dust coated scattered furniture: a broken rocking chair, an upright dresser missing its drawers, and a short, worn trunk with a dented lid. Emma's pulse spiked at the sight of that trunk until she realized it was already open, revealing only a torn pillow inside.

Ian quietly moved to the trunk, kneeling to peer into its corners. "Empty," he muttered, though he ran a careful hand along the inside edge, just in case. He exhaled heavily, resting his palm on the trunk's rim. Emma's chest tightened at the resignation in his posture. She knew how deeply he hoped for a quick find, something to ease the tension strangling his every breath.

Gale drifted toward a battered dresser, the flashlight revealing spiderwebs meshed across its front. She delicately brushed them away. "We've got a few random books in here," she said, tugging open the top drawer. A limp collection of pages slid out, possibly from an old gardening journal. Gale flipped through a couple, then shook her head. "No wards, no hidden compartments. Just scribbled planting dates."

Emma felt a lump rise in her throat. Every false lead hammered her nerves. She pressed her hand to the side of the old rocking chair and ran her fingertips along a splinter. Sadie had once told her that storing powerful objects in the attic was risky, they could attract prying eyes. But given everything they had found so far, Emma thought the trunk must be hidden in plain sight, protected by wards too subtle for them to sense without closer inspection.

Lightning flashed through the high attic window. A moment later came a quiet thunderclap, muffled but insistent. Emma squared her shoulders. "We should check Sadie's bedroom," she said. "The diaries mentioned wards layered over the chest. She might have kept it somewhere personal."

Ian nodded and stood. Gale grabbed a spare rag from a rickety shelf and dusted off her hands. Together, they worked their way down the attic stairs, hearts pounding in unison. The hallway's sconces flickered, revealing peeling wallpaper that had once been floral. Emma passed her grandmother's old photographs on the wall—stills capturing orchard blossoms from decades ago. She tried not to let the ache in her chest slow her steps.

Sadie's bedroom door stood partially ajar. Emma gently pushed it open, then paused on the threshold. Sadie's warm presence lingered; the scent of dried lavender hung in the air. Gale entered turning on the overhead light that cast a glow across the worn wooden floor. "We're looking for loose floorboards or maybe a false drawer," she murmured, gaze sharp.

Emma followed the grain of the wood with her eyes,

searching for anomalies. She recalled Sadie cautioning her once never to pry up any board that bore carvings. That warning loomed in her mind now. She surveyed the base of the dresser, the gap beneath the bed, even pressed a curious foot onto a slightly squeaky plank near the corner. Nothing responded to her weight.

Ian circled the bed, hands pressed lightly to a low bookshelf that held a few of Sadie's older texts. He whispered a brief incantation under his breath. Emma understood he was feeling for wards, a subtle test of the air for magical tension. When he straightened, the furrow in his brow disappointed her. He hadn't found anything obviously concealed.

Then Gale, stepping near the center of the room, sucked in a sharp breath. "Hold on," she said. She knelt and tapped a spot with her fingertip. "This board is off by half an inch. It's not flush with the rest." The flicker of excitement in her voice made Emma's heart leap.

Emma and Ian crowded closer, the three of them peering at the spot—barely noticeable, but definitely out of line. Gale rapped it gently, producing a muted thump. The wood felt more solid than the typical hollow seam. "You think that's it?" Emma asked, voice quivering.

"All I know is that it's suspicious," Gale replied. Without waiting, she reached into her pocket to retrieve a knife always at the ready to nudge it. A jolt of blue sparks suddenly crackled along the board's edge, forcing her to yank her hand back. She nearly dropped the knife. "Ow." She grimaced, shaking out her wrist. "That's some protective ward. Sadie didn't want us messing around here."

"That means we're in the right place," Ian said. He moved to Emma's side, voice hushed. "We have to do this carefully."

Emma pressed a palm against the floorboard just beside the faint glyph that flared. Every line of the symbol looked partially dormant until they touched it, releasing small bursts of magic. She swallowed. "Sadie wrote about wards triggered by a runic sequence. We'll need to combine my incantation with Gale's focus on dispelling them, the way Sadie taught us. Ian, can you steady the resonance?"

He nodded. "Let's try."

Gale took a calming breath. "You do the chant. I'll channel the clarity spell, the focusing one Sadie insisted I practice. And Ian can anchor us if anything gets chaotic."

Emma set her jaw, ignoring the thunder gently rattling the window. She quietly placed both hands on the floorboard. Ian knelt behind her, one palm hovering just above her shoulder, ready to feed stabilizing magic into her. Gale leaned in, free hand inches from the glyph.

Emma summoned her courage, voice trembling at first.

"Let hidden wards submit to truth.
Let genuine hearts unbind this root.
Grant rightful eyes the path to see,
Release the seal and set us free."

The old lines tasted metallic on her tongue, as though the ward resisted letting them pass. She whispered the next lines Sadie had once tucked into a margin:

"By orchard's bond and family trust,
dissolve these locks that gather dust."

She felt Gale's magical vibration shimmer behind her. A gentle hum radiated through the floor, struggling against the layers of wards. The glyph's edges sparked with a harsh white light that flared into the gloom. Ian parted his lips in a quiet exhale, channeling a calm wave of energy to keep Emma's incantation from backfiring. Emma steadied herself, heart racing. She repeated the final line.

Slowly, the glyph carved into the board lost its brilliance, fading until it disappeared like ink in water. Gale let out a breath, revealing that the wooden latch beneath the glyph had become visible. The small metal latch glinted with faint silver runes. Emma gently lifted it, a sense of reverence coursing through her. Within seconds, the board shifted aside without another spark.

Underneath the two loose planks lay a recessed space, just large enough for a single trunk. Emma and Gale peered down into the hole, while Ian helped slide the object up and out. It was heavier than Emma expected. The trunk's exterior was smooth, as though newly polished, but etched with subtle runes near each corner. A faint ripple of magic shimmered across its surface. Emma recognized protective layering, the kind Sadie must have spent hours perfecting.

"Here it is," Gale breathed, eyes wide. "This must be Sadie's hidden trunk."

Ian's hands trembled where they touched the trunk's lid. Emma sensed his hope, recognized the near desperation in his expression. This trunk might finally yield the knowledge that saved him from his nightmares. "We should open it carefully," Emma said, voice hushed. She remembered how Sadie's diaries described advanced wards that could spring illusions if tampered with.

Gale nodded. "We dispelled the surface wards, right? Or do we expect more inside?"

Emma traced the corner of the trunk. "There may be another set, but let's stay alert." She recalled Sadie's final instructions in her diaries, notes that hinted at a dire cost if someone forced the trunk open. Emma bowed her head a moment, silently apologizing to her grandmother for disturbing this. Then she angled her fingers beneath the latch. "Steady me?" she asked, glancing at Ian.

He settled next to her, one knee pressed to the floor, and folded his hand over hers. "Take it slow," he murmured, voice gentle. The thunder outside seemed to subside for a moment, as though waiting for them to proceed. Gale held her breath by Emma's other side, lamp light illuminating every grain in the trunk's wooden frame.

Emma flipped the latch. The trunk's lid eased up with a low creak, unveiling a mild glow from within. She felt an unmistakable surge of old magic. It was neither cold nor hostile—it simply existed, potent and waiting. Her breath caught in her throat. She lifted the lid higher, bracing for a ward's backlash that never came.

Inside, diaries bound in cracked leather rose into view, stacked in a neat column. Beside them lay a cluster of arcane tools: a short rod carved with orchard runes, a small pouch that felt weighted with crystals, and a set of chalk sticks that possessed a faint, almost pulsing aura. Emma recognized the style of Sadie's personal design.

Beneath these items was a handful of loose parchments. Emma saw scrawled text in Sadie's looping handwriting: fragments referencing illusions, wards, and something called the crystal heart. She traced the words with shaking fingertips. The phrase immediately seized her heart—a mention of a lost artifact rumored to break curses. She recalled stray lines from Sadie's older diaries, cryptic warnings that only dire necessity would compel them to seek it. Now, it was clear that Sadie had planned for them to uncover all this in a final attempt at saving Crestwood and, more urgently, saving Ian.

"Oh, stars," Gale said softly, crowding close enough that her breath fanned the back of Emma's neck. She peered at the incomplete script. "You've seen references to this crystal heart before, right?" Her tone brimmed with cautious excitement. "You told me Sadie wrote about big incantations anchored in orchard magic."

Emma nodded, carefully lifting the parchment. Most lines were smudged or written in archaic runes. She could pick out only bits and pieces about harnessing true devotion, synergy of bloodlines, and a reference to orchard roots. The text was nearly indecipherable in places, requiring dedicated study. "She must have hidden the full explanation here," Emma said, voice hitching. "We'll have to interpret it. There's more in the diaries." She glanced around, meeting Ian's gaze. The tension in his shoulders eased slightly, replaced by something like relief.

His voice was husky. "This means there might be a path," he murmured. The shallow bruise under his left eye caught the light, hinting at old battles. "I won't let you risk yourselves for me," he added, though Emma recognized the yearning in his expression. He wanted a solution.

Gale dropped into a seated position beside the trunk, exhaling loudly as thunder gently rapped at the walls. "Hah. This is good news, buddy. Don't even start talking about not risking ourselves. We're all in this. That includes you." She tried a grin, but emotion wavered in her eyes.

Emma felt her own eyes sting. She gently set the parchments aside, exposing the next layer: more pages. The Grimoire's missing spreads, it seemed, lines of advanced illusions and protective spells. Her mind whirled, remembering how Sadie used to scold her for even peeking at complex diagrams. But here they were, no guardian left to caution them except for their own sense of danger. She ran a thumb over a corner of the largest page, catching a glimpse of looping text that read, *Beware illusions of the orchard's darkest hour.*

Her chest tightened. This was truly restricted knowledge.

Ian placed a tentative hand on her shoulder. The small contact steadied her swirling thoughts. Together, they pulled out the diaries and the Grimoire pages, stacking them gently in the trunk's lid. Gale leaned in and touched one battered volume, eyes glancing at Emma for permission. Emma gave a small nod, trusting her friend's caution.

Lightning flared again, illuminating the bedroom with an eerie brilliance. Rain pattered against the windows, not quite a storm but fierce enough to shimmer in the glow. Emma's heartbeat pounded as she realized how drastically everything had changed in a single night.

"This has to be it," Gale breathed, voice subdued. "The beginning of a real cure."

Emma stroked her palm over the trunk's edge. "Sadie must have known we'd need these eventually. I'm only sorry it took losing so much to force our hand," she whispered. She swallowed hard, gazing at the newly revealed diaries and pages that might hold Ian's salvation.

Ian's hand lingered near hers, unspoken gratitude in his eyes. "We'll figure it out," he said, voice raw. "No illusions. No more half-measures."

Gale sniffed back the emotion trembling in her throat. "Agreed," she said, leaning forward to gather the diaries more securely. "Because if Catherine thinks she can keep terrorizing everyone while we sit idle, she's in for a nasty surprise."

The thunder remained, a subdued presence that reminded them of the night's tension. Yet in that circle of lamp light, Emma felt a flow of renewed courage. They had found the trunk that Sadie guarded so fiercely. Inside it, they now held the seeds of a possible future—one where the orchard might cease trembling under the shadow of illusions, and where Ian's curse could be severed once and for all.

She carefully set the diaries back in the trunk, lips pressed together. "We'll decipher what we can first. Then we'll plan," she said. Her gaze locked briefly on the words crystal heart etched in one margin.

And so, they stood there, gathered around the opened trunk in Sadie's bedroom, the missing pages and diaries laid out like fragments of a new destiny within reach. None of them moved from that circle of discovery where lingering hope mingled with the sting of sacrifice. Subdued thunder rumbled one last time, seeming to mark the moment they prepared to embrace. The trunk, and all it contained, had found its rightful owners at last.

THE STORY CONTINUES

The story continues in book three, *Crystal Heart,* coming soon to Amazon.

EXCERPT FROM CRYSTAL HEART

CHAPTER ONE

Emma bolted upright, her heart pounding. How long had she been asleep after the discovery of the hidden trunk in Sadie's room? A haze clung to her mind, as though her dreams had physical weight. Gray predawn light seeped through the small window of her bedroom, illuminating the few dust motes drifting in the air. She pressed a hand to her forehead and exhaled slowly thinking she had probably slept fitfully a few hours after finding the trunk. She, along with Ian and Gale had decided to get some rest before fully investigating the trunk's contents. Before scattering to different corners of the cottage, they had checked on Sadie who was now sleeping more soundly on the floor of the living room.

She had fitfully dreamed of old runes, all swirling in a pale glow that made them glint like shards of starlight. In the dream, she stood in the orchard's heart, and an indistinct figure—someone who felt both ancient and familiar—reached out to guide her fingers along the shapes etched into the bark of an oak. She remembered hearing her long ago ancestor, Lucian Turner's name echo in a voice she couldn't see. Now, awake and trembling, Emma struggled to parse what was real. The lines and loops of those runes were still fresh in her memory, but she wondered if fatigue and stress had twisted her subconscious.

She rose, trying not to shiver. Her bedroom was chilly from the nightly coastal wind that drifted in through warped shutters. She slipped on a cardigan and quietly padded into the living room, where the low embers in the hearth hinted at Gail's or Ian's presence earlier in the night. Sadie was thankfully still sleeping peacefully. Emma poked the fire and quietly threw on a few more logs. The house smelled of rosemary and faint candle wax, a comforting but melancholy scent. Part of her wished she could sink back into bed and pretend she had not just dreamed of Lucian, or that her mind was not brimming with cryptic symbols. Yet something more urgent pushed her onward. Whatever she had gleaned in that dream, it had felt too concrete to ignore.

She spotted her hastily scribbled notes on the kitchen table—pages from Sadie's diaries and the elusive Grimoire sections they had stacked there before slipping into uneasy rest. Biting her lower lip, Emma turned on the overhead light illuminating the spread of parchment and ink-stained passages. She took a steady breath and pulled out a scrap of paper where she had once tried to translate a handful of runic phrases. Scanning it, she noticed how closely the shapes resembled the ones near the bottom margin of the Grimoire text. Her pulse leaped. She had seen these very shapes in her dreams, spinning like a constellation of hidden meaning.

She whispered to herself, "Was this real or just my imagination?" but her voice sounded unconvinced. There was something about the weight of the dream—how it had pressed at her chest, how Lucian's presence still hovered at the edges of her vision—that felt more tangible than a mere nightmare. She smoothed out the pages of the Grimoire and touched a finger to the lines of faded script. Her mind raced with half-buried memories, words that felt lodged in her throat.

Ian's soft footsteps clicked above her, then the boards overhead gave a quiet groan. She glanced toward the attic staircase that led from the hallway. He insisted on sleeping up there although Emma had tried to talk him out of it because of all the dust. He must have sensed her restless energy and had stirred awake at the same moment. For an instant, Emma debated whether to call him. She recalled how worn he had looked the previous evening, eyes shadowed with nightmares. Still, she needed his help. The Grimoire was too daunting for her alone.

She called out. "Ian?"

His answer arrived, muffled but concerned. "Emma? Everything all right?"

"Please come down," she called. "I might have found something important."

While she waited, she set aside the extra diaries, clearing a space at the table for both of them to work. She rubbed her sleepy eyes. Dawn lingered outside: no bird-song yet, just a faint silver glow that backlit the orchard. The trees, stoic in the distance, were a reminder that the orchard itself might hold more secrets than she ever realized.

Ian descended the steps, hair tousled and shoulders stiff under a loose sweater. He paused at the base of the attic steps. In the light, the faint gold flecks in his brown eyes glimmered, bringing focus to the tension scrunching his forehead.

"You're up early," he murmured, voice barely above a whisper. Then he caught sight of the scattered pages on the table and crossed the room in a few brisk steps. "Did you sleep at all?"

She nodded, swallowing. "I did for a few minutes and had a dream. It was... vivid. There were runes, the orchard, and a sense of Lucian's presence. It felt more like a vision than a random nightmare."

He pulled a second chair close, settling beside her. "You think it links to the grimoire text we found earlier?"

She offered him the page of runes she had sketched while they were still bright in her memory. Her fingertip trembled as she circled one shape that resembled a heart bisected by a diagonal slash. "Look here," she said, drawing his attention to a similar symbol in the middle of Sadie's partial translations. "This mark—doesn't it match the stroke in this line about the orchard's hidden relic?"

Ian leaned over the table. She noticed the faint birth-mark on his left forearm and how he pressed a thumb against it unconsciously whenever he grew anxious. Right now, though, his focus was pinned on the runes. He lowered his voice. "Yes. I've seen that shape in one of Sadie's older diaries. Something about the orchard's heart... or was it the orchard's core?"

Emma's pulse skittered with excitement. "It might be the same. It definitely mentions a heart. But these lines..." She traced a row of faint letters that Sadie had copied from the grimoire. "They match my dream's runes almost exactly. I was hoping you'd help me figure out which of Sadie's notes line up best, because if these references are real, we might be overlooking key instructions about harnessing the orchard's magic."

He let out a slow exhale and started flipping carefully through the tattered texts. "We were exhausted last night. Maybe now our minds are sharper. Let's check cross-references to the orchard's synergy spells."

They worked in silence for several minutes, cross-checking each symbol with Sadie's scrawled commentary. One passage spelled out faint instructions for an emotional conduit, conjured by a witch who "pledges her devotion." Another described the orchard's unique wards that awakened only under dire need. Emma's shoulders tensed each time she stumbled across words like *love*, *sacrifice*, or *purity of heart*. She remembered Sadie's repeated warnings: spells reliant on powerful emotion could be as dangerous as any hex if cast recklessly.

She noticed Ian's jaw tightening when he reached a page referencing *bloodline redemption*. His gaze flicked up to meet hers, a mixture of hope and dread in his eyes. Emma knew he was thinking of Alaric Williams, his distant forefather who had twisted illusions to sow chaos. For Ian, the curse was not just a rumor but an everyday threat that lurked behind every dream and anxious breath. The phrase *bloodline redemption* teased him with the possibility of freedom yet dredged up the memory that Alaric's downfall still tainted his name.

She laid a calm hand on his forearm. "We'll figure it out," she said softly. "Whatever these lines mean, we won't let that old darkness define you."

Ian turned his palm upward, intertwining his fingers with hers, just for a heartbeat. "I want to believe that" he said, voice husky. "I do. But reading the words... it's like they're a mirror reminding me what my ancestors did. Sometimes I wonder if I can ever break free of it."

Emma squeezed his hand gently, then returned her focus to the Grimoire text. She cleared her throat, determined to keep an undercurrent of calm in her tone. "Look here: it says, *the crystal heart shall reveal a path to unify orchard and descendant, through a willingness to risk all under love's vow.'* That... that sounds like we can't just find the artifact. We have to channel some sort of emotional offering."

He nodded, brow furrowed. "Love's vow. And a *heart ignited by devotion.*" He pointed at another phrase. "That might match the symbol you saw in your dream. Possibly a sign that the orchard's core only responds to genuine unity. Are you sure you want to attempt that? This text is ancient. Who knows the consequences if we get it wrong?"

Emma's chest fluttered. She recalled past attempts at synergy spells. Each time, the orchard had tested her in subtle ways: illusions of lost loved ones, echoes of heartbreak. She had emerged shaken but more resolute. Perhaps this time, the orchard demanded more from her. From them both.

"It's not about wanting," she said, voice softer than before. "We might have no other choice. If the orchard's relic—this crystal heart—truly has the power to break curses and illusions, then we need it. Especially if we're going to protect everyone from further harm." She hesitated, her thoughts drifting to Sadie resting in the other room. She pictured how her grandmother had looked, pale, each breath a labor. They couldn't let fear paralyze them now.

Ian's expression flickered with the same worry. He set his hand atop the page, covering a snippet of text that referenced heartbreak. "You're right," he said. "But I—my nightmares about harming the people close to me never really fade. If tapping into that orchard magic requires raw emotion, I'm terrified of what illusions might slip through."

Emma eased closer to him, feeling the warmth of his body in the cool morning air. She inhaled the faint scent of sea salt that always clung to him, a reminder of Crestwood's coastal storms. "I know you're scared. I'm scared, too. But you and I've come this far together. We'll face whatever illusions show up. I promise I won't let you stand alone."

He lifted his eyes to hers, vulnerability etched in every line of his face. "Then I'll try," he whispered. "No illusions can be worse than losing all hope. I won't deny how important you—and this orchard—have become to me."

Emma ran her fingers through his hair, brushing back the strands that had fallen into his eyes. Ian blinked, caught between surprise and something deeper. "You're always thinking," she murmured. "Even when we're not talking, I can feel your mind racing ahead."

He huffed a quiet laugh, the corners of his lips twitching. "I can't help it. I want to figure everything out at once. Sometimes, I'm not great at being patient."

Emma smiled, her touch lingering a moment longer before she let her hand drop to his shoulder. "Yeah. Me neither."

Ian turned toward her fully then, studying the delicate furrow of her brow, the way she had always carried determination like a second heartbeat. His hand lifted, fingertips brushing her cheek, tracing the line of her jaw. A simple touch, but enough to make her breath catch. "You're my anchor," he admitted. "Every time I start to drown in all of this—the illusions, the fear—you pull me back."

Emma's throat tightened, but she didn't look away. Instead, she leaned into his palm, eyes fluttering shut for just a second. "And you do the same for me."

Ian swallowed hard, his thumb skimming over her cheekbone, hesitant and reverent at once. Then, with a small, shaky breath, he pressed a kiss on her forehead.

Emma's lips parted in surprise, warmth blooming from where his lips touched her skin. "Oh," she breathed out softly. She felt herself unraveling a bit like she could turn to jelly right then and there. It was the kind of affection that burrowed deeper than desire, the kind that whispered of safety. She wasn't sure how to put that all into words, so she simply said, "Forehead kisses are my kryptonite."

Ian pulled back just enough to look at her, his expression shifting from curiosity to something else entirely. Then, slow and deliberate, he kissed her forehead again, this time letting his lips linger, his warmth seeping further into her skin.

When he finally pulled away, his voice was barely above a whisper. "You are my kryptonite."

Emma let out a soft laugh, breathless and unsteady, because of all the dangers they faced, for all the illusions that threatened to pull them apart, this was real. This was theirs.

A small, tremulous smile curved Emma's lips. She let the moment linger—a fragile bond that told her both of them were ready to risk their hearts, and their lives, if it meant halting the looming darkness in Crestwood. She reached for the large dictionary of runes they had salvaged from Sadie's trunk, flipping through the pages until she found one with two incomplete translations. She translated them haltingly, matching shapes to the scrawled symbols and words in Sadie's handwriting.

One line read: *In the orchard's hush, the awakened relic thrives*, while the next concluded: *Commit with a vow of truth or remain barred from redemption.*

She and Ian exchanged thoughtful glances.

She tapped the edge of the page. "So, we can't cast a

haphazard spell. It has to be... real. Emotionally intentional. There's no faking it or being apathetic with this kind of magic when dealing with illusions. The orchard will know if we're lying."

His mouth twitched in a half-smile. "Crestwood is never simple, is it?"

Emma's laugh held a tired warmth. "No, I guess not. But if the orchard sealed this artifact away, maybe it expected future Turners to unify with someone else—someone who had reason to break an old curse." Her voice faltered slightly. "Seems like that's us."

Outside the window, the sky was turning milky blue, tinged with pink near the horizon. The orchard lay quiet, dew clinging to its branches. Emma felt a surge of determination. She might not have asked for the responsibility that accompanied her family's magic, but it was hers now. Her grandmother's diaries, the orchard's legacy, even the bond she shared with Ian—she had to embrace them if she hoped to save Sadie and shield this town.

Ian carefully lifted the original grimoire page from the table, studying the phrase referencing *heart ignited by devotion.* For a moment, Emma watched him, noticing how the tension in his posture eased whenever he skimmed over gentle references to pure intentions, or love that transcended illusions. Yet every mention of illusions or redemption pinned his jaw tight once more.

After a few moments, he glanced up, eyes searching hers with quiet intensity. "I can't tell if we're supposed to cast a synergy spell or if the orchard itself will weave it once we commit. The text is vague about who leads the incantation. But... I suspect you're the only one truly meant to unlock it."

Emma thought of Sadie's legacy, the orchard's swirling presence that always hummed beneath her feet, and the responsibility she had once avoided—she never wanted to inherit the orchard's burdens. Yet here she was, pressing deeper into its secrets with Ian at her side. And somehow, that realization made the fear less paralyzing.

She set her hand over her heart, remembering the gentle echo of her grandmother's voice urging her not to turn away from magic. "I'll try," she said. "I won't pretend I fully understand how, but if I'm the orchard's descendant, maybe it'll respond. And if love and devotion matter, then we won't be going into this halfhearted."

Ian's lips curved in a quiet, almost shy grin that tugged at Emma's heart. A fleeting comfort welled between them —proof that they had found something precious in each other. He leaned back in his chair, exhaling. "All right. Then let's keep translating. There might be instructions hidden in the lines we haven't deciphered yet."

A new rush of energy flared in Emma's veins. Tired as she was, the swirling puzzle of the orchard's lore awakened her more than any jolt of caffeine could. She searched for a quill, rummaging through the small basket Sadie stockpiled with scraps of parchment and half-dried herbs. Then she flipped to another section of the Grimoire.

The house felt eerily still. No footsteps from Gale, no moan of wind outside. Only a faint crackle from the hearth's last embers. Emma and Ian settled into a focused rhythm, whispering translations aloud before double-checking them against Sadie's notes. Every so often, Emma would pause, eyes flicking up to read the flicker of emotion crossing Ian's features. She found herself savoring the small sparks of triumph whenever they decoded a particularly obscure line.

Time slipped by, the darkness gradually softening as dawn brightened the windows. Pale sunlight crept across the table, casting a golden glow over the scattered pages. Emma blinked at a newly translated passage that made her heart skip:

For a heart ignited by devotion,
a relic opens its unseen corridors.
Past shadows yield in the face of truth,
leading sorrowed heirs to renewal.

She met Ian's gaze, her excitement laced with caution. "This... it's so direct. As if it's promising a second chance, not just at breaking illusions, but at healing bloodlines as well."

He brushed his hand through his hair, expression raw but hopeful. "Then maybe it's what we've needed all along."

Their eyes lingered on each other. In that moment, Emma felt the orchard's presence swirl around them—a gentle, wordless encouragement. If the orchard demanded love, courage, and sacrifice, then she knew she possessed them inside her heart, especially with Ian here. She took a breath, letting the significance of the words settle between them.

He slid his hand to hers, letting his fingertips rest lightly atop her own. There was a softness in that touch that conveyed understanding and the unspoken promise of partnership. Emma inhaled steadily, trying not to let the sudden rush of emotion overwhelm her. The path ahead was uncertain, but not empty. They were forging it together.

Ian's voice came out quieter. "If we trust this relic to accept our devotion, then maybe we do have a shot at redemption—for me, for my family's mistakes, and for everything Sadie fought to protect."

Emma nodded, laying the page gently on top of the diaries. "Then we'll let the orchard see that we're sincere." She stared at the delicately inked lines describing the crystal heart, imagining how it might glow once awakened. A fierce yearning built in her chest, an urge to banish gloom from everyone's life, starting with the man who sat beside her, eyes full of so much hidden ache.

She traced her fingertips over the first line on the page: *Heart ignited by devotion.* The words seemed to brighten in her mind, reflecting all the tension, longing, and hope she and Ian carried. They reminded her that neither orchard spells nor illusions could overshadow a bond forged in genuine emotion.

Though the sunlight strengthened, chasing away the last threads of dawn, an undercurrent of electricity lingered in the kitchen. Emma lifted her gaze to Ian, feeling her pulse roar in her ears. She recalled the many times illusions had unsettled him, threatened to consume him. She remembered the first sparks of closeness they had shared, hesitant but undeniable. And she saw, in his eyes, the same realization: that perhaps their bond was no accident.

Their gazes locked—aware that their growing love might be the key to the relic's secrets. Despite the swirl of uncertainty lingering in the house, the keen excitement of discovery filled them with hope.

OTHER FLORID ROMANCE BOOKS

To be notified of new releases and special promotions from Florid Romance, please join our email list:

https://floridromance.lmbpn.com/about/sign-up-for-our-newsletter/

For a complete list of books published by Florid Romance, please visit our website:

https://floridromance.lmbpn.com/

BOOKS BY KELLI ROBYNS

The Enchanted Orchard
The Orchard (Book 1)
Family Curse (Book 2)
Crystal Heart (Book 3)

BOOKS BY MICHAEL ANDERLE

Sign up for the LMBPN email list to be notified of new releases and special deals!

https://lmbpn.com/email/

For a complete list of books by Michael Anderle, please visit:

www.lmbpn.com/ma-books/

CONNECT WITH MICHAEL ANDERLE

Connect with Michael Anderle

Website: http://lmbpn.com

Email List: https://michael.beehiiv.com/

https://www.facebook.com/LMBPNPublishing

https://twitter.com/MichaelAnderle

https://www.instagram.com/lmbpn_publishing/

https://www.bookbub.com/authors/michael-anderle